Inspired by True Events

CITIZEN WARRIOR
The 4th Branch

by J. Thomas Rompel

COPYRIGHT ACKNOWNLEDGEMENT

Citizen Warrior – The 4th Branch

Self-Published by J. Thomas Rompel, 2016©

Website | www.jthomasrompel.com

Email | contact@jthomasrompel.com

Library of Congress Cataloging-in-Publication Data

10 9 8 7 6 5 4 3 2 1 edition

NOTICE

Acknowledgements

Many thanks to John Young, Marcy Murray and a couple of others who will go unnamed for taking the time to read my draft manuscript and give me great feedback. To my son Tommy and daughter Trisha who have always been and continue to be an inspiration to me. To Renee and Janelle of 'The Writers Studio' who have provided me with skillful coaching in my writing skills. To my sweetheart Linda and her continued love and encouragement. To all the men and women in our military and law enforcement who have given of themselves so we can enjoy our God given freedom. And to all the Citizen Warriors who I know are out there just waiting to be called if needed!

Dedicated to the loving memory of T3

Fate whispers to the warrior,
"You cannot withstand the storm."
And the warrior whispers back,
"I am the storm."

- Author Unknown

X-7 Ranch, Cochise County, Arizona
U.S./Mexico Border

It was a cool, beautiful January afternoon with severe clear blue skies and a slight breeze stirring the wind chimes hanging from the beam on the front porch. The chimes had come from their son Eric this past Christmas. Harold, sitting on the front porch in his favorite chair, listened to the chaotic cadence of the chimes, thinking about days gone by while slowly scratching the head of Sally, their fifteen-year-old German short-hair/golden-retriever mix.

"You're a good old pup," Harold said, looking down at Sally. Panting, she looked up at Harold with her graying chin and cloudy eyes, as if in understanding and then put her head back down on her paws with a sigh. Harold knew her days of chasing jackrabbits were over, yet somehow this old girl could still get up and move around when she needed to.

Harold, feeling the cool breeze wafting across his face, closed his eyes and leaned back in his chair, grateful to have lived a full life. Sitting there listening to the continued tinkle of the wind chimes, he could hear his wife Agnes working inside in the kitchen, preparing supper for the two of them. A tender smile drifted across his face as he thought of the many years they had spent together. They had known each other since childhood, and their love and devotion deepened with each passing year.

Abruptly Harold's serenity was interrupted by the sound of a vehicle approaching from the south. He watched as the fast-moving black SUV with dark-tinted windows made a skidding hard left off the unpaved ranch road onto his dirt driveway. The driver hit the brakes hard, causing the vehicle to skid to a stop in front of Harold's front porch.

"Hey, asshole, I put the 'slow down' sign leading into my driveway for a reason!" Harold said out loud in the direction of the now-stopped Suburban. He watched as the trailing dust engulfed the vehicle from behind, slowly drifting its way toward him. Sally immediately lifted her head and barked as she struggled to get to her feet. She moved behind Harold's chair and then half ran to the steps and down them. She stopped at the bottom, challenging the intruders with a low growl.

The two front doors and the right rear door of the big SUV opened simultaneously. A short man with a black shirt opened to his stomach, a large gold chain around his neck, gold bands on both wrists, silver pointed cowboy boots and a pearl-handled, gold-plated Colt 1911 tucked in the front waistband of his jeans stepped out of the right front door. Immediately following, two tall and heavyset men got out of the other two doors. With the short one leading, they walked over to where Harold was now standing with clenched fists at the top of the porch steps.

"Easy, girl," Harold said to Sally.

The gold necklaces and gold bands on their wrists were a dead giveaway to Harold they were from across the line.

Harold, pissed off and glaring at them, stood there looking down at them as Sally stood her ground, continuing to snarl and growl at them. The two taller men stood back about ten feet to either side of the short man. Both were holding AK-47s.

What the hell, Harold thought to himself.

"I'm Reggie. My uncle is Juan Ortiz. Do you know who Juan Ortiz is?" The short man said, looking up at Harold and then down at the snarling Sally and then back up at Harold again.

"Never heard of him."

"My uncle is the head of the Magdalena Cartel. He told me to come and talk with you."

Looking back down at Sally, Reggie began to take a few cautious steps forward.

Sally did a short charge, growling and baring her teeth. The large man on Reggie's right immediately stepped forward and kicked Sally hard in the ribs. She let out a yelp and turned her attention on the man who'd just kicked her and charged him with jaws snapping. Without hesitating, the man kicked her again in the head, then shot her with a quick five-round burst from his AK47, dropping her on the spot. Reggie stopped and looked down at the dog, whose life was ebbing quickly. He shook his head and smiled, looking back up at Harold.

It took every muscle and cell in Harold's body to keep him from reacting. He could feel a long-forgotten rage surging up inside of him.

Reggie took a couple of steps forward, putting his right foot on the second step and leaning slightly forward with his right forearm resting on his knee, shrugged his shoulders and again looked down at Sally.

"Sorry, amigo. Starting tonight, we're going to be using your road, daytime, nighttime, whenever we please."

Looking down at the short man and then at Sally with a pool of blood forming underneath her lifeless body, Harold defiantly stared at Reggie. The right corner of his lip and cheek quivered. He thought to himself, *like hell you'll use my road!*

In spite of the now fully manifested rage inside of him, at eighty-three years of age Harold had learned that sometimes it was wiser to keep one's emotions in check. He knew these men standing in front of him were evil and dangerous. The safety of his wife was paramount on his mind.

He watched as Reggie again smiled and then, laughing, looked over his shoulder to his right and then to his left, shaking his head. The other two joined in the tormenting.

"Listen, amigo, just so we understand each other. If you contact the Border Patrol or any other *policia* we'll be back. If we have to come back you're not going to like it very much, but maybe your wife will. We'll tie you up and make you watch as we take turns having some fun with her. Then we'll make her watch as we cut off your little man and then your head. After that, we'll kill her and put your little hombre in her mouth. It will give your neighbors something to think about. Huh, how you like that, old man?" Reggie asked, while still leaning forward smiling with raised eyebrows, his left hand now on his crotch and biting his lower lip. Still smiling, again he looked over his shoulder to his right and then to his left at the other two men. He then turned back around, looking up at Harold.

Watching Reggie standing there smiling at him and listening to the other two laughing menacingly further fed the anger and a rage that Harold hadn't felt since the Korean War.

Harold took in a deep breath; *keep breathing and stay frosty*, he told himself. Harold thought about calmly telling them, *just a minute,* and quickly stepping inside and grabbing his M1 Garand rifle leaning against the inside of the front porch door frame with a round in the chamber and a seven round clip in it ready to go.

He knew this man meant what he said, and he also knew he and his wife could not stand against them. Knowing he was outmanned and outgunned, gritting his teeth with anger, Harold said, "*comprende!*" Glaring at them, Harold thought about the silver and two bronze stars he earned in Korea while serving as a Marine and facing much worse odds than these three lowlifes. He wasn't afraid of them or for himself; he was afraid for his wife. He swore to himself that if he outlived Agnes he would hunt down and kill all three of them, starting with the little short son of a bitch.

The three men turned, laughing, and started back to their vehicle. Reggie stopped at the now lifeless body of Sally, shook his head with a chuckle, spat on her, and then made his way back to the Suburban.

Harold heard the short one loudly utter "pussy Americans," just as the doors to the black SUV closed. The driver gunned it, doing a fish-tailing U-turn, driving off kicking up dirt. He made a hard right onto the dirt road, heading back to the gate and fence-line and back into Mexico a quarter mile away. Harold watched them as they drove off and decided from that moment on his M1 Garand would always be on the table next to him when he was sitting on the front porch and never more than two steps away.

He stood there in silence looking down at Sally and then back in the direction of the SUV, continuing to clench his fists. In the Korean War he had been one of thirty thousand Marines surrounded by sixty-seven thousand Chinese soldiers in the battle at the Chosin Reservoir. For seventeen days he experienced lack of sleep, freezing weather conditions and hand-to-hand combat. He'd watched his friends die, with gut-wrenching fear always embracing him. In the years and decades since coming back from the war, he had suffered many restless nights, tossing and turning, re-living those horrid events in his dreams.

He hadn't felt that kind of emotion since those dark times. It wasn't fear of these spineless cowards but rather fear of his wife suffering. In Korea he did battle against brave men who were willing to die for their beliefs. These three men and others like them were nothing but gutless cowards who found false courage only when running with the rest of their kind like a pack of wild dogs.

On the battlefield, he had his fellow Marines to his right and left. Now it was just him and his wife. Harold knew these men had no regard for human life. To Harold they represented the very heart of evil. He was furious he couldn't count on his own government to secure the border and keep Americans safe.

He then thought about his friend and fellow rancher Mike Davis. A few years earlier, Mike resisted the same type of demand. He was a decent and hardworking American rancher and family man. He had been ambushed and murdered in cold blood while thinking he was helping someone who was hurt, lying beside a road on his property. To this day the killers had never been brought to justice.

Harold thought about how Americans and their spineless government in Washington, D.C. had become a joke to the cartels, Islamic terrorists and the rest of the world. The United States was no longer to be feared as it had been under past administrations. Those who meant harm to Americans or who disrespected American culture and laws were no longer concerned with threatening or killing Americans. They knew threats and intimidations backed up by killing or torturing an American worked. Harold knew the enemies of his country no longer feared retribution by the U.S. government.

The citizens of his country had become fearful of their own government. Good Americans were afraid if they stood up for themselves and fought the criminals both on the street and on the border, they would be the ones arrested and punished. There were now over thirty Sanctuary cities in the country getting away with breaking federal laws and protecting illegal immigrants, including many who had been arrested for various offenses.

As far as the Mexican cartel was concerned, they could do what they wanted on U.S. soil without real consequences. If their mules (drug runners) got caught, what always happened? The U.S. Border Patrol would seize the men and their drugs, detain and feed them and then send them back to Mexico.

How could this be happening, he thought? *Why was his government allowing this to happen to him, his wife, and other U.S. citizens? Wasn't the number-one responsibility of the U.S. government under the Constitution to protect and defend its citizens against enemies both foreign and domestic? Was this not one of the basic intentions of the Founding Fathers when they formed this great nation? Since when did the criminals have all the rights and the victims were without?* It was also obvious to him that all three branches of the United States government were corrupt, with the media always looking the other way.

The United States had become a weak and decaying society heading towards third-world status. Spending was out of control; politicians lied and never got called on it. Under the direction of the Justice Department, ATF ran thousands of guns into Mexico to give to the cartels. A president with an alias and an obscure past. A U.S. ambassador along with three other Americans trying to protect him had been killed in Libya on the anniversary of 9/11 with the President and Secretary of State blaming it on a video. The IRS illegally targeted law-abiding citizens and no one was held to account. The list went on and on, becoming daunting and lengthy. *What the hell is going on?*

He knew one thing for sure; he was fed up with the situation. Like millions of Americans, he could see the problem; he just wasn't sure what to do about it.

Agnes had been standing just inside the front porch screen door, off to the side making sure she couldn't be seen; she'd been drawn there after having heard the commotion. Pushing the screen door open with her walker, she shuffled her way out to the front porch. In a short and hurried breath she asked, "Harold, who were those men, and what did they want? I heard gun shots. Where's Sally?"

Harold didn't want to scare her by telling her what just happened. He didn't know what to say; he just looked at her with tears welling up in his eyes. Harold and Agnes had been married fifty-six years, and he knew without saying anything that she knew something bad happened. She pushed her walker ahead to the top of the steps and looked down at the motionless body of Sally, lying in a pool of congealing blood. She started sobbing, slumping into Harold's arms.

"Oh, God, Harold, how could something like this be happening in our country?"

Six-Weeks Earlier
Tucson, Arizona

It was a quiet, older, foothills neighborhood with many of the residents retired along with a few younger professionals with children. By foothills and neighborhood standards, the home on three-quarters of an acre where the two young men from Yemen lived was modest. Yaheem and Aamir kept a low profile and avoided interacting with their neighbors as much as they could. This proved not too difficult as over the decades Americans had grown accustomed to keeping to themselves. In the years since the 9/11 attacks, their neighbors, like many other Americans, had grown complacent and never questioned what the two young Arab students might be up to.

Khaleef al Shammar had been on the Interpol's "watch list" for a number of years. Because of this, he wasn't able to apply for one of the million student visas casually and recklessly issued by the United States to just about anyone who applied for one. Since he couldn't go straight to America, he took a flight from Tehran to Amsterdam. Once in Amsterdam Khaleef knew as long as he didn't leave the secured area he'd be able to get a transit visa. From Amsterdam he flew to Havana, Cuba. Cuba, even though relations had improved, was still no friend of the U.S. They did very little checking on the background of Khaleef. From Havana he flew on to Caracas, Venezuela. Once in Venezuela, it was easy for him to get a visa and fly on to Mexico City, where the second largest Iranian embassy in the world is located. From there he connected with the Magdalena Cartel who in short order brought him to a delivery point where one of his own picked him up and took him to the home of Yaheem al Tayy and Aamir al Tayy.

Yaheem and Aamir did a good job of not arousing any kind of suspicion. As far as their neighbors knew, they were two young students from Yemen attending the University of Arizona with. Both displayed good manners and spoke excellent English. When making the occasional contact with neighbors, they would always smile and engage in polite small talk.

With the arrival of Khaleef, the cell was complete and ready to go operational. One other would be joining them before the initiation of their plan to kill as many American Infidels as possible. It would be an overwhelming attack on the unprotected and unarmed men, women and children at the Southwest Regional Mall.

To the predator Islamic terrorists, America is a target-rich environment of Infidels that must be exterminated! All three of them learned from an early age to hate the non-believers, and they spent their whole lives waiting for the coming moment.

Khaleef and the others would rendezvous with another team of three at the far edge of the west parking lot just prior to the attack. The two teams would split up with Khaleef's team entering from the north entrance of the mall and immediately starting their attack.

The other three-man team would use the west end of the mall for their entrance. Both teams would then systematically work their way toward the center of the mall, joining forces there. Any law enforcement encountered would be neutralized immediately, along with every civilian – man, woman or child. There would be hundreds of casualties on the day of their attack. As they made their way down the concourse, they would also lob grenades into the small stores lining the concourse. Their goal was the complete annihilation of all the American Infidels they could find.

Neither team anticipated any resistance. Upon joining up with each other in the center, all seven of them would then work their way back down the west concourse and, if possible, exit and escape, engaging law enforcement or anyone else as needed. None of them cared if they were killed; in fact, they welcomed death. They looked forward to the pleasure of what they believed would be seventy-two virgins waiting for each of them.

All members of the group with the exception of Khaleef , on multiple occasions, walked through every square foot of the mall concourses. They knew where people would likely run to when the carnage began and where to lob their grenades to inflict the most casualties. They would be thorough in their attack.

Black Friday, the busiest shopping day in America, was upon them. Allah Akbar! God is great!

"It is time, brothers. Allah Akbar!" Khaleef said to his brothers in arms.

They hopped in their SUV after checking everything and securing their gear, since they wouldn't have time once they got to the mall. Khaleef, Yaheemand Aamir each had an AK47 with 12, 30-round magazines. In addition, all carried four grenades. The other team of three men were equipped the same way with the exception of Akman al Hanifia who wore in addition a chest bomb rigged with three pounds of high-intensity explosives. He carried a remote pressure switch in his left pants pocket.

The plan was for Khaleef's group to enter a couple of minutes before the group of three, shooting as many infidels as possible and throwing their grenades into the small shops lining the inside of the mall. It was planned that two to three minutes after Khaleef and his team entered the north entrance the other team would do the same at the west entrance. As they made their way to the center of the mall, they would set up a killing field of fire as they went. No man, woman or child would be allowed to live. Any law enforcement they encountered would be their first target.

They knew it was possible a SWAT team would arrive before they had time to exit the carnage. Allah willing, Akman would rush them, blowing himself up and causing complete confusion and chaos, allowing the rest to fight their way out and back to their vehicles. They would not be taken alive, and it was their desire to be killed in the name of Allah.

Black Friday, 2:35 p.m.

It was an early and cold November Saturday morning as Carter and Paul worked their way through the trees and bushes with their guns at the ready. Carter motioned to Paul that something was moving ahead and to the right. Suddenly they both heard multiple weapons firing; Carter threw himself to the ground in a prone position, while Paul, still standing, shot back. Carter, looking down the sights on his rifle, started firing in the direction of the three individuals shooting at them while straining to get a better view.

"I'm hit," Paul screamed, falling to the ground and going limp.

Carter could hear a voice in the distance yell, "I got 'em." Carter kept firing until he was out of ammo, he quickly reached into his pocket and reached for another roll of caps and loaded his gun. He heard Randy call out to him, "I got you, you're dead!"

"No, you didn't!" Carter yelled back.

...

Driving to the mall, the cool air of late fall had somehow taken Carter Thompson back to his childhood and that little patch of forest near the lake in Evanston, Illinois. He reached over and turned down the volume on the radio a bit and, with a smile on his face, let his mind drift back to that early time in his life. It was no more than an acre but it was the sanctuary where Carter and his friends could play U.S. Marines versus Japs or U.S. Army versus Nazis. All their fathers served in WWII and either fought the Japanese in the South Pacific or the Germans in Europe. Carter's father had been a Marine and spent three-and-a-half years island hopping in the South Pacific.

Each of the kids, when winning the coin toss as to who's going to fight for the United States, always chose whatever branch his father served in. Carter and his friends had grown up hearing stories of the war, especially when their fathers had been drinking.

Carter Thompson, now sixty-four years of age, was a fit man who worked out on a regular basis. Most people were surprised to learn of his age, thinking he was a least ten years younger. Even though Carter lived in an age of lawyers and written contracts, to him a handshake was better than anything on a piece of paper to let you know a person's real character. He kept his agreements, and if he was unable to do so, he would communicate it ahead of time. Coming out of his childhood memories as he drove on, he turned up the volume again on the radio.

"Hello, America, this is Peter Collingham, and I'm here to tell you as a country we're in serious trouble. Our government, led by the corrupt cesspool of the Washington cartel, is growing and expanding and we're losing our rights; the rights our Founding Fathers gave us in the Bill of Rights and the Constitution. The government's number-one job is to keep the citizens of this great country safe which includes securing the damn border from the obvious threats coming across. Our safety, culture and way of life are quickly disappearing before our eyes. Build a wall, put drones overhead or troops on the border. I don't care, secure the damn border!

We have a Congress and President who are ignoring the oath they swore when they took office to protect us, the citizens, from enemies both foreign and domestic. The fact is they don't do that and only enforce the laws that would be beneficial to their personal agendas while ignoring other laws. Our borders, especially the southern one is not secure. I'm not just talking about illegal Mexicans, Central and South Americans coming in; we have Hamas, ISIS, Iranians, Hezbollah, MS13 and you-fill-in-the-blank slithering through our border along with anyone else that wants to bum rush us. Hell, our government can't even do the simple task of securing our cities. Chicago alone is projected to have five hundred seventy murders this year, a city that has some of the most restrictive gun-control laws in the country.

This is a disgusting disgrace, my friends, and we shouldn't stand for it. I tell you right now; the government is never going to do its job. I've had enough, and I say it's time for you, me and every law-abiding citizen to stand up and do what our government refuses to do – go secure the border and clean up the trash in this country…
enough is enough!"

Carter regularly listened to the Peter Collingham show whenever he could; he's one of the top radio talk-show hosts in America with a following of thirty-two million listeners. Carter appreciated his gloves-off approach to telling the truth about the condition of the country and the outright corruption and lack of leadership in Washington, D.C. Carter, like millions of Americans, was frustrated and at a boiling point from watching the destruction of the country by the enemy from within.

Taking in a deep breath, Carter turned down the volume again as he negotiated his way through the heavy traffic; it was the day after Thanksgiving, Black Friday.

This was his favorite time of the year. Even though he hated going to the mall, there was a book that had just been released he wanted. He figured he'd just run in to the bookstore, buy the book and leave, avoiding the masses of shoppers sure to be there. It was midafternoon, and he hoped he wouldn't have any trouble getting a copy of the book.

With one hand on the wheel, Carter's right hand went to his side, double checking the safety on his Sig 226 X-5. He'd put over ten thousand rounds through the gun, all in training. It had an eighteen-round magazine of +P 9mm hollow points, a short reset trigger and was extremely accurate. Carter felt a high degree of confidence in his choice, along with his gunfighting skills which he invested in the last six years. Carter normally didn't carry the 226 X-5, but because he was going to a mall on Black Friday, it was his side arm of choice, along with an extra eighteen-round magazine on his left side.

2:38 p.m.

As Carter turned right at the light onto the road parallel to the mall, he was not surprised at how backed-up the traffic was. After turning and driving a couple of hundred yards, he turned left into the mall parking lot. Seeing the parking lot was full in all directions, he wondered how long it was going to take him to find a parking spot. Turning down the third row he stopped and waited as a family of four got into their car and left; then he rolled into their vacated spot.

He turned off his car, took a deep breath, opened the door and stepped out, double-checking the safety on his side arm with his right hand while confirming that the extra magazine on his left side was secured. It was chilly enough to warrant wearing a tan utility shirt over his polo shirt. This also aided in concealing his pistol which was secured in an inside-the-waistband holster. As had become a habit, he scanned left, right, behind and straight ahead as he made his way toward the entrance of the bookstore on the east side of the mall.

2:46 p.m.

Carter approached the two large doors going into the popular bookstore, pausing as a woman inside pushed one of the doors open with three people following behind her on their way out of the store. Carter then stepped forward grabbing one of the two large doors to let another woman with two children out before going inside.

Five-feet into the expansive and open interior space of the store, Carter stopped for a moment, smelling and appreciating the scent of all those books. He loved bookstores and especially this one. Its hard wood floors, multiple overhead fluorescence lights, endless racks of books and double set of stairs going up to the second level gave it the feel of an old public or university library. He looked ahead at the many tables with books arranged with different genres on either side of the center aisle. Each book on those tables had a sticker on its cover declaring, "price reduced." Continuing on, he was reminded of an obstacle course, only this one was littered with shoppers moving about in a chaotic manner. He assumed they, like him, were on the hunt for a book, magazine or maybe a gift idea for the coming holidays. He could only imagine what it was like further inside the bowels of the mall. Surprisingly, in spite all this chaos, he found himself happy to be there. The holidays were his favorite time of the year.

In the center of the store was an information counter. He decided to take advantage of it to save time to find the recently released book he sought. Standing at a distance, he watched as three female clerks hurriedly moved from one customer to the next. The four-foot-high U-shaped counter with neatly arranged poinsettias on the ends and middle was completely surrounded by customers, two rows deep. Upon seeing this, he opted to forge ahead on his own, find the book, pay for it and get the hell out of there and away from this frenzied spectacle.

As he made his way, he could feel the energy of all the holiday shoppers and the buzz you would expect with a horde of people milling around the different aisles of books.

It didn't take him long to find what he was looking for. He knew it wouldn't be out in paperback yet and besides, he'd rather have the hard-copy edition anyway. Once securing the book in his clutches, he decided to mill around himself to see if there were any other books of interest.

After spending ten minutes on the lower level, Carter made his way up the flight of stairs to the second level. As he arrived at the top of the stairs he went to the right, putting his hands on the banister as he looked down for a moment, marveling at all the people milling around below.

Since childhood he'd had always been drawn to anything that dealt with World War II; the ships, the aircraft and the men and women who served and fought in it. He'd always been a bit awestruck by the courage of these men and women who fought for the world's freedom from tyranny and the oppression Hitler's Nazi Germany and Emperor Hirohito's Japan represented.

He thought for a moment of the contrast in times, then versus now. A year before his father's death, his father made the comment that if he and his brothers knew how things would change in Washington, D.C., there would have been no point for them to have sacrificed so much. Carter thought about his father's comment and understood the truth in it.

Given the level of corruption in Washington now versus then, really, what would have been the point? Carter thought to himself.

Making his way to the World War II section, Carter opened a couple of the books, thinking about his father and how much he missed him and just being able to call him. He recognized that anything having to do with World War II and especially the war in the South Pacific flooded him with memories of his father. After a few minutes, he made his way back down the stairs and into the throng of people below.

After paying for the book, Carter walked over to the coffee shop located in the store. He stood in line for five minutes and then ordered a large iced tea. Looking around, he couldn't find a place to sit, so with drink in right hand and book in left, he casually made his way through the bookstore, heading in the direction of the large opening leading to the center of the inside of the mall.

He stopped in the cooking section, putting his drink and book aside, and briefly opened a book on Cajun cooking. Even though he'd always vowed never to set foot in a mall on Black Friday, he found himself being pulled in the direction of the opening into the mall and the buzz of all those shoppers. As he did so, he finished his iced tea, chucking the cup into a trash can. It amazed him how crowded and busy it was, but then again it was Black Friday.

"So this is what it's like," he said quietly.

Standing in the large opening of the bookstore, leading out to the center of the inside of the mall, Carter took a step forward. Suddenly, in the distance down the concourse to his right, he heard the staccato sound of machine-gunfire, screams and then two muffled explosions. His right hand went under his jacket to his pistol as he stepped back and to the right, leaning up against the door frame while quickly looking out in the direction of the noise.

3:02 p.m.
Purple with Rhinestones

Col. Doug Redman had been home just five days after completing a six-month contract with Spec Force Response, Inc., running security operations in the Helmand province of Afghanistan. It had been his fifth trip over there. His first three tours had been deployments while he was active duty Delta Force. Two years before that, after having put in twenty-five years serving his country with honor and distinction, he retired. It was now time to spend more time with his family. Even though he'd be gone six months at a stretch working for a private contractor, it beat being gone eleven out of the twelve months of the year with the military. Besides, he could make more money working for a private contractor in six months than he could in two years with the military.

Just prior to the launch of Operation Iraqi Freedom, he led a covert mission with a six-man squad. Upon reaching the outskirts of Bagdad at dawn, a young Iraqi girl discovered them moving between the banks of a narrow stream bed. She stood on the bank looking down on the six of them. Colonel Redman and his men had a choice: to allow their mission to be compromised or silence the little girl. Without hesitation, he ordered his men to dump all non-essential gear and head to their alternate extraction point. Just as he finished issuing his orders, she ran the other way, screaming for her father. While the decision to let her live jeopardized the life of his squad, it was the right thing to do. He represented the best of our American fighting men and women that morning.

He was happy and felt good to be home for the holidays and was thinking about how blessed he was as he and his family pulled into the north parking lot of the mall. There was a 4:20 p.m. movie with the latest edition of yet another superhero movie, and he'd promised his wife Liz and two children; thirteen-year-old blond haired daughter Kellie and his tall and lanky fifteen-year-old son Colt, he would take them. Frankly, he was looking forward to it and the family time. He drove in and out of the parking aisles for only five minutes when he spotted a car with its backup lights on. As soon as the car started to drive away, Doug quickly maneuvered the car into the space before any of the other cars had a chance.

Doug and his family walked to the north entrance of the mall. He opened the door and held it for his wife and kids, along with two elderly women and another family.

Wow, was all he could think, seeing all the people. Young teenagers were running and hollering, and along with the other noises of the mall echoing off the hard floor and glass front of the stores lining the concourse, the noise was loud. Looking at his wife, Liz, he smiled and said, "Madhouse!"

He'd never been in a mall during this time of year and was surprised by the hundreds of people moving about. Remembering it was the day after Thanksgiving he thought to himself, *this is the way it's supposed to be; it was after all the busiest shopping day of year.*

They made their way to the entrance of the theater and over to the ticket line. Surprisingly, the line was short for the movie they wanted. Since they had little more than an hour before the start, they decided to go back out to the main concourse and made their way toward the center of the mall. Along the way they passed multiple kiosks with people around them waiting to be sold this, that and the other thing. All of the kiosks seem to be doing a brisk business.

As they made their way deeper into the mall, Doug could see an end to the long line of kiosks. There was a cell-phone carrier at the very end of the row of retail stands in front of the bookstore entrance.

His daughter, Kellie, tugged at his sleeve, "Daddy, can we look at the cell phones real quick?" Doug was about to protest, using the movie as an excuse, when Liz gave him a smile and a wink, which his daughter saw. He smiled at his daughter with a look of surrender. They still had about an hour before the movie begun. He could feel a surge of *time to spoil the princess* coming on.

There were a number of people milling around the kiosk, and he could see there were three salespeople busy helping the customers. *Smart on this company's part*, Doug thought, *they must have brought in reinforcements for Black Friday*. All the phones, all the plans made him want to buy a new phone for himself. To his son, it was a boring affair and he lazily tagged along.

After about five minutes, a young woman in her early twenties asked them if they would like to look at any of the phones. Kellie, never known to be a quiet young lady and seeing the possibility of getting her first cell phone, instantly spoke up and said, "yes!" She grabbed her father's hand and moved to the other side of the kiosk. Doug gave a quick look to Liz as he was tugged along by his daughter to the other side. Liz and his son followed.

Doug stood back a few feet as the young saleswoman showed Kellie the different cell phones. He watched as Kellie held onto the purple one with rhinestones surrounding the edge of the screen. While the clerk was explaining it to his daughter, his wife gave him a nudge of, *let's get it for her*. He smiled and nodded his head *yes*.

"Is this the one you want?" he asked his daughter.

Kellie looked at him and gave him a big hug, saying, "Yes, yes, thank you, thank you, Daddy!"

"I'll take the second one you just showed us," he said as he pulled the credit card out of his wallet, handing it to the saleswoman. His eyes misted up just a bit as he stood there looking at his family and seeing his daughter smile. Liz, catching the moment, smiled at him as Doug looked over to Colt, who rolled his eyeballs and mouthed the words, "Let's go!"

Just as the young woman reached out to hand Doug his receipt, there was a smacking sound and the left side of her head exploded, spaying a red mist and brain matter on a young man and girl walking by. He could hear the all-too-familiar staccato sound of AK47s from down the concourse and what sounded like two grenade explosions and people screaming.

"Get down!" he yelled to his wife and kids, grabbing the three of them and pushing them down behind the kiosk.

Six-minutes earlier

Khaleef and the others were silent as they turned into the parking lot of the mall, making their way to the far west side. Akman and the other two members of his murderous team were waiting for them, sitting in their vehicle with the engine running. As Khaleef's car slowly passed Akman, the two men gave each other a nod. Khaleef then made his way to the north parking lot. It was understood by Akman's team that they were to wait until they got a call from Khaleef to proceed as planned. They would then pull up to the curb and exit their vehicle, shooting infidels as they made their way through the doors leading to the large concourse of the mall. It was also understood that if, after eye contact, they hadn't heard from Khaleef within ten minutes, they were to proceed as planned and start their murderous rampage.

When they were one hundred feet from stopping in front of the north entrance Khaleef called Akman's phone. As soon as he answered they both spoke the words, "Allah Akbar" and hung up.

Coming to a halt, the four members of Khaleef's team hurriedly leaped from the car and began shooting infidels at will. In less than thirty seconds, they were at the entrance and through the doors. Stunned shoppers looked at them in horror. A smile came across Khaleef's face as he noticed the "No Firearms Allowed" sign on one of the doors.

Two of the county sheriff deputies who were on holiday duty realized what was happening at the north entrance to the mall and ran toward the developing carnage. One sheriff managed to get off three shots from one hundred feet away, hitting one of the terrorists before he was cut down by Khaleef. He and his group had the advantage of surprise, overwhelming force and fire power. The deputies were no match for them. The second deputy ducked behind a kiosk, radioing for help and giving a quick report on what was happening. He didn't see the terrorist coming from the right side of the kiosk and putting the barrel of his AK47 two-inches away from his head and squeezing the trigger.

Khaleef and his group, while working their way down the concourse, occasionally threw hand grenades deep into the interior of the small shops lining the concourse. The screams were horrific and the floors on both side and the center of the walkway were quickly being turned to crimson. A woman and her two children jumped up from behind one of the kiosks and started running down the concourse toward the bookstore at the end of the concourse, only to have Yaheem rip them apart with his AK47. Almost instantly the mother and one of the children fell to the hard concrete floor as the little girl, screaming, kept running. Yaheem took aim and hit her squarely in the back of the head.

Over at the west entrance, the same horrifying events were also unfolding. Akman and his two men were making their way down the concourse engaging in the same killing spree he knew Khaleef and his men were doing. The gun shots, explosions and screaming were deafening. On the west concourse, Akman encountered a sheriff who was quickly dispatched by him. As he passed the sheriff's quivering body, he grabbed the sheriff's radio, putting it in his pack. It could come in useful later.

3:12 p.m.

Carter listened again, turning his head in the direction of the noise, and again he heard what sounded like automatic gunfire. He wanted to dismiss that idea, but once more the unmistakable sound of it came in great volleys, and the distant screaming and yelling wasn't stopping. Then he heard two more muffled explosions. He pushed down on his Sig's pistol grip, putting pressure on it to make sure it was firmly in the holster. The last six years of weapons training started to kick in as he pressed himself against the right door jamb of the bookstore. He stuck his head out, taking a quick peek to the right and down the walkway. What he saw confirmed his fears.

While doing so he could feel the rush of air and hear people in the bookstore running to the entrance to see what was going on. He could see and hear the whine of bullets ricocheting off the floor and walls. There was constant gunfire and more explosions. Looking to his left at the gathering crowd he saw a young teenage girl flinch and scream as blood started seeping through her white blouse near the center of her stomach. Instinctively knowing it was more important for him to confront the threat, he turned back around and to the right. As he did so, in front of him and to the right, about twenty feet away on a forty-five-degree angle Carter noticed a man, woman and two teenage age kids huddling down and taking cover behind the kiosk. On the end of the kiosk and to the right of them, he could see a young woman lying face down in a pool of blood forming around her head.

Carter turned to the other people beginning to crowd the large opening and yelled at them to get back and get out of the building, heading to the east. He pondered for a moment if he should take charge of the group and herd them out, when the intensity of the gunfire got louder, moving closer to his position. It would be the safe thing for him to do, and he would have a good reason as to why he didn't confront the killers.

Many in the large group in the doorway started retreating back into the store as Carter turned back to his right and the sound of approaching gunfire. As he looked out, he put his attention back on the family off to his right. He watched as he saw the man reach up and grab a couple of cell phones, turning to the woman Carter assumed was his wife and telling her and the two kids something. He then saw pieces of the kiosk, displays and phones go flying, as rounds from the terrorists' AK ripped into it. He next saw the woman flinch and grab her left arm.

Carter did another quick chicken-head peek to the right and down the concourse, only this time he drew his weapon and had it in a close, high-ready position against his chest. He suddenly found himself confused, shaking and frozen in position while looking out at the family and realizing the terrorist was going after them.

He could see the source of the close gunfire; one of the terrorists was walking toward them while firing his AK47 into the kiosk. Right then, Carter just wanted to run the other direction; but wasn't this the reason he'd been training for the last six years? In case something like this happened?

"Hey, you've got a gun … do something, stop standing there! Help that family, they're about to be killed!"

Carter felt someone shaking his left shoulder and shoving him hard into the door jamb. In the confusion, he looked to his left and down. An elderly woman with pulled-back gray hair and a heavily wrinkled face, no more than five tall, was saying something to him and hitting him on his left shoulder.

Carter looking down at her and could see her lips moving, but he couldn't make out what she was saying.

"What?"

"*Do something!*" She yelled, pointing at the handgun he was holding tightly against his chest.

The woman's voice and the intensity of her command was like a splash of cold water to Carter. He looked at his Sig, back at her, out at the doomed family and the approaching terrorist. He suddenly found himself enraged at what was happening in the mall; they were under attack and there was no doubt in his mind who these terrorists were and why they were there.

3:13 p.m.

Doug was all too familiar with the sounds of automatic AK47 gunfire and grenades going off. He did a quick peek to his left to see how close the terrorists were; one was only about one hundred feet away. It was obvious they were moving in his direction, killing along the way. Doug could feel and hear rounds hitting the kiosk and saw some bouncing off the concrete floor. For now, the rounds weren't going all the way through the kiosk; additional phones and accessories stored inside the kiosk were acting as a barrier and stopping them. Suddenly Doug heard Khaleef's weapon stop firing; he had paused to do a quick magazine change.

Doug took another quick peek and saw Khaleef, now only forty feet away, lock eyes with him just as he finished reloading and charging his weapon. As a rule, when out with his family he didn't carry a weapon, a decision as the chaos was unfolding he cursed himself for. Behind him and to the right, twenty feet away, he could see the large entrance of the bookstore. The terrorist's rounds again started, hitting the kiosk and some were going all the way through. As he turned to Liz, a round exploded through the supply door, hitting her in the upper-left shoulder and knocking her back off balance. Doug grabbed Liz's right hand to pull her back up.

He said, "I'm going to go for it. When I do, I want you and the kids to run into the bookstore and out through the east door."

Though she was in shock and pain, she grabbed her son's and daughter's hands, looked at her husband and said, "I love you."

"I love all of you. I promise we'll get through this!" Doug said.

He knew from his many years as a Delta Force operator that it was better to do something than nothing. He also knew any kind of a distraction you could give a bad guy could buy you a moment in time to close in on him. A human being can't look up at something flying in the air above him and shoot a gun at the same time ... can't happen!

Doug reached up, grabbing a couple of cell phones from the open display. He lurched forward, throwing them up in the air in the direction of Khaleef. He knew if he got his hands on him he'd prevail. Just as he jumped up and to the left in the direction of terrorist, he heard two shots to the right behind him and then one more. A tight, two-shot group of holes appeared at the base of the front of the neck and then one just to the right of the bridge of the terrorist's nose as Doug watched him crumple to the ground. Doug then looked to the right behind him and saw a man about his size and stature moving in his direction with handgun up and eyes forward, looking for more threats.

Out of the corner of his eye and with great relief, he saw his wife and two children run through the opening to the bookstore and on to what he hoped was safety. Whoever this man was, Doug thanked God he showed up when he did. Continuing his already forward momentum, he hurriedly crouched down over the convulsing Khaleef and relieved him of his AK47 along with multiple loaded magazines.

Khaleef looked up at him as if he had a question.

"Fuck you!" Doug quietly said, watching the terrorist looking at him, gurgling and with the life going out of him. He felt the presence of somebody come up beside him.

Moving Out!

Carter had moved to Doug's right side, going to a combat kneeling position while scanning ahead for more threats. After many years of close quarters combat training, everything he was doing was a function of muscle memory. He watched how the man he'd just saved was moving. *He's got to be military,* Carter thought to himself. This was confirmed as he watched Doug grab the AK47, yank open the magazine's pouches and take a handful of them. Doug then grabbed Carter and moved them both back behind the kiosk. They looked at each other. Hearing the continued gunfire, explosions and screaming, without saying a word, it was understood; they were brothers in arms and had a job to do.

Carter looked at Doug. "What do you say we go kill some more of these motherfuckers and put an end to this?!"

"Roger that!"

Doug said looking him straight in the eyes.

"Lead the way; I'll follow."

Carter said, looking at Doug.

The repeated gunfire was getting closer and coming from their front left. Carter watched Doug raise his left hand and with his index and middle finger pointed at his eyes and then left down the concourse, giving him the message to take a look around the right corner of the kiosk while he did the same on the left side. Hearing continued approaching gunfire, his quick peek revealed another terrorist from a distance pointing at Khaleef's now lifeless body and moving in their direction.

He reached over to Doug, tapping his shoulder, holding up one finger and pointing off to the right on a forty-five-degree angle. Doug, having seen another terrorist who was one hundred feet away and looking the other way, came over to Carter's side of the kiosk. Carter gave ground to him, allowing Doug to lead with the AK47.

Doug whispered, "On the count of three, we move out." Carter nodded.

Carter leaned into Doug, feeling him reach back to give a squeeze on his arm. He gave him a squeeze back, and they were off moving forward. The two of them quickly aerated the terrorist closest to them; four rounds from the AK47 and three from Carters handgun.

They both went to a combat kneeling position, looking up and scanning for more threats; in the distance the sound of muffled gun shots found its way to them. Straight ahead and far down the concourse, Carter spotted what looked like one of the terrorists turning into the theater entrance.

3:18 p.m.

Within the first few minutes of the carnage at the mall, Pima County's 911 call center was flooded with a chorus of "911, what is your emergency?, 911, what is your emergency?, 911, what is your emergency?" It was all that could be heard in the basement of Tucson Police Department headquarters, where the emergency-call center was located. It was a typical government-run work space, with individual cubicles occupied by ten operators handling the cacophony of the hundreds of calls coming in.

Within two minutes of the first call, the supervisor at the call center notified the Pima County Emergency Response Team. This team is made up of fire rescue units and the Pima County Regional SWAT Team which includes law enforcement officers from the different jurisdictions in the county. Included in this group is the sheriff's office which also was the primary law-enforcement agency responsible for the regional mall.

Historically, the quickest any SWAT team can deploy and be on scene is fifty minutes on average, and today would be no exception. The inside of the Southwest Regional Mall had become a killing field for the Muslim terrorists.

3:19 p.m.

Bounding and leapfrogging forward, Doug and Carter advanced to the center of the mall. They knew they had to get to the theater and do as much as they could to stop any further carnage from happening. As they crossed the center, to their left they could hear multiple gunshots and another couple of muffled explosions. The familiar sound of a bullet buzzed by Doug's head, followed by the sound of a gunshot. He tapped Carter on his left shoulder and point at a large fountain located in the middle of the concourse. Both of them bolted to their right, with Carter behind Doug, sliding behind the retaining wall of the fountain.

Doug exclaimed, "Holy fuck, they're more of these assholes to our left. I also saw one of them go into the theater straight ahead of us. How many rounds do you have left?"

He watched Carter raise his handgun, pointing the muzzle up while simultaneously pushing the magazine release button and grabbing the bottom of the magazine, pulling it out and looking at the round count holes on the side. With the magazine between his left index and middle fingers, Carter reached to his left side pulling out his other fully loaded magazine and slammed it into the gun. He then put the partially used magazine on his left side.

"I've got around ten rounds left in my mag on my side and eighteen in the mag in my gun with one up the pipe. How many mags do you have left for the AK?" asked Carter.

"Not sure how many are left in the mag in the gun. I grabbed three mags off the dead asshole," Doug explained. He did a chicken head-peak, looking down the concourse leading to the west. He pulled the partially spent magazine out of the AK47 and slapped a full one back in. He then looked around and shook his head, seeing the dozens of bodies on the ground, some lifeless, some crying out, some trying to crawl or get up and away from the madness.

Both could hear gunshots down the west concourse; Doug assumed by the muffled sounds that the terrorists had moved inside the stores lining the concourse.

"What do you want to do?" Carter asked, while looking down the north concourse.

"Let's make our way down to the theater entrance. The people inside the theaters are trapped. I think it's up to you and me, brother. I'm afraid we're on our own. Standard protocol is the police or sheriff deputies aren't going to enter the mall until the SWAT team arrives. This is happening way too fast," Doug said, nodding his head in the direction of the theater.

"By the way, what's your name? I'm Doug."

"Carter."

"Well Carter what you say we go kill some more of those goatfuckers?"

Pain is Good;
It Lets You Know You're Alive

Carter thought for a moment about what Doug just said. This was clearly a highly skilled individual who knew about this sort of thing. Carter knew he was right. At least for now they were indeed on their own. He thought about the old woman who pushed him into action and wondered if she'd made it out all right. *Isn't this the sort of thing my friends and I have been taking time to train for over the last six years*? Carter thought to himself.

He thought about the first terrorist he'd shot and killed. He'd sat out the Vietnam War, was never in the military and thus never in combat. He always hoped, though, if he found himself in a position like today, he wouldn't hesitate. After the freeze-up in the doorway and the old woman yelling and hitting him, the training he'd been through kicked in without him thinking about it. Again he thought back to the asshole he'd dispatched.

Smiling he thought to himself, *fuck him and the horse he rode in on!*

Carter felt a surge of rage and disgust come over him. Looking Doug straight in the eye, he said; "Fuck these motherfucking, cock sucking terrorist assholes, let's do it! I'll follow you; I've got your back."

"Roger that," Doug said. "OK, we're going to move from kiosk to kiosk; you be checking your right, and I've got left. Let's do it!" Carter looked down the north concourse and could see the sprawled-out bodies ahead of them and hear the cries and moaning.

As they got up, Doug took another look down the west concourse and Carter looked straight ahead down the

50

north concourse, and then they began moving in the direction of the theater. About half the distance down the concourse they stopped behind a kiosk and Carter looked behind them.

"Rear clear," Carter said, and they started moving forward again. Just then, two of the terrorists came out of the entrance to the theater. Carter could see their attention was on Doug, and he watched as they started to shoot at him. Carter went to a combat kneeling position and returned fire, hitting the one on the left. Out of the corner of his eye, he could see Doug advance to the next kiosk, engaging both of the terrorists and hitting the one on the right. Carter moved forward to the next piece of cover ahead and to the right of Doug.

Just as he arrived at his new position, he heard Doug call out, "Reloading!"

Carter yelled back, "Cover," and started to re-engage the two gunmen, only this time the one on the right was face down. He could see the remaining one on the left fumbling for something in his chest rig.

He heard Doug shout, "Up!" as he started pumping rounds in the direction of the remaining terrorist. Just as quickly as he started, the slide on his Sig locked back indicating a last round fired or a malfunction. "Reloading!" Carter yelled out as he simultaneously performed a function check. Slap, rack and he was back in business, having cleared a stuck shell casing.

"Up!" Carter shouted out.

Just as Carter completed the task, he heard Doug shout, "moving," and then a sharp and loud explosion. He instantly felt multiple strikes on his left leg, left shoulder and the left side of his neck. It felt like an electric shock, followed by the sensation of a lit match being pressed into his skin where he was hit.

"I'm hit!" he called out to Doug as he watched Doug lurch forward to what was left of the now-armless asshole that had been reaching into his vest. Carter had hit him in the forehead with his last shot a split second after the terrorist pulled the pin on his last grenade.

He watched Doug do a quick three-sixty scan and then move back to him.

"Where are you hit?"

Carter showed him. As he watched and felt Doug hastily examined each wound. He looked down at his left pant leg which was now becoming a reddish dark brown where the small pieces of shrapnel had torn into his flesh. Feeling warm blood running down the left side of his neck he reached up with his left hand and could feel the wound entrance. He then became aware of a stinging sensation in his left shoulder.

"I think we're clear here; all the tangos are down in our immediate area but we've got more to deal with in the other direction. Are you good?" Carter heard Doug say to him.

"Fuck, yes, I'm good! Plenty of fight left in this old dog!" Carter said, assuring Doug he wasn't out of the fight.

Both men knew without saying it, that wounded or not, they had to stay in the fight until it was over. Looking at Doug, Carter gave him a nod n' a thumbs up.

Doug smiled at him, "Hey, pain is good; lets you know you're alive!"

Carter laughed, "True, that!"

It's funny how random thoughts can float up in the middle of a life-threatening event. About five years prior to this, Carter had been at a grocery store doing his weekly shopping. There was a tall, attractive woman whom he'd noticed looking at him, and of course he'd returned the glance. Outside in the parking lot while he has loading his groceries into his Ford Expedition, the woman pulled up in her car. On the back on the glass of his vehicle was a sticker of the name of a company in the firearms industry by the name of "Tango Down." Stopping, she lowered her window and told him she loves to tango and asked him if "Tango Down" was some kind of new dance she wasn't familiar with. Recognizing her innocence, Carter looked at her and then the sticker. He explained to her that he didn't know how to tango and the term "tango down" was a term used when an enemy combatant has been shot and killed. She looked him, her jaw dropped a bit, and she said, "Oh." Then she rolled up her window and drove away. He couldn't help but smile, thinking about that encounter. "Tango down" was one of those terms he always liked hearing for some reason, and now it had a whole new meaning for him.

Smiling, Carter looked at Doug with a nod and said, "I'm good to go; let's go get some!" They both did a quick, three-sixty scan and started moving back in the direction they came from. As Carter started to move he felt a sharp pain in his left leg. *Fuck it!* he thought.

Carter quietly called to Doug, "I've got rear." Looking and scanning as they went, they moved forward, negotiating the littered carnage and kiosks in the concourse on their way back to the middle. From the continued muffled gun shots down the center concourse to their right, they knew there would be more threats to deal with. There were people lying on the ground. Most were motionless, with just a few moaning and moving an arm or leg every now and then. More than once they slipped in the blood on the floor. To Carter, in some spots it felt like they were walking through oil.

Carter watched Doug drop down behind the second to the last kiosk before reaching the center.

"We should call 911 and let the cops know we're in here, what we look like and bring them up to speed on what's happening. I'm concerned they could come charging in, see us and shoot us!" Doug said.

As Doug pulled out his cell phone to call 911, Carter could hear muffled gun shots, though fewer in frequency than before. He could think the only reason for this was that the terrorists had killed most of the victims in the west concourse.

3:24 p.m.

Twelve-minutes had passed since the attack began, and the calls coming into the emergency response center hadn't slowed down. Dolores, a middle-aged, overweight, single mother of three and a seventeen-year veteran with the emergency call center, right-clicked the mouse on the "answer" icon on her computer display.

"911, what is your emergency?" Dolores asked, adjusting her headset and knowing this would probably be another call reporting on what was happening at the mall. Her standard response would be, "Thank you for calling, we have emergency units responding." From there, like the other operators, she would move on and continue to sort out the calls in a methodical manner.

"My name is Doug Redmond. I'm retired Special Forces colonel in the Army and a former Delta Force commander.

"What is the emergency you're reporting, sir?" Dolores smoothly and mechanically said. She wondered... *Why is some retired military guy calling in the middle of all this?* "I'm in the Southwest Regional Mall with one other man by the name of... Carter, what's your last name?"

"Thompson."

She listened as he directed his speaking back to her. "I'm with another man by the name of Carter Thompson. We're both armed and have killed three of the terrorists. Tell your emergency responders the north concourse is clear and to get help in here right away. There are multiple wounded and dead, I repeat there are multiple wounded and dead!"

Even though she was a well-seasoned emergency operator, Dolores was stunned to hear what was being reported to her.

"Whoa! Wait a minute did you say you're inside the mall with another man in a gunfight with terrorists?"

"Yes, that's exactly what I'm telling you."

She told Doug to hold on, muted her phone jack and called out to get the attention of her supervisor. She could see he was looking down at a computer screen and didn't acknowledge her. It was noisier than usual in the call center. Skipping all protocol, she went with her gut instincts, put both her little fingers in her mouth and let out two loud high pitched whistles. When she saw her supervisor look in her direction she waved her hand motioning him over to her.

"Stand by," she told Doug.

"Ma'am, I haven't got time to hold on. Let your SWAT commander know we're in here. I'm six-feet-two inches, two-hundred-fifteen pounds, wearing a light tan jacket, a navy-blue polo shirt and khaki colored pants." Doug paused looking at Carter. "Carter looks like about the same height and weight as me, and he's wearing a long-sleeved tan shirt, black polo shirt and also has on khaki colored pants. We're moving to the west concourse; there's more threats down there... Tell your commander to deploy his SWAT team through the bookstore to the east and another team from the west... *and don't shoot us*! Did you copy all of that?" Doug said in a concerned yet commanding voice.

Dolores could hear the muted sound of automatic gunfire in the background as she came back to him; "Yes, I did, just a sec." The line went dead.

No Time to Wait

Carter knew the average response time for a SWAT team to assemble and get on scene is about fifty minutes. To his knowledge, rarely, if ever, had there been a time when a SWAT team stopped an active shooter or shooters. That was usually the result of either an armed citizen or patrol officers arriving on the scene – they would fill that role. In an event like this, the patrol officers have standing orders to wait for the SWAT team to arrive; in the meantime, the killing continues. The carnage at Columbine High School was a classic example of this.

As they were about to move right and down the west concourse, Carter noticed up and to the left at the entrance to the bookstore there were two deputies, one with a rifle, poking their heads out and looking in the direction of the gunfire. Carter tapped Doug's shoulder and pointed in the deputies' direction. Doug leaned a little bit out from the kiosk, not wanting to startle the two deputies, and gave a quick whistle to get their attention.

3:26 p.m.

Bill Dudley, an eighteen-year veteran with the sheriff's department, heard Doug's whistle and looked over in his direction. Deputy Dudley could see Doug raising his hand motioning them to come over to his position. The deputy, who was also a field training officer, nudged his young partner, Joe Mahoney, who recently graduated from the sheriff's academy. Dudley pointed in the direction of Doug and Carter.

The two of them were the first patrol officers on the scene, having arrived just three minutes after the first 911 calls came in. Just as they pulled up on the east side of the mall in front of the bookstore, a woman with blood on her left arm with a boy and a girl in tow came rushing out of the front door. She ran up to the two officers and was at their car before they could get out. They expected that the woman would be hysterical; however, Liz Redman was not. Though she was in obvious pain, holding her bloody left arm, she started explaining to the senior officer what was unfolding inside as best she could. She gave a detailed description of her husband and a general one about the man who'd saved their lives.

Liz understood police protocol, having served with the Albuquerque Police Department for three years before meeting Doug. She'd left the department to be with her soon-to-be husband and began living the life of an Army wife, moving from base to base and raising a family in the process. She knew her husband, being a career officer in the Army and a Delta Force commander, would be gone for long stretches at a time. He rarely said where he was going or what he was doing.

Liz understood this and never pried. After the attack on 9/11, Doug and his unit deployed to Afghanistan two weeks. For the following ten years he was deployed and gone seventy percent of the time. More than once he came back wounded, only to heal up and head out again. She knew he was a warrior and a patriot, believing in what he was doing for his country, family and the men to the left and right of him on the battlefield. She would always be there for him when he came home and prayed every night he would do so safely. Now that he was a civilian and after all of those years of sacrifice, she was not about to lose him.

As Liz brought the two officers up to speed, various emergency units continued to arrive on scene. She explained to them how she had been shot and that a man from the inside the doorway to the bookstore killed one of the terrorists with his handgun, saving not only her and her children's lives but also her husband's. She had looked back as she ran with her children to safety to see her husband bending over the dead terrorist with the stranger kneeling beside him. She again described what her husband was wearing, height, et cetera and, as best as she could recall, the details of the man last seen with her husband.

Both Bill and Joe served in the military. Bill was in the Army and seen action in Bosnia as well as the first Gulf War. Joe, a reserve combat Marine, had done five tours between Iraq and Afghanistan. It was in both men's nature to act by running towards trouble, and there was plenty of it waiting for them inside the mall.

Protocol Be Damned!

Deputy Dudley knew the standing orders were to wait for the SWAT team. However, he also knew there were two men inside taking on the terrorists by themselves; and that they could use their help and probably needed it quickly. He only hoped they were both still alive. *Fuck the protocol! The worst thing that could happen is we'll both get a letter of reprimand in our file.*

After the hurried briefing by Doug's wife, Bill told Joe to open the trunk of his patrol car. Moving hastily, Bill went to the open trunk, grabbing and putting on his chest rig with four, thirty-round AR15 magazines and two pistol magazines in its pouches. Then he threw the sling on his AR15 Patrol rifle over his head and left shoulder. Knowing it already had a loaded magazine in it, he pulled back on the charging handle, let it go, and racked a round in the chamber. He also double-checked the safety and turned on the red-dot optic that was mounted on the upper receiver with a three-power magnifier sitting behind it. Pointing the barrel of his rifle down toward the ground, Deputy Dudley looked through it to confirm it was on.

...

"Are you ready?" he said to Joe, who nodded in the affirmative while drawing his side arm and moving it into the low-guard position. Bill instructed him to stay close, and they began making their way toward the front door leading into the bookstore. As they were doing so, shoppers were coming out, some bleeding, crying and many yelling, "Help us!" As they went through the doors, they saw an older man collapse. He fell and they heard the thud of his head bouncing on the hard tile floor. A dark red spot started slowly spreading in the center of his shoulders.

The two of them, with Bill leading, cautiously used the book racks as cover, making their way toward the back entrance leading to the inside of the mall. Arriving there, Bill leaned up against the right side of the opening as Carter did earlier. As Bill did a quick peek around the corner to the right, on the ground, just as Liz Redman described, lay a body in a pool of coagulating blood. It appeared to be one of the terrorists.

Tango Down!

As Deputy Dudley was at the doorway and looking in the direction of the sporadic gunfire, he heard a soft whistle. Sixty feet away and to the right of a kiosk he saw a man with his hand in the air trying to get his attention. The deputy immediately raised his AR15 rifle to his shoulder, ready to engage the man should the need arise. He quickly flipped over his three-power magnifier to get a better look at him.

Now, with an enhanced magnified view, he could see what appeared to be two men, one of which fit the description the woman outside gave him of her husband. There were two kiosks between the two deputies and the man who whistled. Bill told his partner to be ready. With his rifle up they swiftly moved towards the closest kiosk.

Nothing like having a combat Marine backing me up! Deputy Dudley thought to himself as he could hear his young partner, Joe, moving in step with him. He knew that to his partner, this should be second nature, having fought in Bagdad, Fallujah, Ramadi and many other towns in Iraq.

After the two of them arrived at the first kiosk, they paused and headed for the one closest to Doug and Carter. Just as they started for the second one, gunfire erupted from their left. Behind him, Deputy Dudley heard the smack of a round on fabric and flesh and then a heavy thump as Joe hit the ground.

"I'm hit, "Joe called out, as the senior deputy spun to his left with his rifle already up to his shoulder looking through the magnifier and red-dot scope. Ninety feet down the west concourse, he saw the terrorist who was shooting at them come into view. Looking through the three-power magnifier, it was easy for Dudley to put the red dot on the guy's chest while squeezing off two quick shots. Then he smoothly moved the red dot on to the terrorist's nose and squeezed off one more round – tango down!

In the heat of the fight, he moved himself out from behind cover and was now out in the open between the first and second kiosk. He looked back at Joe who was grabbing his right groin area.

Joe yelled at him, pointing to the next kiosk; "*Go!*" The senior deputy didn't hesitate and ran, sliding behind just as two rounds buzzed by him. He was now fifteen feet away from the kiosk Doug and Carter were using for cover.

The Plan

Doug was able to see everything that unfolded as the two officers were making their way to them, watching the shot one go down and the lead officer quickly turning and returning fire. The deputy who made it to the kiosk was now close enough to talk to.

Doug watched as the senior deputy reached for his radio and could hear him giving the sheriff department's dispatcher an update of where they were and what was happening. As the deputy was doing so, Doug looked down the concourse. As much as he'd experienced total carnage in combat, he was stunned seeing all the bodies lying on the ground, some of them slightly moving. He felt a rage swelling up inside of him. These were innocent civilians that had been slaughtered by these psychopathic terrorists.

Looking back at the deputy he gave him a "time out" signal, indicating he wanted to talk with him. Doug identified himself, telling him what he'd told the 911 dispatcher. From Doug's vantage point, it was obvious that the deputy was in a better position to look down the center of the west concourse. He watched as the deputy looked to see where the other shooters were. Just like the north concourse, the west concourse had kiosks running down the middle; the terrorists could be anywhere. Doug again got the officer's attention.

"Stay where you are. We're going to get into a better position inside that store with open entrances on both sides," Doug said quietly, pointing to the right and in front of them.

Because it was on an inside corner in the mall and open on both sides, it would be easy to see through to the west concourse. When he and Carter moved to the inside of that corner shop, he wanted to make sure the deputy didn't send rounds their way. Doug weighed doing a quick leap over to the deputy behind the kiosk. He wanted to make sure the deputy understood what he and Carter were about to do, and he was concerned by being overheard by the one of the terrorists, even if he spoke in a normal tone.

Doug turned his attention to Carter, who was watching the corner as well as the inside slant through the shop, and tapped him on his left shoulder.

"I'm going to go talk with the deputy and let him know what we're doing; I'll be right back."

Carter, without taking his eyes off his scan, nodded his head in understanding. With that, Doug made a quick dash over to the deputy behind the kiosk, sliding into him like a baseball player coming across home plate.

Doug again explained his plan, telling the deputy what he and Carter were going to do and where they'd be located. He explained to the deputy that he wanted him to provide cover for them. "Will do," the senior deputy said without hesitation.

After the deputy's affirmative response, Doug turned and did a quick three-step slide back behind the kiosk that he and Carter had been using for cover.

"How are you doing?" Doug asked Carter, nodding his head in the direction of the shrapnel wounds.

"I'm good," Carter responded.

Doug pulled the bolt handle back on his AK, pulled a partially spent magazine out and put a full one in it. As Doug readied his rifle, he watched Carter do a tactical reload, removing the rounds left in the first magazine and putting them in the magazine in his Sig. Looking ahead and scanning, he heard the sound of Carter slapping the now nearly full magazine back into his pistol. Carter slightly pulled back the slide to confirm a round was in the chamber. Then Carter tapped him on the shoulder and gave him a thumbs-up.

3:32 p.m.

Police cars and ambulances continued to wail and pull into all of the parking lots at the mall. By this time, all the news outlets were broadcasting the events unfolding and law enforcement in all cities and towns across America had been ordered to lock down all malls. Just as with the tragedy of 9/11, in the immediate hour after the attacks had begun there would be total confusion, once again demonstrating the government's inability to defend the citizens of the United States.

Doug looked back in the direction of Deputy Dudley, and with hand signals let him know that he and Carter were moving to their new positions. Doug moved in front of Carter and reached back and gave him a squeeze on the arm; Carter returned it. Doug went right, going behind a display counter and making sure the area behind it was clear of anyone. Carter slanted to the left, hugging the wall while making his way to a glass display case. Leaning hard into the wall, he could see down most of the right side of the concourse, and he looked for any movement. He could see only two kiosks from his vantage point and they were across and to the left side of the concourse. Doug, moving into position, was able to look directly across the concourse. If needed, their field of fire would be triangulated with cover down the middle from the deputy.

Only ten feet away, Doug motioned to Carter he was going to make for the first kiosk. Just as he started to move, the sound of gunfire erupted down toward the middle of the concourse, and blood-curdling screams could be heard. It was obvious the remaining terrorists found more victims to kill and taken their attention off the two deputies. They were re-focused on their original mission of killing infidels; innocent men, women and children.

Doug slid into the kiosk with Carter right behind him. "You cover left; I've got right." Doug said.

Carter looked back in the direction of the deputy and saw him looking down the center of the concourse with his rifle and nodding in the direction of the two of them. Because the deputy had magnification on his rifle and could see down the length of the west concourse, Doug set him up to do "overwatch" for the two of them as they moved down the concourse. Having served as a "scout sniper" in the Army, Deputy Dudley understood his role. He also knew to advance forward from his position if he was unable to keep his eyes on Doug and Carter, continuing to provide covering fire if needed.

From the directions of the gunshots and screams, the shooters must have gone into one of the shops to seek out shoppers who were inside hiding.

Dudley watched as Doug and Carter crouched down behind the kiosk, one covering each side. As he scanned toward the sound of the gunfire, he thought he saw movement on the left-side entrance to a women's boutique twenty yards in front of Carter. He trained his rifle and scope on the entrance and also did a quick scan down the center and right of the concourse.

Carter and Doug didn't know how many shooters were left, but from the sound of the intermittent gunfire,

Doug's best guess was there were still at least two to four shooters. Twelve yards in front of Doug's position was a small coffee bar. Doug tapped Carter, telling him he was going to move forward and to the right. He was hoping the deputy could see him and his movement forward. As Doug slid into the next cover, Carter went to the left side of the concourse, making his way to the entrance of a business that was no longer open. Looking inside through the glass doors he could see it was dark inside and empty of any merchandise or displays. The entrances to the stores were recessed inward eight feet, giving him momentary cover.

Reinforcements

Deputy Dudley could see Doug and Carter moving forward and toward the sound of the gunshots. While he knew from Doug's 911 call to the dispatcher that he was a former Delta Force operator, he wondered what kind of background the other guy had. The way he moved and handled himself, Dudley assumed he must have military training in his background. While this was going on, Dudley kept an eye on his partner, occasionally giving him words of encouragement. And he used his radio to give updates on what was happening inside the mall.

As he continued his scan, watching the two men in front of him, from his left and behind he heard someone say, "Dudley, hey, Dudley." Behind him was the entrance to the mall through the bookstore and he wasn't concerned with any threats coming from that direction. He quickly turned and saw three of his fellow deputies, all armed with their AR15 patrol rifles. Bill gave them a thumbs-up and wiggled his radio, indicating he wanted to talk with them. Via the radio and while keeping his eyes forward he brought them up to speed on what was unfolding, as well as Carter and Doug's positions. He told them to stay put as he continued to scan down the concourse for any threats.

Overwatch

As Doug leaned forward to the left side of the coffee bar, he could see the entrance to the women's boutique which was now only ten yards forward and to his left. There was another kiosk directly across from the entrance. More shots rang out and more screaming, followed by silence. He knew that he and Carter had to act fast if more lives were to be saved. He made eye contact with Carter, who was now just behind him to the left across the concourse. Doug pointed to the next kiosk. Carter gave him thumbs-up.

As Doug made his move, Carter turned left, using the empty storefront as a back stop. He was leaning and sliding against it, all the while keeping his handgun up in a high-ready position, looking forward and to the right of Doug in case a "jack-in-the-box" popped up. The entrance to the women's boutique was now just eight feet from Carter as he moved toward it. As he watched Doug bolt for the kiosk, shots rang out to Carter's left as one of the terrorists came out shooting at Doug.

Deputy Dudley now was firmly fixed on the entrance to the boutique. Again he saw movement just inside the entrance, and this time he was sure of it. He trained his rifle on the area. He could see a barrel of a rifle moving forward and shooting in the direction of Doug. Through the magnifier and red-dot scope, he easily made out the detail of the barrel, then the gun and then the evil that was trying to kill the Delta Force operator. As the terrorist's head came into view, the deputy did a smooth, quick trigger press, hitting the terrorist in the right ear with a Hornady Tap 5.56 round, turning the inside of the shooter's head into Jell-O and leaving an exit hole on the left side of his head the size of a man's fist. Threat neutralized!

Carter was just getting ready to squeeze off two rounds when he felt the pressure and buzz of Deputy Dudley's shot whiz by his head and hit the terrorist in the right side of the head. He felt the "thwack" as the projectile made contact. The terrorist hit the hard floor like a heavy sack of potatoes. Carter looked over at Doug, who was holding his left side.

Allah Akbar!

Waving the three other deputies forward, Deputy Dudley advanced with them to the kiosk just to the left of the boutique entrance. One of the deputies looked forward and to the right, while another one covered the rear. Carter was now on the outside corner of the entrance to the boutique. Dudley and another deputy were both positioned with their rifles pointing into the entrance, with a wounded Doug doing the same with his confiscated AK47. All but Carter had a vantage point to see inside the store; they were all concerned with shooting inside the shop in case there were victims still inside.

From deep inside the store they heard a faint, muffled, "Allah Akbar," followed by a large explosion. Carter, Doug and the deputies could feel a tremor underneath their feet and the rush of the overpressure from the blast escaping through the front entrance and out into the concourse along with a wall of dust and debris.

Unknown to them one of the two remaining terrorists had a chest bomb and had detonated it. He was trying to escape with his comrade through an exit leading to the south parking lot but was met by thirty-six law-enforcement officers and a hail of bullets.

Carter, Doug and the four deputies held their positions. With the exception of the moaning of the wounded who lay throughout the mall, it was quiet. Carter moved back and around the deputies and made his way to Doug. Doug had been hit in the left leg and the top part of his pant leg was crimson red.

One of the many courses Carter took over the last six-years was Combat Medical. It was a basic one-day course designed to teach anyone to stop the bleeding of a gunshot wound and keep someone alive until help arrived. Carter quickly pulled off his belt and pulled it tight on the upper part of Doug's thigh to stop the bleeding. All six of them decided to hold their position and wait for more backup to arrive. The senior Deputy Dudley was on his radio, giving directions of approach to his fellow officers outside and to emergency responders. He looked back in the direction of his partner, Joe, who was lying motionless. The veteran deputy let the other men know he was going back to check on him.

Now the inside of the mall was starting to buzz with the sound of sheriff's deputies and other local law enforcement officers moving through the concourses and going into and clearing the inside of the different shops of any possible additional threats. The death toll and the number wounded victims was yet to be counted. One thing was certain, there were seven dead terrorists, each on their way to meet seventy-two virgins… or so they thought.

Carter looked around and then at Doug and said, "What do you say we get the fuck out of here?"

"Roger that."

Carter stood up and reached down and helped Doug to his feet. Carter realized he still had his pistol in his right hand and holstered it. Seeing this, Doug laid the AK47 on the floor in front of one of the deputies. With Doug's left arm slung over Carter's shoulder, the two of them hobbled back in the direction of the bookstore, heading to the exit leading to the east parking lot. Nearing the exit, they could see the flashing lights of patrol cars, fire trucks and ambulances. As they pushed their way through the doors and out into the parking lot, Doug saw his wife and children running toward them.

Gratitude

As Carter helped Doug through the doorway of the bookstore and the two of them limped outside, he felt a sense of euphoria. Though he was exhausted and shaky, walking into the sun's rays gave him a sense of being renewed, almost as if he'd been reborn. He thought about what had just transpired inside the mall – exchanging gunfire and eliminating evil, getting hit by grenade shrapnel and somehow through the grace of God surviving it all. It felt as though a second chance at life had been granted. He was also grateful to have a man of Doug's skills and character at his side. Carter knew beyond a shadow of a doubt that without their combined intervention the carnage would have been much greater.

With Carter still holding Doug up, Liz led them to the fire rescue truck with two paramedics waiting there to take care of anyone coming out of the mall that needed help. When the two medics saw Liz and the children with Doug and Carter in tow, they ran up and relieved Carter's need to help Doug. Immediately they went to work on Doug, putting him on a gurney and cutting his left pant leg open from the bottom to the waist. On the left side of Doug's thigh, it looked like someone had split him open with a ragged-edged knife. It was obvious a round hit him there, going in and exiting out the backside; he was lucky it didn't hit the bone. Doug, smiling, looked at Liz and Carter. "No biggie; it's just a flesh wound."

Less than five minutes behind them, Deputy Dudley emerged from the bookstore. His partner was on a gurney with two paramedics at his side and an IV in the young deputy's right arm. He'd lost a lot of blood, but they thought he'd be OK.

Seeing Carter and Doug at the rear of the paramedic truck, Deputy Dudley walked up to them. "Thank you for what you did in there. You saved a lot of lives!"

"Hell of a team the three of us made," Carter said. "I loved the head shot you made on that asshole coming out of the store shooting at Doug. That was *out fucking standing*! I was just a few feet away when it buzzed by me and hit that asshole right in the ear."

The three of them laughed, giving each other a fist bump. It was more of a nervous and happy-to-be-alive kind of laugh.

Carter was completely fatigued from the whole event, yet he was overjoyed with what they had accomplished. All his investment in training with his two friends the last six-years had paid off. That he was able to fight alongside a guy like Doug was incredible.

Fuck those asshole terrorists; don't fuck with us in our back yard! Carter thought to himself.

Carter overheard one of the EMTs telling Liz he didn't think the round that hit her had hit bone either. Carter, looking at Doug, Liz and their two teenage kids, thought how fortunate it was that everything worked out the way it did.

"What an afternoon," Carter said, smiling at Doug.

"Thanks, brother!" Doug said, looking at Carter.

Doug had spent his entire career in and out of combat zones. He'd battled with Al Qaida, the Taliban and more shithead groups that he could remember and recently with ISIS. Too many times he'd seen men wounded and seen them die. There's a certain kind of bonding and respect that happens on the battlefield. In the heat of the moment our brave men and women aren't fighting for their country, they're fighting for the person to their right and to their left. Doug had fought with countless brave men, always knowing beyond a shadow of a doubt he could trust them. And he knew they knew they could trust him. Whoever this individual Carter was, for Doug he had just joined the exclusive fraternity of warriors. And more importantly, he'd gained a friend.

"No thanks needed, you would have done the same for me."

Doug reached out, gently but firmly squeezing Carter's wrist, looking at him square in the eyes.

"Listen to me brother; you saved not only my life but that of my family. Family is everything to me. It's the heart of the matter of why I do what I do. My job is to keep them safe and because of you they're OK. I owe you!"

There was no mistaking for Carter that Doug was genuinely thanking him from his heart, and he knew he'd just gained a friend for life.

"You don't owe me, brother, and thank you for what you just said, I couldn't do anything else at the time; that evil needed to be stopped!"

Doug listened to him just as he had many times before to other modest warriors. At this point in life he understood that for the most part we have become a nation of sheep. On the battlefield is where the sheep dogs show up, and Doug recognized Carter as one of them. Doug knew a warrior when he was around one.

"I'm buying you a beer as soon as we can get the hell out of here!"

Carter smiled back at him… "I'm going to hold you to it!"

Liz was standing to the side as she watched and listened to the exchange between her husband and Carter. What Doug told him spoke for her. Quietly Liz looked at Carter and said, "Thank you!"

A Beer and Dinner

It's easy to give acknowledgement but sometimes not so easy to receive it. Carter was no different from other people; however, he had learned by this stage in life to listen. He knew that when you listen, you honor and respect the one speaking. He was momentarily overwhelmed with emotion, thinking of the gravity of what he had done for them at the risk of his own life. As he thought back to that frozen moment in the doorway, he realized that if it hadn't been for that old woman in the doorway, he might have run the other way. He was embarrassed and felt a sense of shame knowing it took an old woman to goad him into action. He was troubled by the fact that he'd even thought about running from the danger.

"Carter, I assume you're not still active; who were you with?"

Doug's question brought him back to the present. He could tell Doug assumed he was prior military. At six foot one, a fit two hundred pounds, short gray hair and a strong presence, many times over the years he'd been asked the same question.

"I never served; I was going to join the Marines right after the Tet Offensive, but the short story is I stayed in school with a 2-S deferment. I've owned my own companies all my life and for the past twenty-five years I've also worked as a business coach, helping the owners of small- and medium-size companies."

Doug upon hearing this was confused. Inside the mall right from the beginning he watched Carter kill the terrorist with two quick shots to the base of the throat and then one to right eye. Carter then proceeded to go into a combat kneeling position, scanning ahead and around, while Doug grabbed the terrorist's AK47 and magazines. Everything Carter did in the fight was that of someone with highly developed gun fighting skills. Normal infantry men don't fight like that; that's always been the realm of Delta Force, Seal Teams, Force Recon Marines and Air Force Special Forces. He also deferred to Doug's lead, instinctively moving with him while under fire.

Over the last forty-years or so there has been an all-volunteer military. Out of the conflicts sustained by our troops, some with multiple deployments, there were thousands of experienced combat veterans who, perhaps rightfully, felt they were in an elite class, separate from the civilian populations. Because of this, many active and retired military felt a certain kind of superiority to civilians. They would talk amongst themselves about how a civilian could never do what they do. Some in the military thought they were the real patriots and that civilians were at most a subclass of patriots. Many didn't feel civilians possessed the same kind of passionate commitment to fighting for their family, friends and country the way they did – it was almost a kind of arrogance. Doug tended to share this point of view. But what he and Carter had just gone through frankly rocked his point of view about civilians. Doug had a lot of questions for Carter; what Carter had done and how he performed didn't make any sense to him.

"Carter," Doug started to say just as two EMTs were lifting him and the gurney into a waiting ambulance.

"Colonel Redman, we're taking you, your wife and kids to Northwest Hospital," one of the EMTs told Doug, and he motioned for Liz and the kids to get into the ambulance along with her husband. Because of all the emergency-response training over the years and from the magnitude of what had just happened, protocol dictated they get him to the hospital so the ambulance and paramedics could get back on scene as soon as possible.

"Carter, give my wife your phone number. I'll give you a call later, and we'll set up a time when I can buy you that beer," Doug said, giving Liz a nod in Carter's direction. Carter asked one of the EMTs for a piece of paper, jotted down his number and handed it back to Liz. She then gave him Doug's number.

"You're on. Beer! You cheap bastard, you're buying me a beer *and* dinner Carter said with a chuckle. He figured Doug was either current or prior military and was impressed to learn he was a colonel. He wondered what branch and what he did in the military.

"By the way, thanks for your service!" Carter adds.

While Doug had been thanked hundreds of times when a civilian discovered he was military, he never tired of hearing it.

"You're welcome!"

The EMT men closed the back doors of the ambulance and it began moving out with lights flashing and occasionally the wailer coming on to move people out of the way. Then it pulled out of the parking lot with the siren blaring fulltime, heading towards the intersection two hundred yards away.

3:49 p.m. - Silence Is Golden

Carter felt a tap on his right shoulder; it was an EMT pointing to his left side, which was bloody from the leg up to his shoulder and neck. In all of the commotion, Carter had forgotten about his own injuries. He didn't really even feel them. He was upright on two legs and walking. Besides, many more horrific injuries inside the mall needed these EMTs more than he did. The EMT walked him over to an ambulance, and Carter sat down on the back step to allow him to examine and treat his injuries. As this was happening, Deputy Dudley walked up to him.

"What you and your partner did in there was extraordinary and believe me, it will not go unnoticed by the Sheriff's Department and the community."

Carter didn't want any kind of spotlight on him, and he explained to Dudley that he was just grateful he was there and able to make a difference.

"Very shortly some detectives are going to starting asking you questions. Between you and me, just give them your name, address and phone number and tell them you'll do an interview in twenty-four hours. Don't say anything else. It'll give you a chance to calm down and digest what happened. Good idea to have an attorney with you also."

The deputy saw two detectives walking toward them and turned to Carter.

"We didn't have this conversation, by the way," he said.

Carter grimaced as one of the paramedics was dressing one of his wounds.

"What conversation?"

Carter knew from all his training over the years and from the state-authorized Concealed Carry Class he took years ago, that if he was ever involved in a shooting he should not to do any type of interview with law enforcement, the press or anyone for at least twenty-four hours and never without an attorney present. He was aware there had been multiple examples of an armed, law-abiding citizen using a gun to stop someone in the process of committing a crime. Often in the aftermath he or she starts talking to law enforcement only later to have what was said used against them in a court of law. It's not uncommon for law-abiding citizens to be arrested for having protected themselves or someone else when there was no other choice but to shoot.

Whenever law enforcement is involved in a shooting, the first thing the fellow officers do is get the officer involved away from any kind of interview for a least twenty-four hours; it's automatic for them. It makes perfect sense. After a shooting, anybody is going to be excited, emotional and probably joyous for stopping a bad person doing something violent to someone else or to themselves. In the aftermath of the adrenaline rush, people can say things without considering that it might be used against them later, whether as a defendant in a criminal or a civil suit. It is not uncommon for a shithead's family to sue them for justifiably shooting their psychotic family member.

Forty-minutes had passed since the start of the carnage in the mall. Carter lived just five minutes away from the Safeway shopping center where the assassination attempt on Gabrielle Giffords took place in 2011, and he knew the entire mall probably was going to be yellow-

82

taped off, with no one getting in or out other than law enforcement for a long time. A wave of exhaustion set over him. He just wanted to be on his way and deal with all of this later.

As the two detectives got closer, Carter looked around, noticing all the law enforcement – the recently arrived regional SWAT team and emergency responders – entering through the bookstore on their way to the interior of the mall. He also could see local news vehicles arriving and their boom antennas being raised.

"Excuse me, sir, are you Carter Thompson, one of the men involved in the shooting inside the mall?"

"Yes." Carter said.

"I'm Detective Collins, and this is my partner, Detective Sharpe. We're with the Pima County Sheriff's Department and would like to talk to you regarding the events that occurred a short time ago in the mall," Detective Collins said, as he and his partner fingered their badges and ID hanging around their necks in plain sight.

"Sure."

"Thank you; would you please tell us your full name?" detective Collins asked.

"Carter Davis Thompson."

"Do you have a driver's license or ID on you?"

Carter pulled his wallet out and handed it to him. Both detectives paused, looking at his left arm, neck and then his left leg, now caked with semi-dried blood on his pants and shirt where he had gotten hit with shrapnel.

Detective Sharpe looked at him and asked, "Looks like you're injured; have you had that looked at? How did that happen?"

"I was hit with shrapnel from a grenade going off. I'm OK! I'll get it checked out later. There are many more people with worse injuries that need tending to inside the mall."

"And what is your address and phone number, Mr. Thompson?" Carter noticed a slight shift in tone from the "friendly" to the "getting-down-to-business" tone. He gave them the information.

Detective Collins continued, "We understand you and another gentleman by the name of Doug Redman, who's been taken to the hospital, were involved in the shooting inside the mall, is that correct?"

"Yes," Carter said, thinking to himself how what they did to protect people was already being characterized as a *shooting inside the mall*, rather than calling it what it was; *a terrorist attack by Muslims hell-bent on killing Americans.* Why couldn't the detective have asked, *are you one of the two men who initially engaged the terrorists?* He felt himself getting angry at how political correctness was already beginning to shape this interview and where it might be heading.

Detective Sharpe looked down at his Sig handgun holstered on his right side and at the magazine on his left side. "Why don't you tell us what happened in there? We understand you and Colonel Redman shot and killed four individuals inside the mall. Do you think you might also have shot some innocent people who were trying to escape? I mean, by accident, not intentionally."

To Carter it was obvious where they were taking this interview and he was grateful to have the prior knowledge and training to say no more. He appreciated Deputy Dudley's effort to help him.

"You know, I'm a little tired right now and would be happy to do an interview with you tomorrow, but only with my attorney present. Not right now, though," Carter said, noticing that neither one was happy with his response.

"Just a few questions, it's important we get the facts, you know, while everything is fresh in your mind. Because this is an active crime scene, it really would be very helpful if you answered just a couple of questions." Detective Collins said.

"I understand and appreciate your urgency, but with all due respect I decline your request to talk with you right now. As I told you, I'd be glad to do an interview with you tomorrow with my attorney present."

Detective Sharpe, standing up straight and taking a deep breath, said, "You know, this is an active crime scene, and we can keep you here as long as we'd like, so we'd really appreciate it if you'd cooperate with us now. The sooner you do that the sooner we can get you out of here." By the way," the detective added, pointing at Carter's handgun, "is that the firearm you said you discharged inside the mall?"

It was obvious to Carter these two men were not happy. Law enforcement is used to intimidating people with their authority, and he knew they were attempting to manipulate him through the threat of keeping him there indefinitely. He knew that exercising his constitutional right not to say anything could frustrate and piss off law enforcement.

Carter was aware that law enforcement at all levels sometimes violated people's rights. However, he wasn't going to allow that to happen to him. He thought to himself; *OK, the game called "we're law enforcement and we're going to control you" attempt is over; time for me to take charge of this conversation.* Perhaps when he was younger he would have fallen prey to their intimidation. However, at this time in his life and with his knowledge, no way!

Looking at the two of them with a slight smile, Carter cocked his head to the side slightly and said, "When did I say I discharged my firearm?" Both of the detectives looked at each other, realizing their effort to control him was over before it began.

"Well, you're wearing a gun and one of our deputies and other witnesses said they saw you firing it, so I assume you did," Detective Collins said, pointing at it in an attempt to be assertive.

"Like I said, I'll be happy to do an interview with you tomorrow, but for now I decline to say anything more."

The two detectives looked at each other and then back at Carter. "OK, tomorrow it is. We do have to ask you to surrender your firearm since we believe it was involved in a crime scene," Detective Collins said slowly, being careful with what he said. Maybe they were being tape recorded and maybe not. One thing was clear to both detectives though. This was a person who wasn't going to go along with them right now. Continuing to be careful in his choice of words, Detective Collins cleared his throat and said, "We have reasonable suspicion to believe you discharged your weapon and because of this, we have to tag it as evidence."

Carter knew this was coming. He just hoped he'd get it back as soon as possible. "I don't have a problem with your request. However, I'd like a written receipt with make, model and serial number of my handgun on Pima

County Sheriff Department letterhead and signed by either one of you including your badge number."

Both detectives looked at each other with raised eyebrows and slight smiles. Neither one could deny Carter's request. "We can do that," Detective Collins said, as he nodded to his partner who turned and headed towards a white sheriff's van that said "Forensics" in bold letters on the side. Carter could see him talking with a woman in uniform who went into the van, coming out with what looked like a blue book of some sorts.

Carter looked at Detective Collins and asked him if he wanted to take his gun off him or would it be OK for him to hand it to him.

"If you would carefully take it out, clear it and hand it to me with barrel pointing down, I would appreciate it," the detective said, keeping his eyes on Carter and the handgun. Normally the detective would relieve someone of a firearm himself, but after hearing what Carter and the Colonel had done, instinctively he wasn't concerned for his own safety.

Carter slowly eased his Sig 226 X-5 out of its holster, depressed the magazine release button, pulled the magazine out of it, locked the slide back which ejected the live round that was in the chamber and handed it to the detective, barrel down .

Detective Sharpe returned with a receipt book, writing down make, model and serial number; he even emptied the magazine counting out three rounds of ammunition plus the one that landed on the ground when Carter had racked the slide back. He slowly ripped the yellow receipt from under the original white copy and handed it to Carter.

Holy shit! Carter thought to himself, *only four rounds left out of thirty-six.*

"Am I free to leave now?" Carter asked the two of them.

"Yes, however, if you drove here, your vehicle has to remain where you parked it until the crime scene has been cleared. And honestly, as large as this area is and with all the hundreds of vehicles here, that will probably be overnight and well into tomorrow. Can someone come pick you up?" Detective Sharpe said.

"No problem, I'll find a way home," Carter said as he turned, pulling his cell phone out and turning off the voice recording mode. He wanted to get a couple of things, phone charger, sun glasses et cetera, out of his vehicle on his way out. As he started to walk, he could feel a sharp, throbbing pain in his left thigh where he'd been hit by the shrapnel. Limping slightly and heading away from the mall, he smiled. As horrific as what he'd gone through , he felt euphoria along with an adrenaline hangover. Truth was, he loved the fact he was involved in the gunfight, saving lives, and he was ecstatic that he shot and killed those goat-fuckers!

Holy fucking shit, that was outstanding! he thought to himself.

Outload he said; "Good job, Carter, I'm proud of you!"

Hobbling toward his vehicle, Carter thought about Doug, his wife and his kids and wondered how he was doing. He took out the card with Doug's number and looked at it for a moment and again thought about what had just transpired. He would give him a call in the morning.

3:56 p.m.

At the Southwest Hospital, Doug and Liz were being treated for their wounds. For Doug, it was just one more scar to add to his already accumulated collection from multiple gunfights.

En route to the hospital, detectives Collins and Sharpe discussed how they would approach Doug Redman as well as his wife. They both knew that Doug Redman and Carter Thompson were going to be a critical part of their investigation, and they hoped that Colonel Redman would be more cooperative than Carter Thompson had been in answering their questions.

Doug anticipated questioning by detectives about the events that unfolded in the mall. Like Carter, he too was aware of the importance of waiting twenty-four hours before doing any kind of interview. It went without saying that Liz understood this also.

Inside the hospital the two detectives made their way to the room where Doug and his wife were. They introduced themselves and explained why they were there: to talk to both of them as well as their two children. Before they could begin, Doug echoed what Carter explained to them about waiting twenty-four hours before doing an interview. The two detectives looked at each other with slight smiles and told Doug they understood and would be in touch, handing him their cards. They knew better than to try and ride roughshod on this former Delta Force colonel and intimidate him. Doug's whole demeanor itself was one of *don't fuck with me right now.*

Within a few hours, the remote vans of every news outlet were set up and broadcasting from the Southwest

Regional Mall. Across the country and in every city where there was a mall, local law enforcement was deployed in force. Millions of people were either tuned into their TVs or their radios – the country was in a state of horror and disbelief.

How again could something like this have happened?

"Why isn't our government protecting its citizens?" This became the main question of most of the anchors on the news outlets including the liberal media.

Just as with 9/11, communications between law enforcement agencies, both local and federal, were in breakdown. Supposedly after the events of 9/11 everything was to have been fixed but, as usual with an incompetent government bureaucracy, little had gotten accomplished.

The President was in Hawaii at the time, playing a round of golf when he was notified of what had happened. He thanked the Secret Service agent that gave him the news and asked him to keep him updated; after all he still had six more holes to play.

Civil Disobedience

As Carter got to his truck, he looked around to see if anyone was watching the parking lot to prevent people from leaving. Seeing no-one around, he weighed the detective's order of telling him to leave his vehicle here. but then again the detective didn't know which one was his. Besides, there was complete chaos in the parking lot.

He looked around again, unlocked his truck, started it up, backed out and proceeded out of the lot. It was still too early in all of the confusion, vehicles arriving, sirens blaring, emergency lights flashing and news trucks staking out a spot for anyone to really notice which vehicles were in the lot at the time of the attack. *What the hell, if they tell me to stop, I will. If not, I'm out of here,* he thought to himself as he made his way toward the exit. Carter just wanted to get out of there and go home. He turned right, following an exiting ambulance, headed south one block and then made the left green arrow. Then he was off and on his way home.

Carter drove on in silence, again thinking about the fear and hesitation he'd experienced in the doorway. It made him feel like a coward and some kind of fraud. After all the years of training and the level of skill he had as a gunfighter, he was confused as to why he froze up. He felt shamed and embarrassed having someone, especially an old woman, goad him into action. He hoped that incident of freezing at the doorway and being yelled at by the elderly woman to get him going would never become known. He dreaded the thought of any of his friends finding out, they'd think he might be all bark and no bite. Certainly, he would keep it a secret.

But then again, he'd demonstrated "bite" in his engaging and killing of the terrorists. It was really all too much for him to keep thinking about. He just wanted to get home and away from what had happened.

Carter thought about calling his girlfriend, Kim, to let her know he was OK. She knew he was going to the mall that day, but he hadn't told her what time he'd be there. He knew she was probably at work and might not know of what happened yet. He decided to wait until he got to his house, took a shower and calmed down and relaxed a bit. He needed to gather his thoughts and process the events of the afternoon.

As Carter rolled up his long drive way, he hit the garage door opener and waited for the door to fully open before driving in. Once inside the garage, he entered his house. He closed that door and leaned against it, taking a deep breath of air; he was glad to be home behind closed doors and in complete silence. The memory and sounds of the gunfight, along with the screams and smells, echoed in his head.

Carter undressed and took a shower, allowing the hot water to slowly run down his head and back. He grimaced from the burning and stinging sensation as he washed his wounds. He dried himself off, put gauze and tape on his wounds and then lay down on the bed. He took a deep breath and closed his eyes; he just wanted to relax for a minute.

I love you too!

He could hear a phone ringing in the distance. *Why am I in a dark tunnel with a phone ringing? No, wait, it's not a tunnel. What the fuck ... oh, shit.*

It had gotten dark out. He fumbled for his cell phone.

"Were you at the mall? Are you OK? Where are you?" Kim Rogers was firing questions at him quicker than his clouded mind could answer. He told her he was OK; yes, he had been there, but he didn't explain the details to her. Carter asked if she could come over, and told her that he would explain what happened.

"I'm just ten minutes away. I'm thankful you're OK. It scared me to death when I heard what had happened. I love you!"

"I love you, too!"

Hanging up, he thought about how grateful he was to have her in his life, and he was happy she'd be there soon. Besides, it wouldn't be bad to get a second opinion on his wounds. He didn't trust the idea of talking about what happened over the phone and would share everything with her when she got there.

Carter loved this woman very much; he trusted her and knew she felt the same. He had been married twice before and was still hoping to finally find a woman he'd be happy with. Almost two years into their relationship, he thought she might just be the one. They both enjoyed each other's company and always had fun together. Though confrontation was difficult for him, he always practiced communicating with her if he was upset about something she did or didn't do; and he encouraged her to do the same with him.

On the rare occasion when something happened that was an upset for either one of them, they talked about it. On each occasion they were able to recover and move forward in their relationship. Carter knew that open communication, whether the other person likes hearing it or not, is paramount to the success of any kind of relationship, especially between a man and a woman.

Kim was always dressed to a "T." She was a strikingly attractive, classy, well-read and intelligent woman, possessing a lot of common sense. Standing five feet seven with short blond hair, brown eyes and an athletic figure, when she entered a room, people always noticed. Kim was outgoing and, like Carter, she had a strong presence.

Kim adored Carter and couldn't get to his house soon enough. She arrived exactly ten minutes after hanging up the phone with him. Carter was relieved to see Kim. It felt good to feel her tightly hugging and kissing him. As they walked down the hallway to the bedroom, Carter began describing everything that happened.

"That's so sad and terrible, all those poor people. Thank God you were there to help put an end to those bastards." Kim said with her eyes welling up with tears.

"I'm so grateful you're OK and very proud of what you did! I love you!" The two of them laid down in the bed holding each other tightly.

"I love you, too," Carter said in return. "I'm hungry! What do you say we order a pizza?"

Smiling, she said, "Let's do it."

After they ate the delivered pizza, they went back to the bedroom & watched TV until Carter drifted off to sleep.

Carter awoke early the next day and was glad it was Saturday and that he didn't have any commitments other than to meet with the two detectives. He looked at Kim, who was still sleeping, and thought it would be a good idea to give his friend Dennis O'Neil a call. Dennis was a criminal-defense attorney. After further talking with Kim the night before, and thinking about it more, he realized how important it was to have Dennis with him during his interview with the two detectives.

"Hey Carter, how the hell are you. Good Lord, it's been a long time. What's up?" Dennis said.

He was relieved when Dennis answered his phone and quickly explained his involvement in the previous day's events at the mall.

"You're smart to call me, and I'll be glad to go with you to the interview with the detectives." Dennis told him.

Aftermath

Before he left the mall the previous day, Carter agreed to meet with the detectives at four o'clock at the Pima County Sheriff's Department sub-station; it was only a fifteen-minute drive from his house. He was happy the interview was later in the afternoon. He looked at his watch. It was only eight in the morning, and he was hungry as hell, time for some coffee and food. As he was rummaging around in the refrigerator, Kim walked into the kitchen and gave him a gentle hug and a kiss.

"Are you hungry?" Carter asked, while handing her a cup of coffee and smiling. Kim loved the way Carter was always attentive to her needs, and besides, he made kick-ass coffee.

"Yes, I'm starving! What do you feel like having? Oh, wait a minute, maybe I should do an inventory and see what's available," said Kim.

"Ha, ha. We should be good to go. I did a grocery run yesterday morning. Bacon, eggs, English muffins, cheese omelet? Whatever you want, honey. I'm going to get the newspaper. Be right back, then I'll get cooking."

"No, you're not cooking, I am! Go get the paper. By the way, you look kind of sexy with the limp."

"OK, I won't protest. Better get to cooking then, I'm hungry!" the smiling Carter said, giving her a wink as he left the kitchen. Limping slightly, Carter slowly walked down to the end of the driveway to pick up the Saturday newspaper. Unfolding it as he was walking back to the house, he wasn't surprised to see the entire front page devoted to the shooting. To him it seemed like it happened

96

a long time ago. He thought to himself, *maybe this is what it's like for soldiers in combat after a battle.*

As he was closing the front door, he heard the phone ringing. Carter went to the phone as quickly as he could, feeling his left thigh throbbing with each step. At the same time, it felt good to be moving.

"Hello. Is this Carter?"

"Yes, who's this?"

"It's Doug Redmond. How are you doing, brother? You OK?"

"Hey Doug I'm good. How are you? And your wife and kids? Everybody OK?"

"We're good. I'm a little worse for wear but, hey, that wasn't my first rodeo. Are you available to get together for a bite to eat tomorrow afternoon? I'd like to buy you that beer I promised."

Carter genuinely liked Doug; he could tell he was a strong and solid kind of guy; someone Carter could easily relate to. He also could tell Doug had the heart of a lion.

"You're on. What time is good for you?"

"How about one o'clock at the Grand Union Restaurant?"

"Fine. Wow, what a day yesterday! I look forward to seeing you then."

Carter quickly told Doug that he was meeting the detectives in the afternoon, and that he was taking his friend the attorney along with him.

"Roger that, I'm doing the same at one. Guess I'll warm them up for you. I've also got a good friend joining me who's an attorney. Smart move on your part; the detectives aren't bad guys, but they have a job to do. Hey, we'll talk more tomorrow. Don't trust the phones if you know what I mean."

"I know exactly what you mean. See you tomorrow."

Carter was glad and not surprised that Doug, like himself, didn't feel comfortable talking on the phone. He looked forward to spending time with him the next day. The two of them had formed a bond in the gunfight in the mall, and Carter knew Doug was the only one who could fully appreciate and understand where Carter's head was at about the whole thing.

Now he and Kim heard on a TV news broadcast that at least two of the terrorists had suspected links to ISIS. As he thought about what happened the previous day, Carter felt rage and disgust come over him. These emotions were not just directed at the assholes that carried out their Jihad. Hell, he understood that, for them they were soldiers on the battlefield, committed to killing Americans. No, his rage and disgust had more to do with his own government and their pathetic policy of open borders. He, like millions of Americans, knew the open-border policy enabled anyone, including the enemies of the United States, to come into the country almost completely at will. Once here, all they had to do was to make their way to one of the many Sanctuary cities and live there in protection.

Carter, a constitutional conservative, understood what the Founding Fathers intended in creating this great country. The number-one job of the United States government under the Constitution is to protect its citizens from enemies both foreign and domestic. Every elected official takes an oath to this effect before assuming office. The truth was, elected officials in Washington hadn't really done that since World War II. The open and porous southern border was an example of the executive and legislative branches dereliction of duty.

In the morning newspaper, Carter found a short piece in section B of the paper on how some University of Arizona students had thrown eggs, tomatoes and beer bottles down on the Islamic Student Center on campus. The student center had been there for over thirty years, but the previous year a new student-housing building, fourteen stories high, had been built next door. Each apartment had a balcony, and on the side overlooking the Islamic Center, the easy target proved too much to resist. Some of the students displayed their anger over the mall shootings with the occupants of the Islamic Student Center.

By this time, most people in the country, including many liberals, had grown tired of the special treatment that illegal aliens and Muslims had been receiving. It was an example of a progressive administration over-compensating to make sure nobody's *feelings* got hurt. Many of the college campuses around the country over the decades had become a megaphone for the liberal progressive agenda. What better group to manipulate than young, impressionable college students?

"It's a shame those kinds of things are happening in our country. It's a long way from 'give me your tired, your poor," Carter said to Kim, quoting from the sonnet by Emma Lazarus, engraved on the base of the Statue of Liberty.

Lawyer Up!

Carter's friend Dennis lived only ten-minutes away. When they talked, Carter agreed to pick him up at quarter of three, a little more than an hour before his agreed-upon time to meet with the detectives. This would give the two of them a chance to stop and get coffee, allowing Carter to brief Dennis on the previous day's events and his involvement. He knew he wasn't guilty of doing anything wrong or illegal, yet he wondered, since he was bringing Dennis, if somehow they would think he was hiding something.

Dennis listened intently as Carter shared the details of the afternoon, starting when he shot and killed the first terrorist to Deputy Dudley's shot to the head of the terrorist as Carter was simultaneously pumping rounds into the terrorist's right side. When Carter was finished, Dennis assured him he'd done nothing illegal and acknowledged his bravery under fire.

"After you heard the sounds of gunshots and explosions and looked and saw what was happening, why didn't you turn and run for safety out through the bookstore like everybody else?" Dennis asked.

Should I tell him I almost did run away? How I froze in the doorway, and the old woman, who saw I was holding a gun, admonished me to do something to help? Carter thought to himself.

"To tell you the truth, that thought did cross my mind," Carter paused, weighing whether or not to tell Dennis about the old woman, but decided against it.

"I'm not wired that way, and besides, I could see if I didn't do something immediately, Doug and his family were probably going to be killed."

He heard the words come out of his mouth, but again he paused, reflecting on how he was leaving out the details of being frozen in the doorway and the old woman's intervention. He pressed himself to continue, still leaving out his indecisiveness.

"From that point on, I didn't even think about the danger. I just wanted to stop those sons of bitches as quickly as possible. Besides, it's what I've been training for the last six years. If divine providence calls, my job is to answer. I'm a warrior at heart! I don't run from trouble; I run toward it. It's what I've done all my life. I also believe, for some reason that's yet to be revealed, that God put me there for Doug and his family and put Doug there for me. It was if the two of us had fought together on the battlefield before."

"Wow! Well, good job; I'm proud of you. Thank God you were there. Because of your actions, you no doubt saved many lives and spared people from getting further hurt or killed." Dennis said, smiling and shaking his hand. "By the way, tell me about the training you've been doing the last six-years."

Carter filled him in on the details of how he and his two friends got involved with the Patriot Response Center six-years ago learning combat skills.

"I didn't have any idea that sort of training was available to civilians. Listen, unless specifically asked about this, don't bring it up. What you did was the right thing but I'm concerned it could be somehow used against you, less said the better. I don't want some overzealous prosecutor or the media making you out to be some kind of blood thirsty militia whack job."

"I understand what you're saying, and it makes sense to me. Not to worry, I'm not saying a word about my training."

Dennis went on to explain that even though what Carter did was totally justifiable, he didn't trust any branch of law enforcement. Especially under the current administration in Washington, with the Justice Department's apparent commitment to protecting certain people and programs.

What Carter and Doug had done was yet another example of evidence where an armed citizen was able to stop a crime in progress. For this reason, and with the gun grabbers in Washington determined to do away with the Second Amendment, it's likely the authorities will try and spin it or downplay the importance of Carter and Doug's intervention.

Carter understood this, and it really didn't matter to him. If he could just remain anonymous, that would just be fine with him. He didn't do what he did for fame or glory. He and Dennis finished their coffee and left.

The Interview

They arrived at the sheriff's sub-station as planned at four o'clock. After pleasantries, the detectives led them into an interrogation room which had pale green-walls, a table with two chairs on each side and a recording device on the table. It also had a large and obvious one-way mirror on one of the walls. Carter wondered if there were people behind the glass listening and observing the conversation that was about to begin. He also noticed two small cameras in the corners of the ceiling.

The interview started with the usual declaration by Detective Collins about date and time, asking Carter to state his full name for the record. With Dennis's nod of the head in approval, Carter proceeded to answer the standard questions with either a "yes" or a "no," staying away from providing his opinion. As they progressed in the interview, occasionally Dennis would interrupt, stating Carter's right to not answer based on the Fifth Amendment. This was all new to Carter, but Dennis's thirty-plus years of criminal-defense work had made him a seasoned veteran at handling the questioning process. He could keep his clients from saying anything, no matter how innocent it might sound, that could be twisted and used against them in the future.

Dennis was surprised by the detectives' demeanor. Neither one was being aggressive or accusatory. There was also no attempt on their part to ask questions that could be turned against the person being interrogated. Carter was the ideal client for Dennis; he already knew not to say words like, "I wanted to kill them," or "I wanted to make them suffer." Carter knew without Dennis explaining it to him that statements like that could be spun by some ladder-climbing prosecutor to mean that what he did was premeditated because he hated Muslims and was just waiting for an excuse to kill one. He knew from his training that all he needed to say was, "I just wanted to stop them," nothing more.

Prior to Carter's interview, Doug and Liz with their lawyer in tow had experienced the same kind of respectful treatment. Dennis also noticed that neither of the detectives tried to pit Carter and Doug against each other. What they heard earlier from Doug and Liz matched up perfectly to what Carter was telling them.

Though both detectives worked late into the night and were tired, they had made a point to talk with Deputy Dudley about Carter and Doug's involvement in the fight before their interviews with them. What they heard from the deputy and other witnesses was that what Carter and Doug had done was an incredible act of valor, leading to many lives being saved. The two detectives made a conscious decision between them that they weren't going to try and intimidate or trap either one in saying something that could hurt them later. They also knew how the system worked and understood how county, state and federal prosecutors operated. Besides, both of them, along with everyone else in the sheriff's department, had had enough of radicalized Muslims intent on killing anyone they deemed was a non-believer. Though they couldn't publically say it, they were both glad and proud of what these two men had done.

Dennis was pleasantly surprised that, after a little more than an hour, the interview was over. He wondered if it was because of the acts of heroism his friend had displayed that he'd gotten a pass.

When Carter and Dennis stepped out of the interrogation room, there were no less than thirty sheriff deputies and administrative staff that stood up, clapping and cheering as Carter and Dennis made their way out of the building.

Waiting in the Parking Lot

"How much longer do you think they'll have him in there?" Agent Trevor Blake asked.

"I don't know; shouldn't be too much longer. Pretty amazing what this guy and the colonel did yesterday in the mall. Lucky for the Colonel this guy was there to save him and his family. Thank God for the civilians with the mindset to carry a concealed weapon," Agent Rebecca Harper said, while watching the front entrance to the sheriff department's substation.

"Yeah, but civilians shouldn't be doing the work of law enforcement. I don't like the idea of civilians being armed."

Taking her eyes off the entrance, she looked at her young partner. Agent Harper was old school. She was in her twenty-eighth year with the bureau and knew law-abiding citizens weren't the problem in the country.

"OK, think about what you just said. If it weren't for this guy Carter Thompson, who, even though in Arizona you don't need one, has a concealed-carry permit. If he hadn't taken out the first terrorist, saving the colonel and his family, then the two of them wouldn't have been able to join forces and take out three of the remaining seven terrorists, saving who knows how many lives. Are you saying it would have been better for the colonel and his family to wait behind the kiosk for the police to get there to save them? You saw the video, that asshole was moving in on them, shooting through the kiosk, and would have killed all four of them. No doubt after that he would have continued his rampage on into the bookstore. Tell me that wasn't a good thing the law-abiding Mr. Thompson did!" She turned back and continued to watch the front of the building.

Her partner couldn't argue with what she'd just said. Trevor was part of a new wave of young agents recently brought into the bureau. He served as an Army Ranger, and like many his age did multiple tours in Afghanistan and Iraq. He had been discharged because of the "sequester" implementation. The FBI went on a recruiting effort to hire some of these highly trained combat veterans, and here he was.

"OK, I get what you're saying. But something about this guy has me confused."

"What do you mean?"

"Well, we both watched the videos together and, yes, it was remarkable to watch this guy and the colonel take those assholes out. I mean the way they moved. From the time Thompson shot the first terrorist to the very end, the two of them operated with precision and smoothness. Even after Thompson had got hit with the grenade, he stayed in the fight. What's bugging me is that I understand Colonel Redman, having been a Delta Force operator, having those kind of skills; but where the hell did Carter Thompson learn how to do that? You're not born with those abilities. It only comes about through training and a lot of it. We checked his background, no criminal record, business owner, votes every election... and he was never in the military. Come on, that first guy he shot, a tight, golf-ball size, two-shot group at the base of his throat, and one just to the right of the nose. I went back and timed that sequence. He got those three shots off in less than two seconds, and he's kind of an old guy. So you tell me, Becca, where or how did he learn to do that?"

She turned back toward him while occasionally glancing in the direction of the front of the building. *Why didn't I notice that? Fuck, I must be getting old; but hey, I'm not a combat veteran like my young partner here,* she thought to herself. Special Agent Becca Harper had never been in the military. After graduating from college, she went straight to the FBI training academy in Quantico, Virginia.

"I hadn't noticed that; good job. I haven't a clue where he learned how to do that. I'm glad he was able to, though. Trevor, he was responsible for saving an awful lot of lives. He should be awarded a medal of honor, if they had one for citizens like him."

"OK, maybe so, and you're right, he and the colonel displayed incredible courage yesterday. It's still bugging me, though. I mean, where did he learn those skills? Maybe he's part of one of those crazy militia groups or something."

"Well, bottom line is it doesn't matter where he learned how to do that or if he's a member of some sort of militia group; there's no law against that. I'm just grateful he was there, armed, and that he killed some of those motherfuckers! Hey, looks like him coming out. Let's go talk with him."

Special Agent Rebecca Harper

As they were heading to the parking lot, Carter noticed a man and a woman walking in their direction. She was maybe in her fifties, around five feet seven, short brownish gray hair, wearing a slightly faded baggy navy blue sweat shirt, blue jeans and well-worn black walking shoes. On her right was a younger man keeping pace with her. He looked to be in his mid-thirties, six feet tall wearing a black polo shirt with a tan long sleeve outer shirt over it, tan tactical pants and a pair of tan military style boots. As they came closer, the woman reached into her back pocket and pulled out a wallet, flipping it open to display an FBI shield. Her partner did the same.

"Excuse me, I'm Special Agent Rebecca Harper, and this is Special Agent Trevor Blake. We're both with the FBI. You're Carter Thompson, aren't you?"

"Yes, I am."

Reaching out to shake his hand and looking him directly in the eye, she said; "Thank you for what you and the colonel did yesterday at the mall. It's rare to see that kind of valor displayed."

Shaking her hand first and then the other agent's hand, Carter said. "Thank you. This is my friend Dennis; he's also my attorney."

Dennis nodded his head in their direction.

Carter liked what felt like the genuine openness of the woman, though he wasn't so sure about the other one. He was glad Dennis was at his side. So far, so good; it was a nice meet-and-greet, and he wasn't surprised by the appearance of two FBI agents, given it had been a full-blown terrorist attack.

"Do you want to interview my client?" Dennis asked.

"Not right now. Really just wanted to introduce ourselves and let Carter know if there's anything he needs from us, just give me a call. We'll review his interview with the sheriff's department. Fortunately, there are cameras all over the mall and we've been able to review the whole event. I'm still blown away by what you did, Carter, I know I couldn't have done that. Thank God you were there."

"By the way, I'm curious. You're a civilian, and I understand you've never served. Where did you learn all of those combat skills?" Agent Trevor Blake asked.

"If you'd like to talk with my client, we'd be happy to sit down and talk with both of you. Here's my card. If you'd call me, we can arrange a time that works for all of us to discuss what happened," Dennis said.

"I don't think that'll be necessary, but thank you for offering," Agent Harper said, as she handed Carter and Dennis her card. "By the way, everyone calls me Becca."

Frustration and Outrage

The news coverage on all the media outlets was one constant stream of talking heads reporting events about the carnage in the mall on Black Friday. Security at every mall in the United States had been beefed up, and unfortunately that led to a rise in crime in other areas. Criminals may not be the brightest bulbs on the tree, but they're smart enough to realize when law enforcement on the street is in short supply. 911 operators around the country were constantly bombarded not only with routine calls but also with calls on suspicious activity. America had become a swirling caldron of fear and paranoia. Gun sales were on the rise as well as ammunition sales. Survival stores and websites were doing a landmark business as well.

Fear was the main tool of the Muslim extremists. Led by ISIS, they were successfully terrorizing the souls of the American public. ISIS, partnered with home-grown Muslim extremists, managed to put most Americans into a complete state of panic. What little hope or faith the public had in its government to protect and defend it had all but evaporated. By Sunday morning, less than two days after Black Friday, politicians had jockeyed for position to be interviewed by news outlets all across the country. Even the anchors of the mainstream media could no longer continue the masquerade of misinforming the public. Their commitment to cover for the current administration was quickly evaporating. The anger of the people had risen to a fever pitch after being frustrated by years of observing the decline of America and not knowing what to do about it. It was obvious the Congress was inept and spineless, both on the Democratic and Republican sides. Yes, one could blame the President for the woes of the country, but Congress has been complicit by allowing him to get away with all the lies and deception. But then again, why wouldn't they? Most of the members of Congress were guilty of the same slimy modus operandi. Even citizens in deep denial could no longer tolerate the lack of action to protect them. The mood of the country two days after Black Friday had become dark and angry. Americans had reached a boiling point; they had had enough! Thousands were demonstrating and marching on the White House, demanding the border be secured immediately.

Respectful Anonymity

By Sunday morning, to Carter's relief, neither his name nor Doug's had been mentioned in any of the news reports. The Pima County Sheriff's Department, out of respect and concern for retribution to both of them, declined to give the media their names. And scant details were provided on their actions. Obscurity was fine with him, and he hoped it would stay that way. Carter looked around carefully when he walked down the end of his driveway to get the Sunday paper. He and Kim talked over coffee about what they thought might be happening to the country as the result of this latest attack. As Kim was talking, Carter drifted back to that moment two days ago when his whole world changed.

Like a recorded video, he kept reliving the entire experience, starting with his indecision in the doorway. Even though the events of the whole afternoon were terrible, Carter didn't view it from that prospective. His thoughts contrasted to what was always portrayed in the movies or on TV, where after someone kills a bad guy he feels terrible.

Hell, all I want to do is engage with some more radical Islamic assholes, including any American-born terrorists that victimize the innocent! Carter thought to himself.

He was tired of hearing about neighborhoods being ruled by gangs of thugs. Chicago, a glaring example of this, had become the murder capital of world. Local law enforcement was afraid of getting into trouble or being accused of being racist for doing their job. He was tired of living in an upside-down world.

Both Kim and Carter had their own houses and because of their work schedules they usually spent only one night a week together. They alternated back and forth between each other's houses. This weekend, though, Kim had stayed since Friday night, partly because she wanted to be there with Carter and to help him, but also because she, like the rest of the country, was scared. Kim felt safe with Carter. She trusted him with her heart, and she also knew that no matter what, Carter would put himself between her and harm's way.

Citizen Warriors

It was getting close to noon, and Carter was looking forward to his meeting with Doug. Even though the two of them came from completely different backgrounds, in the days ahead they would discover how much they were alike. One thing for sure was that they were both American patriots who loved their country. Like millions of other Americans, they were angry and frustrated with the federal government's lack of protection. They both were aware that corruption existed in Washington, D.C. for decades. Picking and choosing which laws to enforce had become common-place under current and past administrations and easy get away with while Congress looked the other way.

As Carter was driving to meet Doug, he turned on the radio. Much to his surprise, Peter Collingham was doing a special weekend broadcast. The liberals and most Washington politicians hated him and loathed every broadcast he did. He was one of the people the president blamed for his failed policies.

"Hello, this is Peter Collingham. Well, once again, our president can't seem to use the term "Islamic Terrorists" in referring to the mass murders on Black Friday at a mall in Tucson, Arizona. He couldn't even bring himself to acknowledge and praise the actions of two citizens who risked their own lives by intervening and killing four of the seven terrorists, thereby saving countless others. The level of incompetence and indifference this administration has demonstrated, in my opinion, is derelict and criminal. The president should immediately be arrested and impeached, and a special prosecutor should be assigned to investigate the level of corruption in his administration. He has constantly showed a disregard for the safety of the American public. In fact, I believe he has aided and abetted the likes of ISIS to attack us. They have little to fear from him. It's obvious we've got an American president that is sympathetic and understanding of their hatred for America.

Why hasn't Congress acted to correct his abuse of the Constitution? I'll tell you why; it's because they're all career politicians who are interested in only one thing, getting re-elected.

Will there be any kind of serious military response to these dirty men in scarves who killed the innocent men, women and children at the mall the other day? I doubt it. Our pathetic excuse for a commander in chief wouldn't allow it."

Lowering his voice, he said; "I speak to all of you very seriously now. The Founding Fathers, when creating the Constitution and the form of government they felt would most protect the American citizen from tyranny, established three branches of government; The Executive, Legislative and Judicial branches. However, I suggest to you there's an unspoken fourth branch, and it's not part of the government, it's you the people. I say this because it's your government for better or for worse. In other words, you own the government; it's not the other way around. Everyone in the government works for you, not the other way around. You the citizen are the one to determine if the government is violating the Constitution. The Founding Fathers didn't put the Second

Amendment in the Constitution for hunting or so you could buy a gun to protect yourself from criminals, although you're entitled to do so. No, they specifically put it in so that in the event that tyranny raises its head, coupled with the Legislative and Judicial Branches lacking the will to do anything about it, that we the people would do something about it! The Founding Fathers put the Second Amendment in for you the people to be empowered to take back your country if needed.

I'm not suggesting or encouraging a revolution by force nor asking you to march on Washington, although some of you are already doing that. You should do that with the ballot box. I am telling you this though, and make no mistake about what I'm saying. In spite of the evil events played out on this past Black Friday by forces who want to destroy us, your government is going to continue to do nothing about it other than throw around words about how tragic it was. The government will not call it what it is; Islamic terrorism!

Almost all of our cities have become war zones. As an example, the daily death rate by violence in the city of Chicago is higher than that of our military in combat zones. Disrespect and violence against law enforcement is at an all-time high and covertly encouraged by our President. The border continues to be unsecured. How did those murderous terrorists get into our country? I guarantee that when the dust settles on the investigation, if there is one in the first place, it will show they came through our southern border.

If you want your cities and borders secured, stop waiting. Our government isn't going to do it. It's up to you, the citizen. You are the Fourth Branch, and most of you like me, I know, are at the end of your rope. There are those among us who have the skills and courage as shown the other day in Tucson at the Southwest Regional Mall by those two armed, law-abiding citizens. These were two brave men who chose not just to stand by or run. Among the millions of Americans who listen to me, I know there are warriors present. Since it's obvious to me we will continue to be unnecessarily at risk, I call upon the Citizen Warriors of this great country to step forward and secure our country. Please, for God's sake, make us safe again!"

Carter was more relieved than surprised to hear these truthful and passionate words spoken by the well-regarded talk-show host. Thank God for the First Amendment that allows someone like Peter Collingham to stand up as one of the voices of the people.

Citizen Warrior, that's an interesting thought! He thought to himself as he turned right into the parking lot of the restaurant.

Alliance Formulation

Carter looked at his watch as he pulled into a parking space; it was 12:55 p.m. Just before opening his door, he reached to his right side under his jacket, feeling the pistol grip of his Glock 21 SF., He drew it out of its holster and placed it in the center console. He hated the idea of not being armed, but because he'd be partaking in Doug's promised beer, he couldn't be armed while consuming alcohol. While Carter locked the center console, he thought about his Sig 226 X-5. He knew it would probably be a long time before he got it back from the sheriff's department. His next carry weapon of choice was his Glock 21. Chambered in 45 ACP and using a double-stack magazine with a thirteen-round capacity and coupled with his skill set, it gave him a high degree of confidence. As he opened the door to the restaurant, from behind him he heard a man's voice call out his name. It was a voice he recognized from two days ago. Carter turned with a smile and saw Doug approaching with a slight limp. The two men shook hands and then embraced each other with a brotherly hug, the kind shared by men only when there's a heartfelt connection.

"How are you doing, brother?" Doug asked Carter as he grabbed the door, opening it for the two of them to go in.

"I'm great. Really, couldn't be better; grateful to be alive. How are you doing? How's the leg?"

"Fuck the leg; it's fine. Got a few stiches but, really, it's nothing, I've experienced worse. I'll be a little gimpy for a while but nothing permanent. How're the shrapnel wounds healing up?"

"Hey, pain is good; let's you know you're alive. Right?" Both men laughed and did a fist bump.

Doug gave his name to the hostess. While standing there waiting for her to seat them, Carter took the measure of the man he'd been in mortal combat with two days earlier. *This is a good man!* Carter thought to himself.

It took only a couple of minutes for the hostess to seat them. It was Sunday and the dining section of the restaurant was only half full. The other portion of the establishment was a sports bar, and they could periodically hear the roar of the patrons cheering on their favorite football team.

"Are you hungry? I'm buying; order anything you want," Doug said to Carter as he looked at the menu.

"Well, first I want that beer you promised me."

"Are you ready to order?" The waitress said in a chipper voice as she approached them.

"Order anything you want; it's on me, brother. I owe you big time," Doug said.

"Thanks, really, you don't owe me. I think I'll get a cheeseburger and onion rings if you have them."

"Cheeseburger? No way! They have a really great rib eye here. It's on me, and it's the least I can do for you. Get whatever you want."

"Thanks, really, but a cheeseburger would be great."

"Well, hey, if you don't want a rib eye, why don't you get the surf and turf, prime rib and lobster? It's really good!"

"Thanks, man; let me kick it around a bit."

"We'll take a couple of beers for right now and order something to eat in a little bit," Doug said, smiling back at the waitress as she turned and walked away.

Carter then asked, "How's your wife and kids? Are they doing OK? How's her arm and, seriously, how's your leg doing?"

"Liz is good, and so are the kids. Both of us were fortunate enough not to have any of the rounds hit bone. I'll be a little gimpy the next few days, but what the hell, scars are memories. Thank you for what you did for my family and me. If not for you, we'd all be dead."

"You're welcome. It was no big deal, but thank you for saying that. It means a lot to me. You would have done the same if the situation was reversed."

"Who were you with? My guess is either Army Ranger or Force Recon Marine? I'm retired Delta Force. I assume you're no longer active."

"I never served."

"What? Come on, two to the chest and one to the nose in less than two seconds, are you fucking kidding me? You dropped that guy like the true sack of shit he was. You didn't learn that by going to the local gun range. OK, if you didn't serve then you must have been law enforcement, SWAT, something along those lines. Right?"

"No, never been law enforcement and I'm sorry to say I never served. I went to the Marine Corp recruiting station in Yuma right after the Tet Offensive in the spring of '68 to enlist. I'll share the story with you sometime. Bottom line is, I left not having signed up and stayed in school taking the safe way out. Back then the draft was active and being in school afforded me a 2-S deferment. Frankly, I regret not having joined; I think I missed out on a great adventure. If I could do it all over again, I would join. Big mistake on my part."

Doug looked at him with compassion and said; "You shouldn't feel bad about that. Vietnam was a really fucked-up deal for everyone."

"I know the Vietnam War was fucked-up, and if I'd gone it wouldn't have made any difference in the outcome of the war. At the same time, I feel I let my friends and country down."

"I hear you. Hey, hindsight is always twenty-twenty, right? In my book, what you did the other day more than makes up for that. It was an honor for me to be in the gunfight with you, and I really mean that. We saved a lot of innocent lives the other day, brother!"

Doug then added, "Seriously though, you have me curious and a bit confused. It wasn't just your accurate shooting that I noticed. I watched you throughout the gunfight; you possess some very impressive combat skills for someone who's never served in the military. What's up with that?"

The waitress came back and asked if they were ready to order. By that time Doug had finished his beer, and he watched Carter as he drained his.

"Not quite yet," Doug said, looking at Carter raising his empty glass. "I think I could use another one."

"Make that two," Carter said with a smile.

Carter could tell that Doug was puzzled to hear he wasn't current or former military. Carter knew he'd performed well in the gunfight, but he didn't want to tell him about his initial fear of getting into the fight, nor the fact that an old woman shamed him into acting. Carter resisted the urge to come clean about this with Doug and to tell him that if not for that old woman, he might have left him, his wife and his kids to the mercy of the gunman.

The truth was, he was ashamed of his behavior and wasn't sure how Doug, a combat veteran, would feel about it. The last thing he wanted was for this true American hero to think less of him for his behavior in the doorway.

"OK, if you're not military, and I assume you're not a spook, you got some 'splaining to do, Lucy," Doug said with a chuckle. "You didn't learn those skills in Boy Scouts!

So Carter explained what he and two of his closest friends had committed to six years earlier. After the events of 9/11 and seeing the degradation of the country, especially the last few years under the current administration, they had all come to the conclusion it was time to learn some combat skills.

Carter told Doug about the three of them taking the time and spending the money to spend a weekend at least four times a year at the "Patriot Response Center" in New Mexico and how all of the instructors were former Special Forces guys. Carter and his friends had gone from learning basic combat skills to qualifying for the advance courses offered at PRS. They had completed all the courses, including multiple room-clearing training, deploying both "dynamic and deliberate" room-clearing techniques. PRS also had beginning and advanced long-range shooting classes which was the politically correct term for civilians to develop sniper skills and techniques. Back at home, the three of them would frequently get together on the weekends to keep their skills sharp.

"To be honest with you, I never thought about the possibility of any civilians taking the time to learn how to fight, let alone developing combat skills, but I do understand the motivation. If bad shit happens, as a civilian you're on your own until law enforcement arrives and that could take a long time," said Doug, taking a sip of beer.

Carter looked at Doug, now starting to feel the effects of his second beer, and said, "We don't train to compete, we strictly train to fight. I don't want to fight but if I have to, like the other day, I will fight! There's nothing wrong with a civilian having an edge over the bad guy!"

"Roger that!" Doug responded, raising his glass to Carter and noticing both their glasses were empty.

The attentive waitress reappeared and stood there looking at both men with a smile on her face. "More beer, or are you ready to order?"

Looking at the young woman and then at Doug. "How about both?"

"Sounds good to me."

With that, Carter and Doug gave the waitress their orders, including "just one more round" of beer. They both agreed not to have any more after that since they both had to drive.

As they ate, the two men exchanged their backgrounds, how many children they had and, in Carter's case, how many grandchildren. Doug related that he joined the Army after he graduated from college at the age of twenty-two. He had spent twenty-five years in active duty, retiring when he felt his military pension would be enough to support his wife and two children. Doug had always been good at anything he did and was a natural-born leader. After leaving the Army, he had taken a few months off to transition back into civilian life. As with many combat veterans and especially since he was a former Delta Force operator, he didn't find it easy. The truth was, he was always felt at peace when deploying on a mission, no matter what the risks. He never felt more alive than in those uncertain moments just before engagement with the enemy.

After the few months of doing nothing, he went to work for a personal-security company, escorting executives and their wives and the occasional celebrity on trips. He always carried a side arm when state law didn't prohibit him from doing so. However, he found the work to be tedious and very boring. It was basically an adult babysitting gig. Compared to his life in the Army with Delta Force, it was a complete letdown.

One night at home, he talked with Liz about how he felt about civilian life and his job. Through friends and because of his reputation, he had been approached a number of times to go to work for Response Unlimited. Response Unlimited, like many similar companies, was a contractor to the Pentagon and funded by CIA slush funds. They specialized in providing armed security in foreign countries such as Afghanistan, Iraq, Syria, Indonesia and some countries in Africa.

Doug knew that working for them in many ways was more dangerous than being on a Delta Force team. If he and his partners got into a conflict, they couldn't call in an artillery strike, nor could they call in any Cobra gunships or A10s for close air support. If a threat arose, their immediate course of action was to get out of harm's way as fast as possible. This was the standing orders of Response Unlimited, not to engage any threats, and it was understood and considered as kind of a company joke. Telling a bunch of former Special Forces warriors not to engage the enemy was like telling a dog, "I'm leaving this raw steak on the floor, and I'll be gone for a while; don't you eat it." As soon as you leave, the dog will devour the steak. He can't help it because it's in his DNA.

Liz knew how miserable Doug was working in the private sector. It was obvious he wasn't ready for the quieter life. She had compassion for him and admired the adjustment he'd tried to make for her and the children. Liz was glad he was out of harm's way, and she enjoyed his being able to spend more time at home with her and the kids. She loved him very much and recognized how unhappy he was in his civilian security job. She didn't want him to go to work for Response Unlimited, or any other contractor for that matter since they all were doing the same thing. She also knew these contracting companies provided an important role in keeping Americans safe abroad. The military was stretched far too thin, especially after the president, with the help of a gutless Congress, put the sequestration into effect.

There was no way Liz wanted him to leave again, yet she felt selfish for putting her needs in front of his. It was the kind of relationship they'd always had. Liz knew up front who she was marrying when she fell in love with this man, and she accepted him for who he was. For that, Doug loved her deeply. Even on leave in foreign countries far away, he never cheated on her. He cherished Liz as much as she did him. Liz, with a sigh, hugged him and told him how much she loved him and that she understood. She also demanded that he return in one piece and with no more scars. Doug had smiled, hugged her back and told her how much he loved her, how grateful and proud he was to have her as his wife.

That night had been three-years before the Black Friday events at the mall. He had made the conscious decision after his last assignment in Libya that he was finished with using a gun for a living. It wasn't the same as when he'd left the Army; this was different. He looked forward to the unpredictable future of being a civilian. Contracting paid way better than his full-time Army salary, and between that and his pension he'd managed to tuck away a tidy sum in the bank account. He didn't know what he was going to do next, but he knew for sure he was done with contracting.

Liz was beyond joy hearing this. She also knew Doug well enough to realize that he'd gone through some sort of transformation to now be happily accepting his role as a full-time husband, father and civilian.

What Doug didn't tell Liz because he didn't want to scare her, was that he was troubled by what was happening to his country and worried about the future for their children. This concern on Doug's part was really the seed of an idea that caused him to stay home, so he could be close to his family and take care of them.

One night on his last assignment in Libya with Response Unlimited, he and three of his fellow brothers-in-arms discussed their concerns over a few beers. Deep in their hearts, they all felt a sense of dread for America and were convinced that sooner or later the wheels were going to come off the cart called the United States of America. If it did, they all wanted to be close to home to protect their loved ones. Doug's biggest fear was he'd be in some other country when something bad happened in America, and he wouldn't be there to take care of his family. This was the catalyst that led to his decision to come home and stay home. The events of Black Friday validated his decision.

An Idea Whose Time Has Come

Carter listened to what Doug had to say about his concerns for the future of America and his children. It resonated with him, too. Doug paused after telling Carter all this, and Carter knew Doug now wanted to hear about his life and background.

Carter was fourteen years Doug's senior, but over the last thirty years or so, in many ways they had lived similar lives, except of course Carter was on the civilian side. Carter told Doug about how he had started his first company when he was twenty-six and had not worked for anyone since then. He had owned a number of companies, including a management consulting practice that coached the owners of small- and medium-sized companies. Carter had gained national recognition in his work with business owners because of the stunning success his clients had achieved. Carter was known as being a Vince Lombardi kind of coach; an unrelenting bulldog when it came to his client's success. This strength was seasoned by compassion for what a business owner goes through at times.

Both men understood that while their lives up to this point had been very different, in many ways they were the same. The circumstances were just different. Both of them had several things in common; they were strong and compassionate leaders and relentless when it came to being successful in whatever they did. Defeat was never an option, and the two of them always played to win.

Carter had mutual concern for the direction the country was taking. From his viewpoint, America could not withstand the continued expansion of the government, coupled with its reckless spending.

"Before anything though, the border has to be secured!" Carter said.

127

Turn-About is Fair Play

As Doug listened, he understood that, just like himself, Carter was a patriot and a constitutional conservative. This somehow struck Doug as being odd. He'd always assumed that only those in the military felt that way.

"The Republicans are as bad as the Democrats. If Congress had any balls and honor they'd impeach and then arrest this son-of-a-bitch posing as our so-called president for dereliction of duty and treason. Personally, I'm sick of waiting for something to happen, and I think there are millions of Americans who feel the same way. Congress isn't going to do anything, and to me they're a bigger problem than the president. It's been that way for fifty years, and it's getting worse with each new presidential election cycle. National Security Agency eavesdropping, IRS scandals, Benghazi, the disrespect and disdain for our military and a few other examples of how we have a lawless government with nothing being done about it," Carter said in a deadly serious tone.

"I think all three branches of government are corrupt. The members of the judiciary are nothing more than political appointees nominated by an existing president and rubber-stamped by Congress to further advance their political agenda, whether it be liberal or conservative. The Founding Fathers never intended it to be this way. They didn't create the Second Amendment for hunting – they created it for citizens of this country to deal with the kind of crap we now have in Washington. It's clear and obvious America is now under the control of a "soft" tyranny which, if it's not thwarted, is only going to get worse. Our elected officials are never going to look after our best interests!" Doug could relate to what Carter had just said and found that his words matched how he felt about things. He had never considered the possibility there were citizens who were as outraged as he and his fellow military comrades were.

"Our border is unsecured; we're just forty-five minutes away from a war zone. In the last ten years there's been more than one hundred thousand Mexicans murdered just south of the border. What the fuck, the cartels have control of our own border. They come across whenever they want. And so has the Mexican military, who has made incursions into our interior on multiple occasions, with our Border Patrol agents being told to retreat. This is a foreign military invading our country with none of our military there to stop them. People who live on the border, like the ranchers down there, have to deal with this on a daily basis with no help from the federal government. The illegals and terrorists have no fear and the citizens of our country are afraid to do anything because they'd be the ones to be arrested. The illegals, cartels and terrorists have more rights than we do!"

Carter paused and finished off what was left of his beer. "Hell, the terrorists are smart; they have cells already formed before they get here."

"You're right about the Muslims forming cells. And you're right that our government is never going to protect its citizens," Doug said and then stopped. Carter could tell he had something on his mind.

"Why couldn't we, as citizens, form cells and do what our federal government is too inept or too cowardly to do? I don't think I'm alone in my thinking. Look at the 'Veterans Against ISIS,' a group of American veterans, who are no longer willing to sit by knowing ISIS is gaining ground on the Kurds and slaughtering thousands of innocent people in the process. On their own dime, they've gone to help the Kurds."

Carter pulled his empty mug away from his lips, looking at Doug. Even though he was feeling the effects of his third beer, what Doug had just said was the most logical and best idea he'd heard in a long time.

"I like your idea of citizens forming cells. If you're really serious about this, count me in! Turn-about is fair play!" Carter said, smacking his beer mug onto the table.

"Fuck, yes, I'm serious about this. After watching the destruction of our country while both the Republicans and Democrats in Congress sit by and do nothing, what other choice do we really have? The biggest threat to our children's future is not our enemies, its Washington, D.C. At this point in my life I've had enough, and I think more and more Americans feel the same way."

The two men looked at each other. Doug drained his glass. Carter could see he had something else on his mind.

"Carter, you mentioned you had two close friends and the three of you have taken it upon yourselves to get trained. Are these two men someone you'd trust in a gunfight? And would they also keep their mouths shut when needed?"

"Yes, beyond a shadow of a doubt, I'd trust either of these men with my life and that of my family's also."

Doug had a good feeling about Carter even though he'd only known him for a short period of time. Because of what they'd experienced together and how he performed under fire, Doug intuitively knew Carter was a man who could be trusted and who would keep quiet about things. Doug was a firm believer in, "birds of a feather flock together," and because of this he could only assume that Carter's close friends were made of the same mettle and integrity Carter was.

"I've got three friends, all retired like me and former Special Forces. Two are former Delta and the other one is a retired Navy Seal. Would you and your friends like to join us in some weapons and tactics training? I already spoke with each of them about this, and they're good with it," Doug said, looking at Carter with a slight grin on his face.

Because of Carter's experience over the years with the Patriot Response Center where he was trained by former Spec Operators employed by PRC, he knew the value of this offer. To learn from someone who not only had those skills, but who had also utilized them multiple times in real life on the battlefield would be invaluable.

"Hell, yes, I would, and they would also. We'd consider it an honor to train with you and your friends. We know our gunfighting skills are good, even though we're civilians, but we also realize we still have much to learn, always will. There's no substitute in life for the real thing. Except for the other day, I've never been in a gunfight before, and I know my friends haven't been either. You say when and where, and we'll be there."

Carter knew both of his friends would be on board without asking them, and he looked forward to telling them about the opportunity Doug had just given them.

"We have a friend who owns about thirty-five-hundred acres just north of the Tortolita Mountains," said Doug. "It's all fenced off with a locked gate and only one road leading in and out. Much of it is in a box canyon, and the closest neighbor with a house is over a mile and a half away. About two years ago we helped him set up a pistol, carbine and long-distance range. We set it up according to the latest military specs. The pistol range goes to one-hundred meters, carbine is three-hundred meters and the long distance range goes out to fifteen-hundred meters. We also built a shoot house. The long-range course is set up with different elevations. You can pick your spot anywhere in the canyon, simulating real-world situations. All of the different ranges have reactive targets. The four of us make it a point to get out there as often as we can to keep our skills sharp. Nice and quiet with no one snooping around. Obviously, we have to know we can count on the three of you never to say a word about it"

"You definitely can!" Carter responded. "It's hard to find a spot where you can shoot out to one-thousand meters, let alone fifteen-hundred that you can drive your targets out to. It's a bitch lugging out a seventy-five-pound steel target that far in the desert. A few years ago we found a spot way out on the east side on BLM land. The three of us spent the whole day carrying out targets and target stands along with concrete mix, water and shovels to secure them. The furthest one was eight-hundred yards. After three months of use, we went out there and some fucktard had stolen our targets! You have my word and I speak for my friends, nothing will ever be spoken about it to anyone!" Carter reached out his hand to Doug to affirm his commitment to secrecy.

"OK, let's touch base in the next day or two, and we'll set up a time. I don't know about you, but after the other day I feel a sense of urgency to step up the training. Because our government never is going to do anything, we as citizens need to do something about the threats facing our country. I've been in a lot of combat, and I've got to tell you that the other day shook me up. And I'm not easily rattled. Those goat-fuckers were trying to kill my family. Even though we killed them, I know as sure as we're sitting here that there's more of them on the way to do the same thing to us and other Americans. In the meantime, our government continues to do nothing to secure the border to keep the evil shitheads out! I'm pissed!"

Over the Edge

Carter knew by Doug's demeanor that he was deadly serious. Here was a man who could only be pushed so far. For whatever reason, the other day in the mall had pushed him over the edge. Carter was glad to have become friends with someone who saw things the way he and his friends did. He also had the skills and means to do something about it should the need arise. For these two men, it was one of those moments in life when you connect with someone in a deep and profound way. Somewhere in his soul Carter sensed their meeting was destined and a call to arms.

"I hear you, brother, and I'm with you," Carter answered seriously.

The nice thing about getting pleasantly buzzed on some beer is it allows people to be much more open to sharing their true inner thoughts and feelings. Many times it's also a way for people to get to know each other better.

The waitress came over, interrupting them said as she was picking up their now-empty plates and glasses. "Are either one of you interested in dessert?"

"Not for me. How about you, Doug?" Carter asked, looking at the waitress and wondering if she knew or would even care about the danger facing the country.
"I'm good; just the check, please," Doug said. As he was reaching for his wallet, he reminded, "This one's on me, brother!"

"Thanks. Next time I buy!

The two men got up and left, walking out to the parking lot while simultaneously looking around. Doug noticed Carter doing this and was pleased to see his awareness to his surroundings.

"Doug, question for you. The other day in the mall you were unarmed. Afterward, I thought about that and was a bit surprised. Given your background, how come? I'm not judging you about this; I know to carry is a choice."

Doug knew Carter's questions weren't coming from a place of criticism but of concern. He appreciated that Carter had the trust in him to ask the question, knowing he wouldn't be offended. With the two men facing each other, Doug patted his right side.

"Because we were having a few beers, I left it in my truck. The other day and today will be the last time you'll ever see me unarmed. The truth is, I was so happy to be spending the day with my family, I guess I had a brain cramp. I actually did think about it and thought wearing a weapon seemed like bringing work into my home life. My bad! Never will do that again!"

With that, the two men shook hands and hugged.

"Talk with you in a day or two. I'm looking forward to sending some lead down range with you and your buddies!" Doug said as he got into his vehicle.

Remembrance

On the drive home, Carter thought about the events of the last few days. It was one of those rare times in his life when he knew for certain that his life had taken a new direction. He knew the winds of change can blow at any moment, and it felt like a gale-force wind had just hit him. *I feel like I'm being called to do something, just not quite sure where this is all going to lead,* he thought to himself.

In 1967, President Johnson had made a decision to escalate the American troop strength to five-hundred-fifty thousand in Vietnam. Johnson and his cronies knew the high-school graduating classes of 67' across the country were an abundant source of physically fit draftees. The draft was active then, and a young man of Carter's age and physical prowess had three choices. One was to go to college and carry at least twelve units per semester so you would qualify for a 2-S deferment. This would exempt you from the draft and was good for four years. The second thing a young man could do was to leave the country and head for Canada. For Carter, that was never an option. Third choice was plain and simple, enlist in one of the four branches or allow yourself to be drafted into the Army or the Marine Corp.

At that age, Carter never put much thought into his future: he just lived life day by day. School had always been a slow, boring grind for him, and his sole mission once he got to high school was to graduate. Though Carter was bright, he constantly struggled as a student. Studying is a learned discipline and something no one ever took the time to teach him when he was a young child. When the final   school   bell   rang every day, Carter always felt renewed; it was his happiest moment of the day. Graduating from high school for Carter was the final triumph of *just getting by* and finally gaining his freedom. For him, high school was a requirement. Going to college was a choice.

High-school graduation represented entry into manhood. All he wanted to do after graduating was to get a job, move out of the house and support himself as he headed off into the adventure of adulthood. The conventional wisdom at the time was if you didn't go to college and get a degree, you wouldn't go anywhere in life. This was something his mother pounded into him relentlessly. She was always telling him if he didn't go to college he'd be a failure in life. While he didn't fully buy into her line of thinking, the concern and fear of failing nagged at him in the background of his inner thoughts.

Carter's other conflict was that he felt obligated to help his fellow brothers in the Vietnam War. His father was a veteran of World War II, serving three-and-a-half years in the South Pacific as a Marine. He was always telling him he should join the Marines; *it will make a real man out of you!* Those were the words echoing in Carter's ears after his father's repeated admonitions. On the other hand, his mother constantly leaned on him to go to college. To say he was a conflicted young man would be an understatement.

His parents divorced when he was ten years old, each of them pulling him in opposite direction. Carter felt cowardly and guilty for not serving and helping out his brothers in

Vietnam, but he worried he'd be a failure if he didn't go to college. Not enlisting almost seemed un-American and un-patriotic. Even at that young age, Carter was as red, white and blue as one could get.

While trying to decide whether to go to war, Carter yielded to his mother's influence and spent his freshman year in college in Yuma at Arizona Western College. Unlike most kids who had fun in college, Carter's was the most miserable year in his life. He spent all his time feeling guilty constantly thinking about becoming a Marine and going off to war. He made it a point, though, to get good grades so he could be accepted at the University of Arizona the following year would allow him to escape Yuma and bury the torment of his guilt.

The beginning of his sophomore year in college found him back in Tucson. The thought of going off to war was drowned out by the fun and party time of the University. It was time for sex, drugs and rock and roll! To drown and numb his guilt and fears he smoked pot and drank a bottle of Ripple every night in his sophomore year of college.

As he was driving home, Carter thought about that time in his life and how he always regretted not joining the Marines and going off to war. Just about everyone he shared his feelings of guilt would tell him he didn't miss anything.

As he drove on he thought, *maybe I didn't go to Vietnam because I was being saved for a more important battle. Maybe being at the mall at that place in time and going into battle with a man of Doug's character and background was no accident. Maybe Doug's comment of "why couldn't we form a cell" was a call to battle. Maybe his invitation for me and my two buddies to join him and his friends-in-training was no accident either. Maybe the old woman at the doorway was a reflection of the guilt I experienced for not serving. Maybe this is the time to right the past. Maybe God really does have a plan for us all.*

From Carter's point of view, one thing was certain; there is evil and it's on America's doorstep and alive and well in Washington, D.C. And meanwhile the White House and Congress look the other way. Historically, it reminded him of early Nazi Germany. Maybe it was time to do something about it. He knew for sure he'd had enough, and for his family, friends and country he was ready to lay down his life.

Carter looked forward to calling and setting up a time with his two friends to explain the events and Doug's invitation. He couldn't remember when he'd felt more excited and alive.

Diversity Doctrine –
Dangerous Consequences

"Companies considering contracting with the federal government must be prepared to demonstrate the diversity of their workforce as part of the fulfillment of affirmative action obligations as imposed by federal law. While the requirements are not new, the Department of Labor under the current Administration is placing greater emphasis on ensuring that affirmative action requirements are fulfilled. The strategy laid out by labor secretary Hilda Solis called "Good Jobs for Everyone" puts a strong emphasis on the Department's commitment to increased compliance, investigation and enhanced workplace representation of all covered groups." Jamie Goretick and Joanne Waters, *Executive Counsel*, The Magazine for the General Counsel, CEO & CFO.

Dynatherm Corporation was well-known and well-regarded by the Defense Department. Amongst other things, the company specialized in producing lightweight and efficient explosive material used by the U.S. and its allies in their arsenal of surface-to-air missiles. DOD also used their warhead components for many of the air-to-ground and hand-held, shoulder-fired weapon systems. Because of its expertise in this area, Dynatherm had a number of contracts with the U.S. federal government. The Department of Defense was their main customer.

Because Dynatherm was a U.S. government contractor with more than fifty employees, they are required to submit a Diversity/Affirmative Action Plan to the Department of Labor. Like other companies its size, it didn't have a choice in the matter. Long before the sequester was announced, the current administration began radically downsizing America's military. This directly impacted most contractors to the U.S. government, and Dynatherm was no exception. After all, what were they to do? Seventy-three percent of their business came from contracts with the United States government.

The Department of Labor, as directed by the White House, was instructed to ratchet up the pressure on defense companies doing business with the government. Three years prior, the Department of Labor in an audit of Dynatherm, determined the company was not in compliance with the Diversity Doctrine. In a letter from the Department of Labor and personally signed by the Secretary of Labor, the company's chief counsel was told they had thirty days to correct the problem or all of their government contracts would be immediately cancelled. The issue was the fact that their minority hiring ratio was off by .02 percent. Immediately they had to hire nine minority employees or risk losing billions of dollars in contracts which would put them out of business. In the past, the average time from start to finish for hiring a person took sixty to ninety days. This was to give ample time for all of the references to be followed up, as well as a rigorous background check on each applicant for obvious security reasons.

The board of directors instructed Joe Cannon, the head of Human Resources and Development at Dynatherm, to "just get it done!" The glaring problem was the window of time allotted to accomplish this. He understood the politics in the company as well as the gravity of the situation, and he knew he would be out of a job if the task wasn't accomplished on time. Throwing all precautions to the wind, he instructed Susan Welch, who headed up the screening process for new hires, to go into the minority "dead file" (those people who for one reason or another couldn't pass a background check) and find nine "reasonable" candidates and hire them *now*. She knew the term "reasonable" was code for hire "any warm body as long as it was a minority." When Welch protested, raising concern for security breaches, Cannon explained the situation.

He promised her that within ninety days of fulfilling the Department of Labor demands, they would thoroughly investigate every new hire. Any problem areas in the backgrounds of the new hires would be investigated. If the issues were not satisfied, the individuals would be terminated.

Joe Cannon had worked his way into his position not because he excelled at his job but because he excelled in the fine art of company politics. Golf outings, cocktail parties et cetera, Joe was always there, rubbing shoulders and yucking it up with the company CEO and CFO and their immediate subordinates.

Welch looked at him skeptically when he told her the plan. She knew it was all bullshit, but she was a single mother raising two children, so she thought wiser not to protest any further. Cannon had a history of declaring great plans for the future and never following through with them.

She was also keenly aware that newly hired employees had forty-five days in which to join the union. If they did so, they would be protected from any future grievances the company might have against them. Rubber stamping their background check was no exception, as per union contract. It was Dynatherm's responsibility to get that right, not the new hires.

Rashid Abdul Romani was one of the recent rejected applicants pulled out of the dead file. Since he was African American, he qualified as a minority. When HR ran the original background check on him, it came back with "no history," which is grounds for rejection. Rashid, along with eight others, otherwise fulfilled Cannon's requirements. Rashid reported to his new employer within five days of receiving a phone call from Welch, who offered him a position.

Praise Be Allah

Immediately after hanging up the phone from Dynatherm, Rashid called his uncle Jamal Romani who praised him and Allah for his accomplishment. Romani would be reporting to work at Dynatherm Munitions production plant in Chattanooga, Tennessee, the following Monday. Smiling as he ended the call with his nephew, Jamal said, "Allah Akbar!"

Rashid, alias Mike Green, was raised in the Near North Side of Chicago in a Chicago Housing Authority project called Cabrini-Green. Cabrini-Green was originally built in the 1940s and at one point housed fifteen thousand residents in mid- and high-rise apartment buildings with over thirty-six hundred units. Over the years, decay and neglect created hazardous living conditions for the residents.

Like many adolescents living in Cabrini-Green, Rashid was the product of a fatherless home. In spite of his mother's best efforts, he gravitated into the gang culture. By the time he was fourteen, he'd been arrested eighteen times on charges ranging from petty theft to attempted murder. Many of Rashid's family members also lived in the housing project. Jamal (alias Pete Green) was Romani's uncle and ten years his senior. Jamal was an influential force in Rashid's life. Jamal was also a gang member of long standing, and because of him, Rashid followed him into the gang life.

He always felt safe around Jamal and trusted him. He was the closest thing to a father figure in his life. When Rashid was fifteen, Jamal was arrested and sentenced to twenty years for the murder of a rival gang member.

Rashid felt lost without him and would visit him in Joliet Prison as often as possible. While in prison, Jamal "saw the light" and became a devout Muslim, abiding by the prison rules and becoming a model prisoner. After eight years, he was paroled for good behavior, vowing never to return to the criminal life.

Following his early release from prison, Jamal returned to Chicago and immediately started attending the Ribah Mosque. He became a devout listener of the preaching's of Iman Mohammad Ammar al Quraysh who immigrated in the nineteen nineties to the U.S. The Imam had direct ties to a then-unknown splinter Islamic terrorist group which would become known as ISIS. Jamal invited Rashid to join him, and quickly his nephew became a devout Muslim, following the teachings laid out in the Koran.

For Rashid and Jamal, being a Muslim came first, followed by being black, oppressed, victimized and a mentality of entitlement. In terms of importance, being an American wasn't even a consideration. They both become radicalized Muslim Americans, viewing everyone else as infidels. They firmly believed that the end of the infidels was coming. The vision of everyone in their mosque was that one day soon Sharia Law would rule America and the world. All of them were there to do their part to promote this end and would help in any way they could.

It was not farfetched to understand their thinking. Under the administration's foreign policies, the rest of world now believed America had become weak. They believed they had a believer in the White House who was indirectly aiding and abetting the Muslim extremist quest for world domination. To accomplish this, first they had to bring America to its knees. Creating terror was their primary strategy.

When Rashid Abdul Romani, the former Mike Green, assumed his new belief and identity, he applied for and received a Social Security number. He secured this with the aid of a forged birth certificate and a fraudulent work history supplied by someone in the mosque. Mike Green, along with his criminal record, no longer existed. With a new Social Security number and driver's license in hand, as per Jamal's instructions, Rashid had applied to the Dynatherm Corporation in Chattanooga, Tennessee. It was at this facility that all of the explosive materials were manufactured. Rashid had no history, no criminal record, but he was a minority. Now, with Susan Welch's new marching orders from Joe Cannon, not having a work history no longer mattered.

After two years of exemplary work, Rashid Abdul Romani applied for and was transferred from the shipping department to the manufacturing department of Dynatherm. In his new job, he was responsible for mixing the components RDX2 and pouring the material into round ceramic molds with a half-inch diameter hole in the middle for a thirty-six-hour curing process. The hole in the RDX2 molds is where the detonators are placed when it's time to arm the warhead. There were four different sizes of molds. The completed material, upon removal from the molds, weighed ten, twenty-eight, thirty-five and sixty-five pounds, respectively. RDX2 was an extremely explosive material, making conventional C4 or Centex look like lady-finger firecrackers. A half-pound charge of RDX2 could easily level an average house.

After curing, Rashid would extract the RDX2 which would have a clay-like consistency. You could hit it, throw it or put a torch to it, and it would do nothing. Upon removing the material, he would put the cured molds of the RDX2 on a pallet that would then be moved by another worker to a secured storage room. The inventory of all the different molds was constantly in flux. On rare occasions, the molds would break. When this happened, Rashid was instructed to dispose of the molds in a secured container for incineration at a later date. The molds, along with the RDX2, were supposed to be constantly inventoried for security reasons. However, this wasn't always the case.

Once in his new job, and with instructions from his uncle Jamal, Rashid intentionally dropped one of the ten-pound molds. It broke almost perfectly in half. Rashid appropriately reported the incident and then went to the secured container to dispose of it. Instead of putting it in the trash container, he carefully (after making sure no one was watching and he was out-of-sight of the overhead cameras) placed the two pieces of the mold on the floor behind it. Later, when his co-worker was on a break, he went by and scooped up the two broken pieces and put them behind his work bench. The next day, he grabbed the two pieces and took them into the employee bathroom. Once safely behind the closed door of one of the bathroom stalls and with no cameras present, he super glued the two halves together. No one was in the bathroom, and he slowly opened the door, making sure no one was in the area. Then Rashid went back to his work bench with the now-complete mold on his left side away from the view of the camera. Over the course of the next six months, when he was preparing the sixty-five pound molds, on two occasions he was able to pour off enough material so as not to be noticed into a ten-pound mold. He was confident

Allah would aid him in his task, and because of this he was never nervous or worried about being discovered.

At the completion of close to six months, Rashid successfully smuggled out of Dynatherm's munitions production facility three ten-pound donuts of RDX2. At this point, he called his uncle to report his accomplishment. Jamal then drove from Chicago to Chattanooga that week to pick up the RDX2 from him. Rashid never once wondered or questioned how or for what the RDX2 was going to be used. All he could think was, "Allah Akbar!"

Acceptance

Doug talked with his three friends – Conway Armstrong, Mike Buckholder and Rocco Rossi – about his part in what happened the day of the mall shooting. He told them about his running battle with a well-trained civilian named Carter Thompson. He shared with them the details of how Carter saved him and Liz and his kids. Even though he knew his friends trusted him and would go along with his ideas, he felt it was important to have them buy into his plan of including Carter and his two friends in their training sessions.

Doug wondered why he wanted to include Carter and his friends; he wasn't sure, but he felt compelled to do so. Doug was not what some people might call a religious man, but he was very spiritual. There was no question for him that God had an impact on his life. As far as Doug was concerned, when Carter showed up the other day – when he did and the way he did – it was a matter of divine intervention. Carter saved him and his family along with countless others. Doug was certain that God delivered Carter to him at just the right time, and he knew somehow that the two of them would be connected for life. It wasn't just that Carter was important, it was somehow that the two of them acting as a unit was really important. But he just didn't know for what and how God was going to use the two of them.

The four men were all sitting around the table in Doug's home office when Conway looked at Doug and said, "Boss, you know I completely trust you, and if you feel solid about it, then that's good enough by me."

Conway, also former Delta, was a big, burly kind of guy. He stood six-feet-three, with a short military buzz cut and weighed in at 262; he was soft spoken, mild-mannered and a dry sense of humor. Doug served with him through multiple tours of duty and seen how Conway would transform into a killing machine if it was needed. It didn't matter to him in a fight how he dispatched the enemy – guns, knives or bare hands – whatever was the most efficient at the time. One time when they were doing an entry into a hut in Afghanistan, Doug watched as a Taliban fighter trained his rifle on Conway, who was just three feet away. Conway moved like a cat just at the exact moment the Taliban pulled the trigger, knocking the rifle out of the way and then grabbing the guy and twisting his head a hundred and eighty degrees, dropping him to the floor. *Was that face down? No, it was face up, with the front of the body twisted the other direction, lying on the floor.* Doug smiled, thinking about that moment and remembering the dumb look on the Taliban's face. Conway reminded Doug of the pictures of the Viking crusaders, swinging their swords and axes as they charged into battle.

Rocco, a former Navy Seal, stood six feet tall and was thin and wiry. He was fast, jumpy, intuitive, smart, well read and as loyal a friend as one could have. Doug expected Rocco, in his usual manner, to ask many questions – which he did.

"How old is this guy? What does he do? Do you really think you can trust him? What about his friends? How old are they? Are they all in good shape? OK, we know this Carter can and will kill someone when needed, but what about his friends? Why weren't they in the military?"

Doug answered every question as best he could. Rocco responded, "OK, let's see how it goes. I'll get behind it conditional on his two friends don't prove themselves to be fuckups!"

"Fair enough," Doug said, nodding his head and smiling at Rocco. He also hoped Carter's two friends were of the same grit and caliber that Carter is. His gut told him they'd be OK. Doug wasn't surprised by Rocco's response and expected it. He also knew if Rocco became confident in their abilities and characters, he would get behind them one-hundred-and-ten percent. Rocco was the kind of man who, when he became your friend, was your friend for life and one that would lay down his life for you or your family.

Doug nodded to Rocco and the three of them looked at Mike, the fourth member of the team. Mike was five feet nine, with short gray hair and a heavy beard. He was stocky, a former Army Ranger with a "can-do" attitude no matter what the circumstances. Mike was the coolest one in the group. He was part of a unit spending two tours in Iraq defusing IEDs. Doug knew Mike longer than the other two. As far as Doug was concerned, there was no one cooler than Mike under extreme pressure. The old expression, "He has ice water in his veins," was a perfect description of him.

Mike quietly looked at the three of them. "I'm in; let's see what these three civilians can bring to the party. I'm ready when the three of you are to train them."

"If you guys are good to go, let's get out to the range with them a week from this coming Saturday. I'll give Carter a call later today and confirm he and his friends can be available that day. I already know what Carter's skill set is with a handgun, and if his two friends are half as good as he is, it will save us a lot of time bring them up to

151

speed. I wouldn't be surprised that they're also proficient on the AR15," Doug said.

Doug promised them as soon as he connected with Carter he'd let them know. He called Carter later in the day as to their plans. Carter was ready to go and said he would get back to Doug as soon as he confirmed with Garrett O'Keefe and Mick Kilroy.

Friends

As soon as he hung up the phone with Doug, Carter called Garrett and Mick. The three of them had already met, and Carter explained about the mall events, his lunch with Doug and the invitation for the three of them to train with Doug and his men. Both of them were excited about this, and Carter had no doubt when he called to confirm the date a week from Saturday to train with Doug and his guys that they'd jump at the chance.

While training together the last six years, the three men made the seven-hour trip over to New Mexico and back many times. This afforded them plenty of time to talk about their concerns for the country and its future. Garrett and Mick were the same age and twelve years younger than Carter. Like Carter, they didn't train to compete but to fight should the need arise. All three of them were successful in what they did in life. Other than their immediate family members, very few people knew how well-trained in combat skills these civilians had become. And they wanted to keep it that way. They didn't want to fight; however, if something bad happened, they'd be there to answer. Garrett and Mick always carried a concealed handgun on their side and an extra magazine, just as Carter did. Because they spent so much time together, in the spirit of true Patriots, they became like one unit in the dangerous ballet of live-fire training at the Patriot Response Center.

Training Initiation

As Carter anticipated, Garret and Mick would make time to be available to train the following Saturday. They would bring four-hundred rounds each of handgun and AR15 rifle ammunition, knee pads, elbow pads and all the other gear they used when training at PRC. Doug told Carter they wanted to start by evaluating their close-quarters combat skills.

Because Carter's house was on the way to the range, it was agreed Garrett and Mick would be there at six o'clock in the morning, and they'd go in one vehicle. From Carter's place they would head up Oracle Road to the Oracle Junction, where they'd rendezvous with Doug and the other three at seven o'clock. About a half mile up the Florence Highway on the left-hand side was a rest stop with a covered picnic table and benches, making it easy to find.

Right at seven, Carter and the other two rolled into the rest stop where Doug, Conway, Mike and Rocco were waiting for them in one vehicle. Carter waved to them and before he could even stop, Doug waved back and pulled out of the rest stop, heading north on the Florence Highway. Carter followed close behind.

It was a beautiful December day, forty-three degrees, severe clear and sunny with no wind in the early morning air. After about twenty minutes heading north on the paved two-lane highway, Doug turned left onto a narrow dirt road which was heavily covered in desert brush on either side. After another fifteen minutes heading slightly southwest, with branches scraping the sides of Carter's Ford Expedition, they came to a stop at a locked gate and cattle guard. Looking in both directions, Carter could see sections of barb wire attached to Ocotillo branches, serving as vertical supports for the fence line and reaching beyond what he could see. About every thirty feet there were also steel fence posts driven into the ground, serving as additional support for the fence.

When Doug pulled to a stop in front of the gate, Rocco, who was riding in the right front seat, jumped out unlocked the gate, pulling it open so both vehicles could pass through. Once Carter's trailing vehicle was far enough forward through the gate, Rocco closed and locked it and then jogged back to Doug's truck. As they continued on down the dirt road, Carter could see a small mountain range getting larger as they approached the northern end of it. After another ten minutes they veered to the left, and the rutted narrow dirt road began going up a hill. Rounding the top and on the other side, Carter could see the opening to a box canyon and some small buildings at its opening about a quarter mile away.

Doug's vehicle came to a stop in front of the old ranch house. Mick, who was riding in the right rear seat of Carter's truck, hollered out, "Holy shit. This is bad ass!" In front of them they could see a gun range to the left and another to the right. Carter figured one must be for handguns and the other one for the AR15. He could see the latter went out to what looked to him to be three-hundred meters. Straight ahead was the box canyon with a foot trail going up to it. The canyon was thickly covered with Palo Verde trees, desert broom, barrel cacti, Cholla and saguaro cacti dotting both sides of it. In the base of the canyon, Carter could also make out mesquite trees and cottonwoods. He assumed that during the winter rains and summer monsoons water flowed down the dry river bed at the bottom of the canyon. Off in the distance he could see what he assumed to be white twenty-by-twenty-inch steel targets, spaced at what looked like one

155

hundred yards apart, heading up and into the canyon as far as he could see.

The sixteen-hundred-square-foot ranch house had been there for eighty-three years and was built out of the local rocks and topped by a pitched tin roof. It had a kitchen, a large main room and three other rooms that once served as bedrooms. Outside, fifty feet away, was a large concrete patio – the ramada – which also sported a tin roof. Underneath there were two large picnic tables and an open fire pit with a brick barbeque and chimney off to one side. Another two-hundred feet away and to the left was what Doug had told Carter about; a five-room "shoot house," where they did their house-clearing exercise, using "Simunition" ammunition in their guns on targets and mannequins placed in different spots. From time to time, they would go force on force with the use of Simunitions. It was the closest thing they could do to replicate a real gunfight.

After everybody exited the two trucks, Doug gave Carter and the other two a quick overview of the layout. He then pulled all of them together in the covered patio area and had everyone introduce himself and briefly outline his background. After that was complete, Doug then went over the plan for the day.

The day went quickly, and they all broke for lunch right at noon. This gave all seven of them a chance to sit down over a meal and get to know each other, apart from being on the firing line. The drills that Doug and his men put Carter, Mick and Garrett through were almost identical to the ones they had learned at PRC, including the command jargon. At the end of the day, they headed back to the patio area to debrief. Carter, Mick and Garrett got there first. Doug, Conway, Mike and Rocco huddled for a

156

few minutes at the AR15 rifle range which had been their last training station of the day.

The four of them watched as Carter, Mick and Garrett made their way to the ramada, sitting down at one of the two picnic tables and unloading their gear onto the adjacent table. They could see that the three of them were tired but could hear their spirited voices talking in the distance.

"Well, gentlemen, what do you think of our three civilians?" Doug asked, looking at the other three.

All three of them agreed they were surprised by the level of skill displayed in the live-fire training, both on the pistol range and the rifle range. Equally important to Doug and the others was Carter's, Garrett's and Mick's understanding of the different drills presented to them. They were also impressed with their choice of gear. The three of them had SBRs (short-barrel rifles) with suppressors attached to them. In addition, each rifle had a weapon light, an angle fore grip, a PAC III infrared aiming device mounted properly on the top rail of the hand guard and a mount for either a three-power magnifier or a PVS-14 night-vision optic which would sit right behind the Aimpoint Micro T-1 red-dot scope.

Carter and the other two took full advantage of the availability of the battle gear available to the general public. In addition to their weapons and accessories, they also acquired full chest rigs with level-four ceramic plates in the containment pockets. If Doug and his friends didn't know any better, they would have thought they'd been outfitted by the Department of Defense. It was obvious these three not only learned combat skills with their weapons but could use those skills to defend their families, friends and country. Carter, Mick and Garrett, like many other Americans, anticipated the decline of the country and readied themselves in case of an economic collapse or anything else that could befall the country.

While Doug had the benefit of having been in a gunfight with Carter, it was apparent that his two friends appeared to be just as skilled. "Given how things are going in America, I think it would be a good idea to get these guys up to speed as quickly as possible. I feel comfortable with all three of them if the rest of you guys are. They will bring a totally different dimension to our training and understanding of the civilian world. Personally, I like the idea that they're not prior military. It would be interesting to hear how they view what's happening to our country. I'm also confident they'll bring additional resources and knowledge. I wonder how many more are like them out there in the civilian population?" Rocco said earnestly, looking at Doug and the other two.

"You bring up a good point, Rocco. We really don't know what it's been like for the civilians in the country, especially in recent years. If you guys are available, and if they're willing, I suggest we do this again for the next five or six Saturdays in a row except for a break during the holidays. What do you guys think?" Doug asked.

The three of them agreed with Doug's idea and could see the value in meeting frequently. They walked down to the patio where Carter and the other two were waiting for them.

Doug let them know how pleased he and his friends were with the skill level they'd demonstrated. Then he asked Conway, Rocco and Mike to offer any critique or comments. The three of them did so and also acknowledged their surprise that civilians like them were willing to take the time and spend the money to get the right gear and training. Doug went on to tell them his idea to meet for the next five-weekends, with the exception of Christmas and New Year's, for additional training. He let them know that at the end of that period the four of them would assess their progress. It was also agreed that on the third and fourth Saturday they would meet and train at night.

Whenever possible, operations by our nation's special forces are carried out under the cover of darkness. Carter and the other two were aware of this and welcomed the idea of night training. They had participated in night training a few times at PRC and were familiar with the problems presented by the darkness. Besides, they understood most bad things happen at night, and the three of them wanted to be trained for all conditions.

Carter, Mick and Garrett gave thumbs-up for the idea of training for the next five weeks with the four of them. They thanked Doug and his friends for taking the time to work with them. They also assured them – as previously agreed – under no circumstance would any of them acknowledge the existence of the training site or the affiliation with each other. As they broke up, all of them shook hands. Doug and Carter gave each other a hug.

As they were driving out, Carter, Mick and Garrett couldn't stop talking. To say they were pumped up would be an understatement. They couldn't wait until the following week, wondering what they'd be doing next.

Progression

The seven spent the next three Saturdays training together. Then they broke for Christmas and New Year's as planned. During the training weekends, they got to know each other better. Doug, Rocco, Conway and Mike all moved into a space of trust and respect for these three civilians. As they progressed, all seven of them were becoming a cohesive and well-choreographed unit. Carter, Mick and Garrett were honored to be in the presence of these four combat warriors. They continued to learn advanced tactics and other little nuances about the gunfight. While Carter proved himself with Doug on the day of the mall shooting, there was no doubt as the weeks progressed that Mick and Garrett possessed that same set of skills, grit and determination.

Apple Pie

In between week four and five, Garrett got a disturbing phone call from one of his oldest and best friends, Eric Grimm. Eric lived in New Mexico, but grew up in southeastern Arizona on his family's X-7 Ranch. Garrett learned of a recent conversation between Eric and his eighty-two-year-old father. Harold, Eric's father, reluctantly told him about a recent incident when three cartel members drove up to his ranch house threatening him, Eric's mother and killing their old and beloved dog, Sally.

Over the course of the last few years, Eric was aware that vehicles driving up from the south came through the gate of the ranch since it bordered Mexico. Out of frustration, Harold repeatedly called the Border Patrol about the constant trespassing and incursion onto U.S. soil by these drug-runners and human traffickers, but for the most part he was ignored. On only two occasions in the last four years had the Border Patrol intervened. They took into custody a group of Mexican nationals along with their drug loads only to send them back across the border the next day.

Eric's father told him what these three men said would happen if he didn't stop contacting the U.S. authorities; they would rape, torture and kill Eric's eighty-one-year-old mother, make his father watch and then kill him. Reluctantly, Harold also told Eric the cold details about Sally's death.

Harold Grimm told his son he wasn't going to live in fear anymore and that the next time he was threatened, he was going to put his M1 Garand to good use and kill those sons of bitches. If they got him and Eric's mother, so be it. From Harold's point of view this was his land and his country, and he'd had enough of waiting around for the United States government to secure the border and protect its citizens; it was obvious they weren't going to.

Eric told Garrett that he pleaded with his father not to do anything rash, and his father finally agreed. Harold and Eric's mother always treated Garrett like a family member. Garrett loved hearing Harold's stories about his experiences in the Korean War and had the utmost respect for the man and his wife. As far as he was concerned, Harold and Agnes were *salt of the earth* Americans, and that included his friend Eric. Garrett knew his friend well and could hear the concern and fear in Eric's voice; he also could hear the outrage in his core.

Why was it people like Eric's parents and others who lived along the border, working hard all their life, couldn't live in peace? Garrett thought to himself.

Garrett told his friend Eric, "I'm sorry to hear that's happening to your folks. Hey, I'll drive down this weekend and see how they're doing. Let them know I'm coming; I don't want to surprise your dad and have him open up on me with that M1 Garand. But I'll only go if you can promise me your mother will have one of her apple pies waiting for me – you know, with the well-done crust, extra sugar and cinnamon on top."

They both laughed, but more to relieve the tension of the gravity of the situation. Eric let him know he'd pass the message along to his mother and thanked Garrett.

When Garrett hung up the phone, he was enraged. Not just at the assholes threatening Eric's parents, but because the U.S. government was allowing this to happen in the first place. The U.S. citizens living along the border not only were living in fear, but they also had to deal with a tremendous amount of trash and human waste being left by these invaders. Their land – the washes, creeks, river beds and surrounding areas – were becoming dumping grounds. The problem of illegals coming across had been happening for years, but recently the amount of traffic and violence on both sides of the border rose dramatically. In a short span of just ten years, more than one-hundred thousand Mexican nationals had been murdered by the cartels throughout Mexico. There was a war right on the southern border of the United States, and no one really was even talking about it.

Garrett thought, *I wonder how long it would be tolerated if the politicians in Washington, D.C. had trash and human waste discarded on their property. Probably for as long as it took to dial 911 and have law enforcement show up to stop the people doing it and arrest them.*

After about an hour of mulling over his conversation with Eric and the threat his parents were living under, he called Carter. If nothing else, he just needed to vent and have someone lend an ear to the problem. He felt compelled to do something, but he wasn't quite sure what he could do to solve the problem.

"I'm glad you called me, Garrett," said Carter. "I'm sorry this is going on for your friend and his folks. This is fucking bullshit! I'm not sure what to do. However, I think it's worth discussing on Saturday when we're with the rest of the team. Maybe Doug and the others will have some suggestions."

Taking It to the Next Level

After digesting the conversation he'd had with Garrett the previous day, Carter gave Doug a call. He told him about the situation with Eric's parents. He asked Doug if at some point in the day on Saturday he could talk to the whole team about it and get their feedback.

"I'm not sure what to do, either. However, I trust that as a team we'll figure it out. Let's do this over coffee first thing in the morning before we start training," said a concerned Doug.

Doug knew better than to move into live-fire training with two team members worrying about a problem. Clear and resolved minds are always safer on the firing line. After a number of weeks of getting to know Carter better, Doug admired his strength and leadership. He knew true leaders were not only tough and strong, but also listened with compassion to those around them. It was out of Carter's respect and love for his friend Garrett that he was prompted to do something. The fact that Carter trusted to bring it up with Doug and friends said volumes about how far they'd come as a team in such a short time.

As Doug thought through the problem and how it correlated with where they were in their training, he made the decision to change what they were going to do the coming Saturday. He now felt it was time they focused on room-clearing techniques and strategies. After this weekend two more training session remained before the end of the month, and Doug now had a sense of a new direction for the group. He and the other three were pleased with Carter, Garrett and Mick's progress.

It was obvious to Doug and the others that Carter and his friends understood the importance of working as a team under induced live-fire stress. The four of them recognized these three civilians were warriors like them. Aside from the level of training and experience, the only real difference between the retired Spec Operators and Carter and his guys was that Doug and his group had "been there, done that" in real time in places far away from home.

Enough is Enough

It was a cold and crisp January morning with light frost on the ground in the Arizona desert as Doug and his guys rolled into the training facility. On the way, Doug briefed them on Carter's request and what was going on with Garrett and his friend's parents down on the border. They arrived a half hour early. Doug wanted to get a fire going and had Rocco and Mike arrange seven chairs around the fire. To Doug, there was something very spiritual and symbolic for men to talk around a fire at the beginning of the day. It didn't matter to him how long it would take for them to hash out this problem. He also realized that bringing this kind of discussion to the team could only strengthen their relationship. They had an opportunity to solve a real-life problem together as a team, where there was a clear and present danger to a Korean war veteran and his wife.

Doug had his own ideas about how to handle it, but he wanted to hear from the rest of them. *Maybe this is why God had Carter show up in my life when and where he did,* he thought to himself.

As Carter, Mick and Garrett pulled in, they could see the smoke rising up in the air from the fire pit of the meeting area. It was easy to make out Doug and the others standing around the now-roaring fire. En route that morning, the three of them discussed Garrett's friend's parent's situation down on the border. Carter let them know he'd told Doug the problem and requested time as a team to talk about it. Garrett was grateful there was a least the possibility of a resolution to Eric's parent's problem with the cartel but couldn't imagine

166

what that could be. "Thanks for bring it up to Doug and asking for their help. I never thought we'd really be discussing a real-life problem that hits so close to home," Garrett said to Carter.

Carter had his own ideas of what the seven of them could do. He just didn't know if he should speak it. *But then again, why shouldn't I say something,* Carter thought to himself.

Carter smelled the mixture of burning mesquite and coffee wafting its way through the early morning desert chill, as the three men walked towards the fire and meeting area. He was genuinely moved by the thought of the seriousness of the conversation they were about to have. It was as if an ancient war council was about to meet. He closed his eyes, taking in a deep breath. For just a moment, he thought he could feel the presence of ancient warriors around them.

Since the seven of them had met multiple times first thing in the morning, they were accustomed to giving each other a handshake and brotherly hug all rolled into one motion. They became, in a very short amount of time, a band of brothers, forged in mutual respect for each other and love of God, family and country. For this group of seven men, there had not been any head-butting criticism of each other, no testosterone-induced fits of insecurity or any other form of personal competition which are often witnessed when a group of highly focused, competitive men get together. But then again, Doug made sure the training was focused on developing their gunfighting skills and never about competing with each other.

After the usual good-natured bantering and the filling of coffee mugs, they all took their place around the fire. Doug motioned to Carter to sit next to him. Doug spoke first, explaining to the entire team the purpose of the meeting. When Doug finished, Carter spoke, underlining what Doug said and then invited Garrett to repeat the details of his conversation with his friend Eric about his parent's situation.

Garrett told the story about the three Mexican men approaching from the south and driving up to Harold Grimm's ranch house. And that the ringleader threatened to sexually assault and kill Harold's wife and then torture and kill him. Garrett left nothing out, including the details of killing the old family dog.

Garrett then went on to relate about Harold and Agnes being good and generous people who had always been kind to him. Growing up, they meant a lot to him. He next explained the old rancher's background as a United States Marine. By the time Garrett was wrapping up, it was obvious that all seven of them were pissed off and angry. The fact that two decent, elderly Americans were being terrorized by cartel gang members, and that they didn't have trust and faith in the U. S. Government to protect them, was unacceptable and disgraceful.

Garrett, because of his familiarity with the ranch and the nearby border, also detailed how close the town of San Miguel was to the Grimm ranch: just a mile or so, on the other side of the border. He had heard it was now being used and controlled by the Magdalena Cartel.

Doug, Conway, Mike and Rocco immediately understood the strategic importance to the cartel of this location. It was obvious this was one of their staging areas for their human and drug smuggling. Harold Grimm's ranch was perfect for them. The cartel's use of fear and intimidation in the absence of any real consequences by the U.S. government was typical.

Fear and intimidation had been used throughout the ages to achieve strategic ends. In almost every war in every era, fear and intimidation was used with great success. From the Taliban in Afghanistan threatening local villagers, to the Viet Cong threatening villagers in Vietnam during the Vietnam War, to Hitler's Nazi Germany, to the Japanese in Indochina to its current, effective use by ISIS in Syria and Iraq, it had always proven an effective tactic.

The only difference this time was the United States was not at war with Mexico. However, it is obvious that the Mexican cartels are at war with the United States. This war wasn't about taking territory, it was about money and power – at the expense of the American citizens and their way of life.

For Doug, Mike, Conway and Rocco the easy answer to the problem was "stupid-simple." Just go destroy the enemy. In this case, the enemy was the Magdalena Cartel.

Rocco was the first to speak this possibility: "Fuck those assholes. The only reason they do this is because our government isn't protecting people like Harold and his wife who live along the border. If this shit was going on in Washington to some of the congressmen and their wives, they would put a halt to it immediately. I say it's time we go do a little "meet and greet" with those assholes in San Miguel and let them taste some American wrath! Give them a little payback for threatening the Grimms and killing their dog!"

Each one in the group except Doug had something to say, with all of them echoing Rocco's sentiment. As they went around the circle, declaring their revulsion over the situation and their desire to do something, the fire seemed to burn and glow even hotter as Carter watched it. He shared their sentiments, and he understood that Rocco, Conway and Mike were dead serious about doing something about the problem. He also noticed Doug's silence and wondered what he was thinking.

Carter thought about the moment in the doorway when he froze up and the old woman appeared. Immediately he pushed that thought out of his mind. He felt strength, confidence and courage in this group. It was as if something was missing in his life. Besides, he'd never been one to let someone else fight his fight or a friend's fight alone. He was resolved that if they were going to go up against the Mexican cartel, he'd be there. He was tired of sitting on the sidelines complaining about our own government not keeping Americans safe. He felt that if God tapped him on his shoulder to step forward, then as a patriot and in defense of the country he was compelled to do so.

Doug sat there, waiting for everyone to finish what they had to say. When they were all done talking, they looked at him, waiting for any wisdom or guidance he might have.

As he sat there listening, Doug thought about everything that had transpired in the country since the current president and his cronies had taken office. He also reflected on the lack of action by prior administrations in the securing of the border. He remembered that day he and Carter fought side by side in the mall and how their relationship morphed into putting them all around the fire on this January morning.

What were the seven of them training for? Why did I take these three civilians into our confidence? Doug thought to himself, while looking at the group.

In Doug's life as a leader, he rarely needed a lot of time to process all the implications and potential consequences of future actions – the reaction of U.S. authorities or injury or death to any of the team members. However, this was one of those times he felt he needed to think. Doug was fairly confident about the direction he wanted them to go in, but he just wanted a little time to process such an important decision. Sitting there with all eyes on him, everything became clear to him. He thought about the disintegrating state of the country and its values, and about what was at stake for the future for his children. The government is never going to help someone like the Grimms, it was time to act!

"Carter, would your house be available Wednesday evening at seven for all of us to meet and discuss this further?" Doug asked, knowing Carter's place was a wife- and kid-free environment, making it easy for them to have privacy.

"Absolutely!" Carter said.

Doug looked at everyone, making sure all of them would be available; all answered in the affirmative.

"OK, then, Wednesday night it is; we'll continue this conversation then. Everyone leave your phones in your vehicles for this meeting, and Carter you do the same."

All of them understood the seriousness of this matter. Better to play it safe. You never know when big brother might be listening.

Simunition

Once they'd completed their discussion, Doug began explaining to them the scope of the training they'd be doing that day. That done, he told everyone to get their gear on, including their weapons which should not be loaded. He also asked them to leave the bolts to their AR15s and all ammo in their vehicles. Doug didn't want any live ammunition of any type in their possession for the room-clearing practice they were about to do. He'd brought along Simunition paint-pellet rounds, along with the bolts needed to operate and fire them in their rifles. In addition, he had a number of Glock 19 semi-automatic handguns set up to shoot only the Sim rounds.

In the morning, they switched off between doing dynamic and deliberate entries into the shoot house. Doug, along with Rocco's help, set up targets in each of the five rooms, including a hostage target in one of the rooms. Mike and Conway would work with Carter and the other two on their entry techniques and room-to-room search. Their task was to engage the appropriate targets as they went until they got to the room with the hostage and the two terrorist targets, taking them out first and then simulating rescuing the hostage.

During their lunch break, other than a discussion about their entry and room-clearing techniques, the group didn't say much. Understandably, each of them was deep in thought about the earlier conversation. The mood of the morning's training was more serious than usual and also without much talking. Each and every one of them was upset and angry about the Grimms's situation.

In the afternoon session, Doug positioned Mick and Garrett on the perimeter of the building, about twenty yards out, with both of them in full view of the two doors leading in and out of the building. Rocco took Carter and set him up on the roof of the ranch house, overlooking the shoot house about seventy-five yards away. From this position, it was easy for Carter to have a panoramic view of the shoot house and beyond. Rocco explained to him that his job was to run *overwatch* for the entry and perimeter team. If anyone looked like a bad guy, Carter was to dispatch him, preferably with one shot to the head, thereby silencing the individual immediately.

Once Carter and the other two were in position, Doug told Mick and Garrett to close their eyes. Doug then radioed Carter to turn around and look the other way for thirty seconds, giving Mike time to hide behind a large woodpile twenty-five yards west of the house. At the end of the thirty seconds, Doug, Rocco and Conway did a dynamic entry into the shoot house with Mick and Garrett on the outside perimeter and Carter on the roof top seventy-five yards away.

After turning back around, Carter could hear the muffled sounds of the Sim rounds inside the building. He hadn't seen Doug and the others make their entry into the shoot house and wondered if one of the four of them would be playing the role of a bad guy approaching the house from any direction. Looking through his fixed-four power red dot scope, he scanned the building and the surrounding area. It was easy for him to see Garrett and Mick with their rifles in a high-ready position, trained on the corners of the building where the doors were located.

Alone on the roof top, Carter could feel the pulse of adrenaline going through his system and felt his breathing

173

increase. He inhaled, taking a deep breath and thought to himself, *slow down; relax; breathe!*

Carter continued to look through his scope, scanning the surrounding area. After what seemed like a long time but in reality was only two minutes, he thought he saw some movement near a woodpile located twenty-five yards west of Garrett's position. Carter now focused his attention on this area, looking intently to confirm any signs of movement. He knew from his training the pitfalls of tunnel vision. He made a point to lift his head up every now and then for a quick view of the surrounding area – behind him and then back onto the scope – returning his attention to that woodpile.

The woodpile was about five feet high, thirty-five feet in length and ten to twelve feet in width. As Carter continued to focus on it, he again saw movement. He had the scope on his rifle zeroed in at one-hundred yards, the same distance separating Carter and the potential target. At the rifle range, at that distance, Carter consistently produced a tight, golf-ball sized group, dead center of the target.

From his position, it was easy to see the thin barrel of a rifle starting to protrude from the far corner of the woodpile. Carter readied himself, watching as more of the barrel became visible. He then saw a hand, arm and the left side of a man raising a rifle up to his shoulder and pointing in Garrett's direction.

He could see Mike was the one with his rifle up. In less than two seconds, Carter took a deep breath in while putting the red illuminated chevron reticle of the ACOG right in the middle of Mikes head; then he let his breath out

three-quarters of the way. Upon completion of the exhalation cycle, Carter smoothly squeezed the trigger, hitting Mike just above and to the front of his left ear.

Carter saw Mike flinch when the Simunition round hit him and then watched as he pretended to fall down, playing dead. For most people, getting shot with a Simunition round in the head would have them crying like a baby, but not Mike. Carter wanted to holler in excitement but knew his job was to continue to run overwatch until the mission was complete. Carter felt a sense of pride and satisfaction in having done his job.

"Tango down!"

After another few minutes, Doug and the other two emerged from the building, hollering at Carter to come down and join them for a debrief of the mission. Doug and the other three were pleased with the performance of Carter, Mick and Garrett. All three had done their job, with Carter saving the life of a team member.

During the rest of the afternoon, Doug ran two more scenarios in the shoot house, positioning Carter, Mick and Garrett on the outside perimeter and switching their positions each time.

At the end of the day, they huddled for their final debriefing. It was noticeable to all that a certain kind of chemistry and teamwork further developed between them throughout the day. The previous four sessions of work together suddenly started to jell. Instead of seven individuals working together, they were becoming one well synchronized unit.

As they broke their huddle, they gave each other a handshake and hug. All of them were looking forward to the evening meeting on Wednesday night at Carter's house and hearing what Doug was going to suggest they do to help the Grimms.

Negative/Positive

Carter, with Mick and Garrett in his vehicle, led the way out of the canyon and down the ranch road, turning right when they reached the Florence Highway heading back to Tucson. They couldn't stop talking about the day's events and the level of training they'd done with Doug and the other three. As Carter drove, he thought about the day, the early morning conversation and the kind of training they did. He wondered if Doug was preparing them for a real mission. If he was, Carter was fully on board and knew both his two friends would be also, even though they might have concerns about possible consequences.

"Are you two OK with where I think helping the Grimms might be headed? I am, even though I've got some concerns that make me nervous," Carter said.

"I'm good with whatever we decide to do to help them. And yes, I hear you about being nervous about this," Mick answered.

"Of course I am. Carter, thank you for bringing it up to Doug so I could explain about the Grimms's situation. They're like a second set of parents to me. I'd do anything for those two, and I mean anything!" Garrett said in an earnest tone.

Carter pondered the meaning of what Rocco said around the fire that morning about doing a "meet and greet" with the cartel shitheads living in San Miguel. By now, he knew Rocco well enough to realize that this wasn't just idle, tough-guy talk.

"OK, so here are my concerns. Any of the seven of us could get injured or killed. Assuming that doesn't happen, the reaction of the U.S. authorities makes me nervous, even though we'll be on Mexican soil. I can't imagine how anyone would know it was us that did the "meet and greet," but you never know. I don't want to end up in jail on either side of the border. Then I think about what if those were my folks being threatened and who didn't have a means of sufficiently protecting themselves; I would definitely take care of the problem. Since we can't count on our government to protect the border, then it's time citizens like us step up and do something. OK, so that's on the negative side of things. One the positive side, I'm comfortable about the idea of doing something to help the Grinms because we're doing it with four highly skilled and competent combat veterans," Carter finished.

"I hear you, brother; ditto on the concerns and ditto on confidence being partnered up with Doug and company," Mick said.

"Flat-ass ditto for me, too!" Garrett said.

"Sounds like we're all in. It's time to let the cartel know there are Americans who are no longer willing to tolerate their bullshit and are going to do something about it. The time has come to put them and anyone else who wants to do harm to America on notice; even though the United States Government is too pansy assed to do something, there are citizens who aren't afraid," Carter said, in a matter-of-fact tone.

Wednesday, 7 p.m. – Carter Thompson's House

The usual greetings were exchanged as all the combined team members entered Carter's house. Carter had plenty of coffee, soda and water on hand, and everyone knew to help themselves. Once everyone was assembled comfortably in Carter's living room, Doug reminded them to make sure their cell phones were left outside in their vehicles. It was understood anything discussed in the meeting was not to be shared with anyone outside the group under any circumstance.

"A little over six weeks ago this man to my left appeared out of nowhere as if God put him there at the right place and time. He saved me, my wife and my children and countless others in the battle we waged together against the Islamic terrorists we now know were affiliated with ISIS. That fateful and eventful meeting between us is the reason the seven of us are together tonight."

Looking at Rocco, Conway and Mike, Doug said, "The three of you and I know the level of courage and trust it takes to be on the battlefield with live rounds flying around your head and the threat of injury or death present at all times," Doug continued, again looking in the direction of Carter.

"Just as I would with the three of you, I would go into battle with this man any time, any place. It is because of Carter and his trust in the two of you," Doug said now, looking at Mick and Garrett, "that I trust both of you. I've watched the three of you in our training sessions. The four of us are impressed by your all around skills and understanding of the gunfight. Before meeting the three of you, we didn't know there were American citizens out there with as big a commitment to this country as we have. Our hats also go off to you in recognition of your spending the time and money to get some training over the years.

"After our discussion Saturday morning about the situation at the Grimes ranch, and especially with Harold being a veteran and all, I know we all agree he and his wife deserve better. All of us sitting in this room know our government isn't going to help them."

"You're right, and Harold Grimm knows this, and it's why he doesn't bother reporting the threats on their life. I know him well. If that old Marine didn't have to worry about his wife, I guarantee you he would have blown those assholes away the day they pulled up to his house," Garrett said, interrupting Doug.

"I have no doubt. The truth is, though, that their situation is hopeless without somebody helping them," Doug said, looking at Garrett.

"Roger that!" Conway said.

"It's because of this I say, why don't we step up and help them?" Doug said, as if pointing to the eight-hundred-pound gorilla in the room.

"Hooah!" Mike, Conway & Rocco spoke in unison.

Looking at Carter, Mick and Garrett, Doug went on.

"Rocco, Mike and Conway know what I mean when I say let's do something. The truth is, the only way to deal with an evil like the cartel is at the end of a gun. It's the only thing they understand.

If we're a "go," there will be danger and great risk involved, even possible death. We also run the risk of getting caught by either Mexican or U.S. authorities. I say, for the lives of those two senior Americans who deserve to live in peace, we go send a message to the cartel. To me, it's worth the risk; what do you say?"

Immediately Carter felt a sharp twinge in his gut. While he knew this was the right thing to do, he couldn't shake the fear he'd freeze up again when it counted. And this time there wouldn't be any old woman around to shame him into action. He again felt an urge to communicate the truth about the mall shooting, but the shame of it stopped him from saying anything. The wrinkled face of the old woman again appeared in his thoughts, pushing and commanding him to do something. He could hear her voice as if she was standing next to him. He took a deep breath.

"You can count on me. I'll do whatever you need me to do!" Carter said. He silently prayed to God for strength and to remove the doubts and fears he had.

After last Saturday's morning meeting around the fire, Carter thought long and hard about possible courses of action to address the Grimms's problem. Every time he thought about it, the only solution that logically made sense was the one Doug was offering. He realized there could be some real serious consequences of getting caught by either U.S. or Mexican authorities. Getting caught by U.S. authorities could mean a lengthy prison sentence. On the other hand, getting caught by corrupt Mexican authorities would mean being turned over to the Magdalena Cartel, ending in probable torture and death. He also realized that getting wounded or killed in a shootout with cartel members could be an outcome. Weighing all this, Carter came to the conclusion to act if there was an opportunity to do so. Besides, he had confidence in Doug and the others in making this a successful operation. Carter looked at his two good friends.

"You know I'm in!" Garrett said.

Mick, looking at all of them, said, "You can count on me, too! I'm tired of just sitting around complaining about how bad things are in this country. The way I see it, if somebody doesn't stand up against evil, it's predictable we're going to lose what's left of our country. It's not right the Grimms are being terrorized like this and it's all because our government – Congress in particular – isn't protecting its citizens. And… oh yeah, killing their dog? Damn right, I'm in!"

Doug looked at all of them with a smile. "OK then, let's do this!"

He knew what they were going to do was the right thing and felt confident about the men he'd being doing it with.

"This coming Saturday, we'll do a dry run on the mission. In the meantime, I have copies of satellite photos for you of San Miguel, courtesy of Google Earth; fortunately, they're only a few months old." Doug waited for everyone to get a copy in his hands before proceeding.

"As you can see, there's only seventeen buildings in the whole town. Five of them are adjacent to the main road, leading from the Grimm ranch straight through town heading south and connecting to Mexican Highway #38. What's nice about this setup is that all the buildings are located on the east side of the road, giving us an approach from across the road on the west side. That's open desert with lots of trees, cactus and so on that we can use for cover and concealment. Directly to the south, about a half mile down the road, there's what appears to be a gas station."

Doug thought it odd there was a gas station near such a small town and wondered how that came to be. Then again, how convenient for the cartel to have a gas station so close to the border; it was handy to top off their tanks for their many illegal runs into the United States.

Good and current intelligence on an objective always insures a higher probability of success to any operation. Doug and the other three understood the importance of this from their military background. But as civilians, now they didn't have access to militarized aerial drones and didn't have any local ground intelligence. What they did know was the cartel was operating out of San Miguel, and they needed to figure out which buildings and structures they were using. Even though he figured they weren't using more than two or three structures, it was essential for them to get their eyes on the area to verify which ones and how they were being used.

Doug went on explain the need to first run a reconnaissance operation on the town and surrounding area to determine where the cartel was located. Since Garrett was familiar with the territory around the X-7 Ranch, Doug asked him if he'd go with him and Rocco the next night to get eyes on the objective. Garrett felt a rush of adrenaline at the thought of doing this and without hesitation answered in the affirmative.

Doug then asked Carter, Mick, Mike and Conway to follow them down, providing backup if needed. They would use Carter's SUV and stay on the U.S. side of the border. All of them agreed. Doug fully understood the need and value to have everyone involved one way or another in an operation like this.

After clearing it with Carter, they agreed they'd meet at his house at eleven o'clock the following night for mission planning. Then they'd leave at midnight which would put them across the border around 2 a.m. They'd take Doug's SUV and Garrett and Rocco were reminded to bring their night-vision gear. San Miguel was only a mile-and-a-half south of the X-7 Ranch. They planned on crossing the border at the cattle guard and gate on the Grimm's ranch that separated the two countries. They'd then drive for approximately a half mile and go off-road, leaving their vehicle as concealed as possible. From there, they'd approach the village on foot. Even though they'd be carrying weapons, there was no plan to use them; they were strictly for defensive reasons if by chance they were detected and had to fight their way back across the border into the United States.

Doug asked Garrett, "Garrett, would you tell us what you know about the terrain we'll be going into?"

Garrett advised that the terrain in that area was well covered by desert fauna – mesquite trees, Palo Verde trees, cacti, and all kinds of other desert vegetation. He assured them there'd be excellent cover in their approach to the little town.

In his teenage years, on weekends he and his friend Eric went across the line countless times, hunting rabbits with their twenty-two caliber rifles. Back then, nobody from either side really cared who came and went across the border. Many times they'd walk to San Miguel, going into the little general store to get some relief from the heat with an ice-cold strawberry Mexican soda.

It didn't bother Carter and Mick that they weren't asked to go on the surveillance mission the following night. Both of the men understood Doug's logic in choosing Garrett for tomorrow's mission since he was familiar with the area. They trusted Doug's decision and were confident he knew what he was doing.

While driving home from Carter's house, Doug thought about what was unfolding. He noticed neither Carter nor Mick had any kind of reaction to Garrett being asked to go with Rocco and himself. This was a good sign; Carter, Garrett and Mick trusted him and the others. Trust between all seven of them was paramount for this to be successful. That Conway and Mike didn't have a reaction was not a surprise to Doug. They were both professionals who would understand and support his selection of Rocco and Garrett for the next night's operation.

7:33 p.m. –
Central Mexico

The driver pulled into a truck stop in Parral, Mexico, en route to his destination of a nuclear disposal site on the outskirts of Mexico City. He'd had been driving for eighteen hours and was too fatigued to drive any further. In his truck and unbeknownst to him, he was carrying a shipment of cobalt-60 from a hospital in the northern city of Mexicali, Mexico, to a radioactive waste storage center south of Mexico City. He didn't notice the two Chevy Suburbans pull up about one-hundred yards to the south of the truck stop or the six heavily armed men approaching from the left and right rear of his truck.

Alliances

The Magdalena Cartel controlled most of northwest Mexico, all the way to the US/Mexican border. They were responsible for about eighty percent of all the drugs being smuggled into the United States from west Texas to just west of Tucson and through the Tohono O'odham Indian Reservation. Along with prolific drug smuggling, the cartel also controlled all the human trafficking into the U.S., including Islamic terrorists at twenty-thousand to thirty-thousand dollars a head.

Among those being smuggled into the country by the Magdalena Cartel are individuals linked to Al Qaida, Hamas and ISIS. Once in the country, these people are connected to the extensive network of support. After 9/11, coming through the southern border of the U.S. was the pathway of choice for any terrorist to gain entry.

Juan Ortiz, head of the Magdalena Cartel, had established and organized an effective chain of command. The cartel's method of enforcement was always swift and brutal. No one living in Mexico dared go against them. Juan Ortiz made sure both military and police leaders were paid off to look the other way. Occasionally, when a police chief attempted to enforce the laws by trying to keep Juan Ortiz and his group out of his town, he was killed quickly and always in broad daylight. Just as with the Muslim extremist groups, fear was the greatest ally the Magdalena Cartel had at its disposal.

Abu-Ali al-Anbari reported directly to the grand leader of ISIS, Abu Bakr al-Baghdadi. They had great disdain for Al-Qaida and viewed them as being weak and too politically motivated. Through the direction of Abu

Bakr al-Baghdadi, Abu-Ali was given the task of organizing and carrying out an attack on U.S. soil. Their method of destruction would be the detonation of a dirty bomb in a large city somewhere in America. Both men and their lieutenants knew the most reliable way to accomplish this was through the southern border of the United States and specifically between Douglas and Nogales, Arizona. Once the material was across, it would be delivered to one of the many active cells already in the U.S. Their act of Jihad would dwarf Al-Qaida's pathetic attempt on 9/11 to destroy the U.S. economy and bring America to its knees. With the detonation of their dirty bomb, Allah would smile down upon them!

The Iranian Embassy in Mexico had multiple contacts with all the Mexican cartels and let it be known that two million U.S. dollars would be paid for the delivery of any radioactive material to the head of the respective cartel. Juan Ortiz, having been a dependable source for smuggling terrorists into the U.S., was fully aware of this. For two months he made plans to procure such material and deliver and collect the funds. He also agreed to see to it that the material was delivered to the awaiting courier on U.S. soil. Juan knew the dangers of transporting nuclear material and planned on using lower-level subordinates to smuggle it into the U.S. He didn't want to risk any of his lieutenants being exposed to lethal radiation should there be an accident.

The truck about to be hijacked in Parral had exactly what they needed – cobalt-60 – a radioactive material used in cancer therapies. Inside the truck were eight containers, each with a depleted uranium (DU) shield encased within a steel housing and fixed in position by retaining bar assemblies and polyurethane foam in the interior void space. The exposure device is contained within a protective carbon steel sleeve. Inside of each container was a container of welded construction.

Cobalt-60 could be used to make a dirty bomb, and any conventional explosive material would be sufficient to disperse the radioactive material into an aero form. Depending on the direction of the wind and the size of the blast, it literally could, for example, shut down most of the island of Manhattan, making it uninhabitable for decades to come. It would be the ultimate blow to the U.S. economy and cause untold panic and fear, totally undermining the government. Chaos would reign.

Wet Spot

"Abre la puerta!" one of the hijackers said, tapping on the passenger door window of the truck with the barrel of his rifle. The driver awoke with a start as flashlights pointed inside the van. He didn't know exactly what he was carrying in the van – it wasn't his job to ask. Earlier, when he arrived at the hospital in Mexicali for the pickup, workers at the hospital loaded the eight containers into the back and told him to be careful and not to touch or disturb the load. He opened the door and was immediately grabbed and dragged outside; another rifle pointed at him, and he was told if he valued his life to say nothing. The driver knew better than to do anything but comply. Other people at the truck stop, seeing what was going on, looked the other way or left the area. Calling the police would be a waste of time, for it was always assumed the local police would be in on it. This hijacking was no different.

Once the van was seized, the two Suburbans came racing up and slid to a halt, kicking up a cloud of dust. One of the large SUVs turned around, backing up to the rear of the delivery truck. Four men got out and seized the containers inside, transferring them to the awaiting Suburban. The leader of the group considered killing the driver but instead he ordered one of the men to tie the driver up.

"You understand what will happen to your family if you identify any of us or our vehicles," the leader of the group said to the driver, who was shaking with fear and grateful to still be alive. He had stained his pants.

"Si!" Nothing more was needed to be said by the driver.

All the men got back into the Suburbans, turning them around and heading north out of town. It would take roughly twelve to thirteen hours driving straight through to get to the town of San Miguel. Five minutes after the Suburbans were headed north, Juan Ortiz received the call he'd been waiting for. He would be in San Miguel waiting for the Suburbans and the delivery of his two-million-dollar package. Juan Ortiz, like most of the Mexican cartel leaders, was a psychopath. He smiled at the thought of all that money! He didn't care what the Islamic terrorists were going to do with the cobalt-60, he just wanted the money.

By the time the hijacking incident made it into the news cycle a week later it would be reported that the hijackers didn't know what was in the truck and were only interested in stealing the truck itself. It was also reported the cobalt-60 had been recovered. A nice spin, Mexico style, and for sure to never be investigated any further by the U.S. mainstream media, or even Fox News for that matter.

1:00 a.m. Thursday Night – Carter's House

Carter had a fresh pot of coffee ready by the time everyone started arriving at 11:00 p.m. As the protocol was already established, everyone left their cell phones in their vehicles.

By 11:10 p.m., everyone was seated around the large glass table with steaming mugs in their hands. Rocco, as per Doug's request, had a topographical map of the area along with the satellite photos he'd acquired of the X-7 Ranch, including San Miguel and the areas south of the ranch.

The map revealed what Garrett had told them about the terrain leading up to the town. The surrounding area was rolling hills separated by the many dry desert washes. There was only one way in and out of the town, either from the north or the south. In the satellite photo, they spotted an area about a half-mile north of San Miguel which would be a good place for the three of them to hide their vehicle. Another plus was that any noise from the truck would be out of earshot. Garrett, knowing the area well, gave thumbs-up. Because of the hour, they hoped no one would be awake.

In Doug's planning, he included the possibility that there might be one or two cartel sentries on duty. But he also wouldn't be surprised if there was no one guarding the cartel buildings, since up to now they probably hadn't been bothered by anyone. They just continued to run their drug-and human-trafficking operation without any interference from anyone, let alone from the Mexican authorities who were paid well to stay away. Because if they didn't stay away, it would be a sure death sentence for them and their family members.

After Doug briefed everyone on their approach, they did an equipment check: firearms, extra magazines, tactical vests, night vision gear, radios, et cetera. Because there was no plan to engage any of the cartel members, they would be traveling light so they could move quickly if needed.

As planned, Carter, Mike, Conway and Mick would follow Doug and the others to about a half-mile north of the Grimms's ranch house. They would look for a place to pull off the road and park out of visual range. This would put them in position if Doug, Rocco and Garrett got into trouble and needed them to come in and reinforce them. It would also be close enough to be in radio contact with the recon team. Once the two vehicles turned onto the X-7 Ranch road, they would turn off all the lights to their vehicles and use their night-vision gear to negotiate the road. During the day, Mick rigged kill switches inside the two vehicles to the taillights and interior lights to disable them when the brake pedal was depressed or doors opened.

After a final equipment check, Doug, Garrett and Rocco got into Doug's SUV. Carter and his group got into his truck. They left Carter's house right at midnight and made their way to I-10, getting on at the Orange Grove eastbound entrance. Garrett knew from previous trips to the ranch that it would take about an hour and forty-five minutes to reach where the ranch road intersected Arizona State Route 80. From there, it would be only a short, fifteen-minute drive to the cattle guard and gate at the border. Once there, it would take them about five to ten minutes to get to where they were planning on pulling their truck off the road. Then they'd travel the rest of the way to San Miguel on foot. By two-thirty to two-forty-five, they would have eyes on San Miguel. If all went according to plan, it would take two hours for surveillance of the town, putting them back at Carter's house by around six-thirty to seven a.m.

1:47 a.m.

With Doug's vehicle in the lead, they reached and turned off onto the ranch road. Both he and Carter turned off their headlights and hit the kill switches, while simultaneously pulling over to the right side of the ranch road. After everyone donned his night vision gear, Doug did a quick radio check between the two vehicles. Except for the on-the-hour radio check, there would be radio silence until Doug and the other two were coming back from their reconnaissance of San Miguel.

After Doug and the other two drove off, Carter waited for the agreed-upon ten minutes and then put his Ford Expedition into four-wheel drive. The four of them proceeded down the ranch road and turned right, down a sandy wash. They drove for a quarter of a mile and came to a halt north of the ranch house. They would be hidden enough so that if anyone were heading either north or south on the ranch road they wouldn't be able to see them.

As Doug eased his vehicle up to the cattle guard and gate, Garrett hopped out and lifted the chain latch and pulled the gate open. Doug drove across the cattle guard and into Mexico. Once the SUV was far enough past the gate, Garrett closed and secured the gate and then got back in the vehicle and gently closed the door. Using GPS coordinates from Google Map, Doug proceeded on as planned and within about ten minutes came to the turn out they were looking for. He turned to the right and continued on in the desert terrain for a couple hundred yards. When certain they were in a well hidden place, he turned it around to allow for a quick exit if needed.

The three of them exited the SUV, using great caution to close the doors as quietly as possible. Doug and Rocco, being well-seasoned veterans of this type of operation, whispered to Garrett that they would stay put for five minutes and listen for any sounds that didn't belong in the desert. After five minutes of waiting, Doug signaled to the two of them that he was going to do a quick radio check with Carter.

Carter, Conway, Mick and Mike were all outside of their truck in the wash under mesquite trees when Carter's radio ear bud came alive with the sound of Doug's voice.

"Desert Bloom, this is Desert Look; how do you read me?"

"Loud and clear. I repeat: loud and clear," Carter said, keying his mike.

"Roger that; will check back with you as planned. Out!" Doug said.

Both teams were relieved to know the radios were heard loud and clear. If they weren't able to make contact with the hand-held radios, then they'd go to cell phones for backup. Doug purchased cheap throwaway cell phones at Wal-Mart on his way to Carter's house that night so that any possible NSA monitoring of cell phone use could not be traced back to them.

As planned, one hour from the first radio check Doug would do another. Exactly five minutes after that hour, if there was no contact, Carter and the others would wait an additional ten minutes for another radio check from Doug or the either of the other two. If that didn't happen, then Carter would attempt to initiate contact with his cell phone. If still there was no contact, then the four of them would immediately drive to the border crossing and park. They would then proceed south on foot as fast as possible to reinforce Doug and the other two if needed.

Standing there quietly in the dark Carter, could feel adrenaline going through his system. He hoped there wouldn't be any problem, but if there was, he hoped he'd be able to prevent anyone from getting hurt.

12:17 a.m. –
San Miguel, Mexico,

San Miguel is a small village with a total of seventeen buildings, all but two of which were homes. Across from the five buildings on the other side of the road, there's a cattle fence and open desert, leading up into the hills that are about one-hundred-and-fifty yards west of the village. Down the road to the south, about a quarter mile away, was a Pemex gas station. There were hundreds of these government-owned gas stations in cities and small towns and along the highways in Mexico. Normally, a village the size of San Miguel wouldn't warrant one but at Juan Ortiz's request to the executives of Pemex, one materialized there at the expense of the Mexican taxpayers. The executives were reluctant at first, but after a few drinks and a half-a-million dollars each, they installed one just south of the town.

With the exception of the cartel activity, there was very little traffic in and out of the quiet and sleepy San Miguel. The population of the town consisted mainly of ranch hands, *caballeros*, who worked the half-dozen ranches in the area. Along with the ranch hands were their families. Other than that, there was not much reason for anyone to go to San Miguel. This all changed when Ortiz and his thugs moved in and took over the town. The road heading north went to a cattle gate and through the X-7 Ranch, which belonged to an old man and his wife, Harold and Agnes Grimm.

Besides the Pemex gas station, the other two commercial buildings in the village consisted of a small cantina and an even-smaller general store next to it. Since the next largest town with a Pemex gas station was seventy kilometers away, this served as a convenient stop to fuel up their vehicles for their many runs into the United States and across Harold Grimm's ranch. These frequent runs north were used for the transportation of either drugs or people. The recent push for amnesty offered by the President of the United States made the human side of trafficking very busy and profitable. Because of the president and congress's complicity, hordes of illegal aliens were streaming into the United States along its southern border.

The residents of San Miguel understood this and were aware of the cartel's presence as well as the nature of its business. At any given time, there were at least three to ten cartel members residing in two houses next to each other on the main road. A few of the local young women were forcibly obliged to take care of the cartel members whenever they wanted sex. And there were many young girls and women from Mexico, as well as countries in Central and South America passing through as part of the human trafficking side of the business.

Contrary to the belief by many people in America, although these women originally wanted to come to the United States for a better life, most of them ended up being sold into the prolific sex-trafficking trade in America. By the time they'd arrived at the U.S. border, the thugs of the Magdalena Cartel had used and abused them. Most of these women arrived despondent, broken and compliant by the time they reached the U.S.

Juan Ortiz spent most of his time between a posh section of Hermosillo, the capital of the state of Sonora, and the seaside resort of San Carlos, located just two hours south of Hermosillo. It was established in the late 1960s by an American married to a wealthy Mexican woman. In 1968, the movie *Catch Twenty-Two* was filmed at Algodones Beach just north of San Carlos, putting it on the map. With its coastal mountains, sprawling beaches, great scuba diving and sport fishing and sitting on the Sea of Cortez, it had been developed into a popular vacation getaway for both Americans and Mexicans.

Juan Ortiz left early in the morning from his seaside villa in San Carlos to head to San Miguel. It was about a five-hour drive, and he wanted to be there when the two vehicles carrying the hijacked containers of cobalt-60 arrived. Reggie Ortiz was his young nephew and entrusted by his uncle for the management of the human and drug trafficking in and out of San Miguel. For the senior Ortiz, there was too much at stake not to personally oversee the management of the sale of the cobalt-60. The buyer was waiting for his phone call and would pay two million dollars for the delivery of four of the canisters.

Reggie was respected and feared by the other cartel members he managed. He was psychotic, sadistic and could be extremely violent and ruthless in dealing with anyone who got in his way or he deemed disloyal to his uncle.

Juan was pleased with the way Reggie ran things on his behalf. Reggie surprised him by showing homicidal restraint recently in dealing with the owner of the ranch they used as their entry point into the United States. He really was expecting the same kind of outcome Reggie produced with another American rancher, Mike Davis, who was causing a problem for them by not co-operating. Though Juan knew rancher, Harold Grimm, was old, he expected him to resist any attempts on Reggie's part to force him to keep his mouth shut about their comings and goings through his property. He knew if the rancher didn't comply, Reggie would have killed both him and his elderly wife. Juan was pleased that didn't happen because that would have brought the attention of the U.S. authorities and media just as it did with Mike Davis's death.

Around five o'clock in the afternoon, the two Suburbans with blacked-out windows came rolling into San Miguel, stopping in a trailing cloud of dust in front of the house where Juan Ortiz awaited them. Juan stood on the front porch as Reggie walked out to meet the occupants of the Suburbans. After confirming with the captain of the crew who hijacked the cobalt-60 containers that they were safe and secure, a smiling Reggie looked over to his uncle and gave him a thumbs-up.

Juan watched as Reggie and the captain of the crew walked back to the lead Suburban, opening the back doors to allow Reggie to look inside. All of the containers were placed in the front Suburban, and Reggie instructed them to leave them where they were. As per standard operating procedures, the two Suburban's stopped at the Pemex to top off their fuel tanks before coming into town. They were ready to travel in either direction at a moment's notice.

Juan, although just as ruthless and psychotic as his nephew Reggie, was good to his men and their families as long as they showed loyalty. He called to Reggie to take the men to the adjacent house where hot showers and food was waiting for them. The two houses the cartel controlled had long ago been converted to quarters for the men who worked for Senior Ortiz. Both buildings could house and feed up to twelve men and also facilitated their play time with the many young women they forced to have sex with them. Besides having a well-stocked kitchen, each house also had an ample supply of alcohol. The men of the cartel liked their liquor and never could seem to get enough of the good times.

As the newly arrived men made their way to the two houses, Juan motioned Reggie over, instructing him to call their contact in the U.S., Ammar, and let him know the shipment was ready. They were ready for the transfer and delivery.

Madkhal Mosque – Tucson, Arizona

A little more than seven weeks had passed since the attack at the Southwest Regional Mall, and for the media it was long past being an item. Because of this and the subsequent typical contradictory statements by the president and his staff, the whole country was thrown into a state of turmoil. By the end of the nine weeks, any concern for additional attacks had all law enforcement, both local and federal, in a state of numbed alertness. Immediately after the mall attack, the president, after finishing his golf game, went on national television and proclaimed, "It was a horrific act and the crime will be thoroughly investigated. Whoever was behind this will be brought to justice and tried in a court of law." As usual, he didn't use the words "terrorist" or "Islamic extremist," though it was glaringly obvious who perpetrated these attacks.

Ammar al Shammar knew that for a Muslim, the safest place to be after the mall attack was at the Madkhal Mosque in Tucson. He knew the Justice Department had standing orders to local and federal law enforcement agencies to take a "hands-off" approach to these obvious hotbeds of terrorists. The president wanted to show the rest of world, and especially those in the Middle East, that with him in charge, they would be dealing with a more tolerant America. Besides, if law enforcement were allowed to do their job, rooting out terrorism might be considered racist.

Inside the mosque was a walk-in safe. All of the smuggled firearms, RPGs, explosives, et cetera were stored inside it. Only the Imam knew the combination to the safe. In addition to the large assortment of firearms and explosives was a large cache of money, including the two million that was needed to purchase the hijacked cobalt-60 from Juan Ortiz.

The call came in to Ammar at around eight in the evening; it was Reggie informing him they were ready to deliver the four canisters of cobalt-60 in exchange for the two million dollars. The two agreed on a rendezvous point approximately one mile off the exit of I-10 to Hwy 191, down a dirt trail heading east for half a mile. They'd met there on two occasions in the past, when other Islamic extremists were delivered into the country. It was a good spot, far enough away from I-10 and Hwy 191 that they wouldn't be noticed. Reggie and his two men would meet Ammar around two-thirty in the morning with the cobalt-60. Reggie reminded Ammar of the two million, and Ammar assured him he'd have the money with him.

Reggie would take the same two men who had accompanied him on his previous visit to the Grimm Ranch. All three men would be armed with AK47s, along with ten, thirty-round magazines each. At the slightest sign of trouble, they would not hesitate to fight and then move as quickly as possible back into Mexico.

Juan and Reggie both knew who Ammar and his associates were as well as their intentions to bring America to its knees. As far as they were concerned, it wasn't their problem. It was the problem of the United States to deal with these terrorists. All they cared about was the money, and for the last couple of years, that had been very good – at twenty to thirty thousand per head to smuggle Muslims into the U.S.

Ammar called the Imam, letting him know the items they'd been waiting for were ready to be picked up. The Imam was pleased to hear this; within five minutes of Ammar's arrival at the mosque, the two of them stepped into the safe room together. Ammar retrieved the two black utility bags with the one million dollars stuffed inside each one. Along with the two bags, he also grabbed the Geiger counter placed next to them.

Once outside the safe room, the two men went into the Imam's office and closed the door behind them. Ammar picked up the yellow Geiger counter and flipped on the power switch to make sure the batteries were at full charge. While they never been double crossed by Juan Ortiz, both men knew the only way they could be certain that the four containers had cobalt-60 in them was with the use of the Geiger counter. They knew the Magdalena Cartel could be every bit as ruthless as they were. The only difference between them and the cartel was that what the cartel did was always for money. What the Islamists did had everything to do with dominating the world and the establishment of Sharia law.

Ammar had an hour-and-a-half drive to the rendezvous point, so he left at twelve-thirty in the morning. Their plan, in the making for three years, was coming together. The recent mall attack sent America into a state of panic, fear and paranoia. He and his other Muslim terrorist buddies fully believed that following up quickly with the detonation of a dirty bomb in a major city would cause the American people to lose what little faith and trust they had left in their government's ability to protect them. They also recognized that rendering acres of a large metropolitan area uninhabitable for decades to come would further damage the already fragile U.S. economy. They believed that "As America goes, so goes the world" was true.

"Allah Akbar," was all Ammar could think.

2:32 a.m.

It was easy walking for Doug and the other two as they came to a hilltop overlooking San Miguel. Doug could tell from the satellite image that it should be an ideal spot to observe the little village and surrounding area. Again using GPS coordinates, Doug, Garrett and Rocco reached the back side of the hill to the top and were in position within thirty minutes of leaving their SUV. Well hidden and with a thick blanket of stars overhead, the three lay prone and broke out their binoculars. They started surveying the town which was only about one-hundred-and-fifty yards down slope.

Right away, their attention was drawn to one of the two vehicles parked outside the two center buildings lining the street. There were six men milling around it. Rocco set up a "super ear" listening device and eavesdropped in on their conversation. Though they were talking in Spanish, which Rocco didn't understand, occasionally Rocco would hear a word or two spoken in English.

All three saw two men, each carrying something out of the smaller of the two buildings and putting the items into the lead vehicle. They then watched as they saw the same two men go back into the building and come out again, carrying what looked like the same thing. Again, the items were placed in the same vehicle. Each time the two men passed, the other men gave them a wide birth. They moved way out of the way as if the other two had Ebola or some other infectious disease. Doug and Garrett and Rocco couldn't help but wonder why they were doing that; it seemed very odd.

The two buildings were well lit but the rest of the town was dark, except for a single streetlight north of the group of men. The three Americans also could see off to the south the glow of the lights from the Pemex gas station.

Doug and Rocco assumed that activity this late at night had to be cartel members. As they continued to watch, they noticed one of the men talking on a cell phone. After the man took the phone down from his ear and put it in his pants pocket, all of them went into the larger of the two buildings on the left. This building was just as well lit on the inside as it was on the outside. Doug and the other two were curious about what was carried from the smaller of the two buildings on the right. And why all the activity so late at night?

The three of them held their position and continued glassing, using their binoculars to look for any other activity, but they could find none. Exactly an hour after the first radio check, Doug keyed his microphone; Carter came right back to him, confirming the radio check.

Forty-five minutes later, five men came out of the building on the left. Three of them had what appeared to be AK47s and got into the same Chevy Suburban the suspicious items had been placed in. Even at this distance, in the quiet of the night they could hear the sound of the engine being started. The headlights came on, shining a cone of light ahead in the darkness as the vehicle hurriedly proceeded north. Doug hoped their hidden vehicle would be undetected by the men in the Suburban. Because they left in such a hurry, it was obvious to Doug and the other two that something was up. They all sensed it had to do with the four items in the back of the Suburban.

"Desert Bloom, this is Desert Look, a black Suburban with three men armed with AK47s just left San Miguel, heading fast towards your position. Make sure your night vision goggles are on and stay in blacked-out mode.

When they pass you guys, let them get ahead about a half mile or so, and then follow them. Stay with them until the Suburban arrives at a destination. Copy? Over." Doug said keying his mike.

"Roger that; we'll keep you advised.

Desert Bloom out."

Doug wanted to take this opportunity to use Carter as the go-to guy on the radio, plus he felt it was important as another part of his training. Doug was confident Carter would be proficient on the radio, and he also trusted his ability to navigate with his vehicle in a black-out mode using only his night vision gear.

It was now obvious to Doug, Rocco and Garrett that these two buildings would be the focus of their next late-night visit, when they would return to give a little payback for terrorizing the Grimms. Doug looked at his watch and saw it was close to four o'clock. The original plan was to extract and rendezvous with Carter and the others and head back to Tucson. However, with the first Suburban heading north, things changed. Doug figured they should exit the area quickly, as he didn't know if and when the second Suburban would be heading back their way.

From their hilltop vantage point, when they looked to the north they could see the taillights disappearing into the darkness of the thick desert underbrush and terrain. Doug had been through multiple deployments with plenty of experience on the battlefield. His intuitive sense paid off more times than not. In this case there were all kinds of red flags going off.

Doug wondered... *Why three armed men and why leave in such a rush? Where were they heading, and what's in the vehicle?*

Doug again keyed his mike, letting Carter know they'd be heading north and coming back across the border.

4:10 a.m.

Barely ten minutes passed when Carter and the other three could see the headlights of the Suburban heading in their direction up the ranch road from the south. In the stillness of the night, it was easy to hear the sound of the engine and tires interacting with the dirt road as it blew by them, doing a good fifty plus miles per hour. Waiting for the Suburban to get some distance ahead of them, the four men standing in the still, cold desert air could feel and smell the slow drifting dust that reached them in the Suburban's wake.

They got back into Carter's Expedition, easing their way toward the road and turning left as they watched the glow of the Suburban's taillights through their night-vision goggles. Looking through the goggles, Carter was impressed by how easy it was to see any glint of light, making it easy to follow the Suburban. Trailing behind, Carter maintained a consistent half-mile separation. In the green glow of the night vision goggles Carter could easily see the I-10 freeway five miles away and could make out the dim glow of headlights heading east and west. After a short five minutes, Carter saw the brighter glow of the brake lights coming on as the Suburban made a right-hand turn, heading eastbound off the ranch road, a mile before the entrance to the freeway.

Carter slowed his vehicle down and came to a complete stop on a rise in the road bed. The road and surrounding terrain sloped down, heading in the direction of the freeway. This vantage point gave them an excellent observation point. After the Suburban turned right onto what they assumed was some sort of dirt road or trail, it continued on for three quarters of a mile as they watched. At that time, they saw another set of headlights in front of it flash its headlights on and off three times, pause two seconds, then flash two times and then one time after pausing another two seconds in between. The Suburban then slowed to a stop in front of the other car, turning its headlights off.

"I wonder who the hell that is, and what are they up to," Conway quietly said.

What if we get discovered? What if whoever is in those two vehicles starts shooting at us? Carter thought to himself. He became conscious of his grip tightening on the steering wheel as he thought about what could happen when Mike said, "Who knows? Something isn't right."

Carter keyed his mike, letting Doug know their position and what they were observing. Rocco was just getting back into the vehicle after closing the gate, putting them back into the United States, when Doug heard Carter's report. Doug told Carter he wanted them to hold their position with lights out until he caught up with them. In the meantime, if the Suburban or the other vehicle started moving back in the direction of the ranch road, Carter was to head toward the freeway with lights on and wait for further instructions. Carter responded in the affirmative.

Hand-Off

By the time Reggie and his men arrived at the meeting place, Ammar was there waiting for them. In the dark, Ammar could make out Reggie and the silhouette of the two other men as he walked to the back of Reggie's Suburban. The rear doors were already open. Before handing over the two million, Ammar wanted to confirm the contents of the canisters inside the vehicle. He flicked on the switch to the Geiger counter and moved it over each of the canisters in a back-and-forth motion. With each pass, the Geiger-counter needle moved, confirming the low-level emissions from the containers. Smiling, Ammar looked at Reggie, motioning him to his vehicle. Reggie nodded to his men to grab the canisters so they could place them in Ammar's SUV.

Reggie unzipped both the bags, looking inside to confirm the contents. He assumed each bag contained one-hundred bundles of hundred-dollar bills, equaling ten thousand each. He quickly counted out twenty-five bundles and placed them on the floor in the back of Ammar's SUV. He then took the remaining bundles from each of the duffle bags and measured them against the stack of twenty-five, assuring the total amount. He then had his two men count the bundles to double check. After a short period of counting and putting the money back in the bags, Reggie and one of the other men lifted them out of Ammar's vehicle and carried them back to their Suburban. The third man stayed back holding his AK47, watching Ammar.

With both duffle bags secured in the Suburban, Reggie called to the third man to get in the vehicle so they could leave. In the meantime, Ammar got into his SUV, started the engine and was already rolling up behind the Suburban as the two vehicles started to pull out.

4:15 a.m.

Since the doors were open on both vehicles, the interior lights served to silhouette the men moving around. Though some distance away, through his binoculars and night-vision goggles, Carter could see the rear gate of the Suburban open up, and he watched as two of the men each carried something to the other vehicle and then return to the Suburban and repeat the process one more time. He next noticed that someone got out of the waiting vehicle and handed what appeared to be two bags to one of the men in the Suburban.

"What do you think? Drug hand-off?" Carter asked the other three who were watching the same events unfold.

"I'm not sure. I thought the cartel usually moved drugs in small bales. Maybe meth or cocaine? Your guess is as good as mine. Whatever it is, I guarantee you it ain't legal!" Mike said.

"It'll be interesting to hear what Doug and the others saw in San Miguel. Maybe they know what was in the Suburban." Conway said.

After another few minutes of watching, Carter's team saw the headlights of both vehicles come on. The SUV that had been waiting drove around the Suburban and headed westbound, back toward the main road. The Suburban made a U-turn and followed in the same direction.

"Desert Look, we've got lights on and movement from the two vehicles. They're heading back to the ranch road. We're going lights on and heading in the direction of I-10 as planned. Out," Carter said after keying his radio.

"Roger that. We're right behind you and will also be going lights on, trailing you by a couple of miles. Give me a report when you get to the freeway entrance. Out," Doug replied to Carter.

"Will do. Out."

With the lights still out, Carter reversed his truck down the hill so they'd be unobserved when he turned the headlights on. With lights on, he punched it, going over the rise on the road and down the other side, heading north toward the freeway. He was hoping to get past the side road before either of the other two vehicles got there. As they came over the top of the hill with their headlights on, they saw the two vehicles, still on the side road, both come to an immediate halt, turning their lights off.

4:16 a.m.

Ammar was pleased the four containers of the cobalt-60 were in his SUV. He carefully negotiated the dirt trail heading back to the main road, thinking of the destruction the detonation and disbursement of his lethal cargo would cause for the infidels of America. While in the middle of this thought, in the distance and to his left, he saw a vehicle approaching from the south on the ranch road. He slammed on the brakes, sliding to a stop. He turned off his headlights, put it in park and took his foot off the brake pedal. He prayed to Allah that he hadn't been spotted and if he had, that the vehicle heading north wasn't Border Patrol or any other type of law enforcement. He had all the necessary documents with him, yet he dreaded the idea of having to go through any type of ordeal like that. Even though he was in the country illegally, he smugly knew enough to evoke his Fourth Amendment right which prohibits any unlawful searches without probable cause.

Reggie and the other two in his Suburban could see Carter's approaching vehicle and immediately stopped a hundred yards behind Ammar. After exchanging the cobalt-60 for the money, his men put the two million dollars in three different backpacks. If needed, the three of them would abandon their vehicle and flee on foot with the backpacks to the border which was only few miles away. They would fight their way back across the border if necessary and could care less if they killed a few Border Patrol agents or any other law enforcement in the process. The dirt trail they were on at this point was narrow, and they knew Ammar's vehicle would act to block any other vehicle trying to get to them, and that would give them time to run.

The occupants of both vehicles were relieved when the truck on the ranch road sped past where the dirt trail intersected it, heading in the direction of I-10.

4:20 a.m.

In the distance ahead, Carter could easily see I-10 with the headlights of vehicles moving east and westbound. About a quarter mile behind them in the rear view mirror, he watched the first SUV come out of that side road and turn right as if following him. The second one, the Suburban, appeared and turned left, heading back south toward the border.

Doug's gut feeling told him the Suburban would turn back and head south in their direction once it came out of the side road. From Carter's reporting, it was obvious some sort of hand-off just occurred between the two vehicles. He decided to continue on in a blacked-out condition and looked for a place to pull off the road to avoid being detected by the occupants of the Suburban if they did come their way. After pulling off the ranch road and parking a quarter of a mile in a mesquite grove, they watched as the second vehicle turned and headed back in their direction, just as Doug predicted. As the vehicle passed them heading south, they could see it was the same Suburban they observed leaving San Miguel heading north. Whoever was in that Suburban was heading back across the border into Mexico.

4:21 a.m.

Carter crossed the overpass of I-10 toward the westbound entrance ramp. He slowed down, coming to a stop just before the entrance to the ramp, wanting to see which direction the other vehicle was going to go. Just as he did so, he saw Ammar's vehicle approaching and turning onto the eastbound ramp. Carter felt compelled to turn around and follow him, but then he remembered the whole purpose of their mission tonight was to do recon on the cartel in San Miguel in preparation for a "meet and greet." He realized that after tonight he was all in with no turning back and smiled at the thought of it.

Carter keyed his mike to let Doug and the others know their position and the direction of the SUV. He waited for a minute and then keyed the mike again – nothing; he waited a few seconds and radioed Doug again, but still no response. Carter grabbed his cell phone, pulling up Doug's number on speed dial, and by the third ring Doug picked up. Carter gave him a status report on the other vehicle and was relieved to hear the Suburban passed Doug's position without incident. Doug reported they were on their way and would meet up with them at Carter's house.

All seven Americans in both vehicles couldn't help but wonder what the hell that activity between the Suburban and other vehicle was all about. It was obvious it was a rendezvous, but beyond that, it was a mystery. What was the rendezvous about and with who?

4:22 a.m.

After turning onto the eastbound ramp to I-10, Ammar called Imam Mohammad Abdullah al Hamadan, of the Madkhal Mosque in Tucson to let him know the package was picked up. Though it was almost dawn, the Imam answered the cell phone on the first ring. In the pre-planning of this attack the Iman was chosen for the procurement of the cobalt-60 and arranging for a trusted driver to make the rendezvous with the cartel.

Once the cargo was in hand, Ammar was next supposed to head to an Islamic training camp twenty miles northeast of Santa Fe, New Mexico. It was an eleven-hour drive from where he was now. He would rest there overnight before driving straight through to Dearborn, Michigan, to deliver his deadly cargo to his awaiting brothers.

After heading east on I-10 for a little more than an hour, Ammar began to squint as the sun came up over the horizon directly in front of him. It was a new day, and he was grateful Allah allowed him to receive the toxic and deadly cargo he had on board.

6:11 a.m.

By the time the four of them pulled into Carter's driveway, the sun was climbing up the horizon. Though he'd been up all night, Carter felt alive and energized. During the drive back, they talked and wondered about what they observed that night.

"Who's up for coffee?" Carter asked, going through the front door of his house.

After filling their coffee mugs, they sat around in Carter's living room which still had the same furniture arrangement from the previous night's briefing. They were anxious for Doug, Rocco and Garrett to get there so they could hear what they learned while in San Miguel.

Twenty-two minutes later, Doug and the others came rolling up the driveway. The three of them hopped out of Doug's SUV and made their way into Carter's house.

After the new arrivals helped themselves to coffee in the kitchen, everyone took a seat in the living room. Doug proceeded to tell Carter's group what his team observed and also confirmed which buildings they would target when they returned for their "meet and greet."

"There's been a few times while running an op when something clearly wasn't right. The rendezvous the four of you witnessed last night was one of those times. I don't know what the three Mexicans carried in their vehicle or who they met up with, but my gut feeling is that it wasn't drugs – much too small of a load for that. Something just doesn't add up. The quick trip north, the rendezvous with another vehicle, and then one heads north and eastbound on the I-10 with the suburban heading back to Mexico. Whatever that was about wasn't good! Doug said.

All seven of them discussed the situation for another ten minutes until it became obvious all they could do was speculate about it and nothing more.

"I think we need to find out what we can and as soon as we can. I know we discussed paying a little visit to the cartel in San Miguel next week, but now I think we should get down there ASAP! If everyone's available, I'd like to go back down there tonight. We got enough intelligence from last night, and our target looks relatively easy to hit. Everyone on board?" Doug asked, scanning the team.

Doug wanted to get another training session in on room clearing at the canyon range before going back down to San Miguel. But he felt a growing sense of urgency to go that night. Long ago he'd learned to trust his gut instinct and, when possible, act on it. Over the years it kept him and his fellow brothers-in-arms alive.

Doug was impressed by how smoothly last night's mission had gone, and he felt a sense of pride for having blended a combination of civilians and retired Special Forces together so quickly. He was equally impressed with how well Carter, Garrett and Mick performed under stress the previous night.

Carter, Garrett and Mick looked at each other and nodded their heads. Two of them would have to make arrangements to change some personal plans, but there was no way any of them were going to miss out on this adventure.

"We're in!" Carter said speaking for the 3 of them.

Conway, Mike and Rocco also gave thumbs-up to Doug's request to go that night. They all agreed to meet back at Carter's house at ten o'clock that night, and then they would basically run the same schedule as the previous evening. The big difference was that tonight all seven of them would be crossing the border and fully geared up. Now, because Doug and Rocco had seen the target, together they would develop a detailed plan for the night's mission.

Thursday, 8:32 a.m. – Las Cruces, New Mexico

After three or four hours of driving, Ammar pulled into the parking lot of a McDonald's in Las Cruces, New Mexico. From there he would continue down I-10 and turn north on I-25. This would take him through Albuquerque and then up to Santa Fe. He had never traveled in this part of the world before and was relying on the GPS in his phone to guide him. Though the training camp wasn't on the map, he'd been given coordinates to put into his phone.

Ammar thought about using the drive-thru of the McDonald's; however, nature was calling. He was able to find a parking space close to the front door. Getting out of his vehicle he shivered in the chill of the cold January air. As he walked through the front door to the fast-food chain, he hit the button on the key fob, double-checking to make sure his vehicle was locked.

The southwestern town of Las Cruces was very conservative, and folks there were not accustomed to seeing Middle Easterners. Standing at five-feet-five with a slight build, wearing black sandals, white socks, black pants, light tan jacket, Ammar was dark skinned and with an unshaven, heavy beard. He looked remarkably like Mahmoud Ahmadinejad, the former president of Iran. The three local construction workers sitting toward the back of the restaurant certainly didn't miss seeing Ammar walk in. He could feel their eyes following him as he went into the men's bathroom. He prayed to Allah they wouldn't come into the bathroom and give him trouble.

After relieving himself, he walked out of the bathroom. One of the three men brushed past him, making a point to bump into him with his shoulder and sneering, "Your kind ain't welcome here, you little goat-fucking asshole."

Ammar knew he was no match for anyone of these men and regretted he wasn't wearing a suicide vest. After getting bumped, he just kept walking without saying a word and hoped no more would come of the encounter. He thought about his cargo and the destruction it would soon cause and smiled to himself thinking... *If only they knew of the horror I'm going to help rain down on the infidels of America!*

As he stood in the line to order, the other two got up and stood behind him – right behind him.

"What the hell is that odor? It stinks in here. I wonder if I can get extra bacon on my burger," one of the men said, and all three of them snickered.

Ammar got his order and quickly walked back to his SUV. The three men followed him outside, taunting him all the way. He got in, started it up and drove out of the parking lot, turning right to head east. He started looking for I-25, which he knew would soon be coming up on his left. As he drove off, he wanted to scream something at them but decided against it because he didn't want to draw any more attention to himself.

He was going to top his gas tank off in Las Cruces, but because of the incident at McDonald's, he decided to wait until the next town. He knew from his GPS that the little town of Notroso would be a good place to fuel up, and it was only thirty-five miles away. Angry and lost in thought about what happened, he almost missed the only gas station in Notroso when it appeared before him on his right. He quickly pulled in and, zipping up his jacket against the cold wind, he got out and grabbed the fuel nozzle on the pump.

After fueling up, he drove on, making another pit stop at a gas station in Albuquerque. By this time, Ammar knew the bulk of his journey to the training camp was behind him; the GPS said only an hour and a half to go.

Five-minutes out of Albuquerque, his "check engine light" came on. He started losing power and pulled over on the right shoulder of the highway.

Ammar was upset as he called the number given to him by the Imam for his contact at the training camp. A voice came on the other end. Ammar identified himself, explaining he was stopped alongside the road with his vehicle wasn't working. The voice got his location, said someone would be there soon and hung up.

Ammar reached down and turned on his emergency flashers and sat back to wait. He was tired. He thought about how it had been a long thirty-six hours with no sleep as he listened to the methodical staccato sound of the emergency flashers.

He woke up with a tapping on his driver's door glass. It was a New Mexico Highway Patrolman.

"Sir, can you hear me?" The officer asked, as Ammar woke up from his short nap. He nodded his head in the direction of the officer.

"Sir, are you OK? Would you mind rolling down your window? May I see your driver's license, vehicle registration and insurance card? How much have you had to drink?" Ammar gathered himself together. He knew from his training that if he encountered law enforcement he should take a pro-active approach. Since the events in Ferguson, Missouri, law enforcement was very wary of falsely accusing minorities.

"I am a Muslim, and it is against my religion to consume alcohol, so, no, I haven't been drinking. My car stopped running. and I'm waiting for a tow truck to arrive. I'm afraid I fell asleep."

Ammar reached into his glove box and pulled out all the necessary documents and handed them to the officer. He knew they would be there in the event something like this happened. The officer walked back to his patrol car and returned in five minutes, handing the papers back to him.

"You have a good day, *sir*!"

A little more than an hour passed when a tow truck appeared, coming from the north making a fast U-turn. It pulled ahead of Ammar's vehicle and then backed up to within a few feet of the front of the SUV. A man jumped out of the tow truck, walked over to Ammar and told him to put it in neutral. Within ten minutes, he loaded the SUV onto the flatbed of the tow truck. He told Ammar to get in the cab. With a lurch, they were off, heading north.

The tow-truck driver, Tameez, was the mechanic for the training camp. Other than a nod and a short greeting, the two of them didn't speak to each other on the way to the compound. This was fine with Ammar, as he was tired and distressed about his vehicle breaking down. This slowed down his mission, and he didn't feel like talking to anyone. He assumed the tow-truck driver was unaware of the deadly cargo they were hauling. As a general rule, Islamic terrorists are very good at keeping things on a need-to-know basis at all times. One thing for certain, though, was that Ammar and Tameez shared a deep-rooted ideology and religious belief that all infidels must be exterminated.

Thursday, 5:48 p.m. –
Islamic Training Camp, N.E. New Mexico

The drive was uneventful, and within an hour and a half, they pulled into the compound. After hopping down from the cab of the truck, Ammar turned and saw an older man in his sixties approaching him with a smile. Qulaib al Hanifia was the elder of the training compound and the only one that knew the purpose of Ammar's appearance there and the nature of his cargo. Qulaib was thin, and taller than Ammar and Tameez, standing at six feet, two-inches. He had a turban on his head, shamaz wrapped around his neck, blue sweater, tan vest and long white dirty pants. Even in the winter cold, Qulaib was wearing only sandals – no socks. His long, flowing, red beard gently bounced as he walked toward the tired courier. Qulaib welcomed Ammar with a hug and a kiss on each cheek and then invited him to his quarters for tea. As they walked to the main building, two other men appeared and helped Tameez unload Ammar's vehicle.

On the east side of the main house was a newly built garage, large enough to accommodate up to four vehicles, complete with a hydraulic lift. Once Ammar's SUV was unloaded off the tow truck, the three men pushed it into the garage and up onto the lift. Tameez got in and tried to start it, but to no avail. The motor would turn, but the engine wouldn't fire. Ammar's vehicle was a fifteen-year-old Toyota 4Runner with one hundred and sixty-three thousand miles on it. Though the ISIS affiliate had plenty of funds and could afford newer vehicles, they preferred older ones to keep a low profile. Tameez pulled the hood latch on the inside and jumped out, as one of the other men lifted the hood.

It is common in all of the Islamic training camps around the world to have individuals with expertise in many different areas such as weapons, communications, internet and engine mechanics. This strategy enabled them to keep a low profile in the community and stay off the radar as much as possible by not bringing people in from the outside who were not part of their movement.

After an hour, Tameez came into the main house to explain to Ammar and Qulaib that the vehicle needed a new fuel pump and relay. It was too late by that time to go to Albuquerque to get parts, but said he would go first thing in the morning. He assured Ammar he'd be on his way by tomorrow afternoon. Although the news made Ammar feel even more anxious, he knew he must surrender to the reality of the situation. He would use this time to rest up before proceeding on his long drive to Michigan. He pulled his phone out of his pocket and called Tahmeed al Bahra'a, his contact in Dearborn, to inform him of the delay.

At eight o'clock, everyone assembled for their evening meal in the rectangular-shaped dining hall on the north side of the yard. Inside were multiple long tables set up with buffet style serving areas and a large kitchen behind the serving area. It could easily accommodate up to fifty people for a meal.

After their meal they would hold their evening prayers before retiring for the night. There was always at least one person – always with an AK47 nearby – left on duty to guard the facility for the night. In the three years since the training compound had been established, none of the locals, or anyone else, ever caused a problem. They knew even the red-neck locals were afraid of getting in trouble with local authorities if they disturbed them in any way. With the aid of left-wing liberal attorneys, the White House administration and a compliant media, millions of Americans had been turned into sheep.

When they first opened their training camp, there were at least four men on guard duty at night. It didn't take long for them to learn there was no need to fear any encroachment on their facility. At this point, they didn't feel a need for more than one or two guards at night.

Thursday Evening, 10:00 p.m.

By ten o'clock that evening, everyone was seated in Carter's living room with a mug of coffee in hand. Carter, at Doug's request, set up a white board so he could diagram the road, fence and approach to the two buildings in San Miguel that were their primary targets. The objective of the mission was straightforward – confront any Magdalena Cartel members they found at gun point and impress upon them not to fuck with any more Americans. Also to let them know if they set one foot across the U.S. border, they would be hunted down and forced to pay a heavy price. The Americans would let the cartel members know that even though the U.S. government wasn't doing anything meaningful to stop them, American citizens were no longer willing to tolerate the cartel's criminal activity in their country. It was time to send a message that some Americans weren't going to just sit around waiting for U.S. law enforcement to secure the border.

Doug further explained that while they all were going to be armed, the intention was not to start shooting anybody that looked like a cartel member. But at the same time, Doug made it clear that if anyone starts to point guns at them, they need to do whatever is necessary to protect themselves and their team members.

For Doug and the other three retired operators, pre-mission briefings were something they were used to. For Carter, Mick and Garrett, this was a first. Carter had asked Mick and Garrett to arrive at his house an hour early. He wanted to make sure there was no doubt in Garrett's or Mick's mind about what they were about to do. Their lives were about to change, big time. For Carter, it felt right. But if either of them had reservations about this, he would understand; and he was not concerned that either of them would compromise the veil of secrecy if they decided not to go.

Arriving right at nine, an hour earlier as planned, Garrett and Mick walked into Carter's house with all of their gear, including their side arms in drop leg holsters. Carter greeted each of them with a hug. He could tell by their demeanor that they were going to be good to go, but he'd learned a long time ago, even with good friends, never assume anything.

The three old friends went into the kitchen, and Carter grabbed the coffee pot and filled three cups with the steaming, dark brew. They all stood there in the middle of the kitchen, and Carter looked at them both with a steady gaze.

He announced, "What we're about to do is going to change our lives forever. I understand the potential downside, but I'm resolved and ready to go. The truth is, I've been looking forward to doing something like this for years now. As you both know, I sat out the Vietnam War – a decision I've regretted ever since. Maybe God was saving me for something else. Maybe this is a chance to redeem myself in my own mind. Either way, I'm crystal clear this is exactly what I need to do, and I'm glad it's with the two of you." Tears began to well up in his eyes as he felt a rush of love, trust and respect for his two friends standing before him.

"Do either of you have any concerns or considerations about tonight?"

"Yeah, I've got one big concern," Mick said, with the corner of his mouth starting to turn up in a smile at Garrett and then Carter. "If we have to run, will your old fat ass be able to keep up with the rest of us young pups?" The three of them burst out laughing.

"Fuck you and the horse you rode in on!" Carter said, busting out laughing and flipping Mick the bird. "Love you guys! Let's do this!" The three of them hugged.

Carter again remembered freezing up in the doorway at the mall and the fear that almost overcame him. Again he thought about the old woman; he could see her face, hear her voice and feel her pushing him, while yelling and pointing at his gun, "Do something!"

Breathe, you'll be OK. You'll deal with it if it comes up.

"Why don't you guys get your gear and let's double check each other before Doug and the others get here?"

They were almost finished with their gear check when they saw headlights coming up the driveway. Through the large picture window in his living room, Carter watched as Doug's SUV rolled to a stop. He could hear the sound of the doors opening and closing as he went over to the front door to greet Doug and Rocco. Just then, two more sets of headlights appeared, and Mike and Conway came up the driveway behind them.

Five minutes after everyone got their coffee, each took a seat in the living room. The conversation went from a guys-in-the-locker-room tone to total quiet, waiting for Doug to start the briefing. Carter had set up the three-by-five-foot white board on a stand with a selection of four different colored markers. It was positioned in the front center of the room so everyone could see it.

Without saying a word, Rocco got up and began drawing a diagram of San Miguel and the buildings in the immediate area they would focus on. Then Doug, using the satellite photos he'd handed out earlier as a reference, pointed to the layout Rocco had drawn, putting a circle around the five buildings on the east side of the road leading in and out of the village. Then he drew another circle around the two buildings believed to be controlled by the cartel.

Across from the buildings on the west side of the road was a cattle fence running north and south. To the west of the fence line was open desert dotted with mesquite trees, cactus and other vegetation, and the terrain rose upward to the hill that Doug, Garrett and Rocco had been on the night before. Rocco had laser measured the distance from the top of the hill to the two targeted buildings and found it to be right at one hundred and fifty-two yards.

Doug went over their planned approach to the top of the hill, which would duplicate what they did the previous night. He explained he wanted Carter and Mick to set up seventy-five yards apart and twenty-five yards to the west of the fence line on the other side of the road and directly across from the two main buildings. He, along with Mike, Rocco and Conway, would go in to deliver their message. Doug wanted Carter and Mick positioned on a forty-five-degree angle to each other so they could triangulate their covering fire if needed. They should also be able to see either side of the two buildings. Because of Garrett's long-range skills, he would be set up on the top of the hill, providing overwatch for the rest of them. He was aware of Garrett's 6.5 millimeter Grendel sniper rifle and asked him to bring it along. Doug knew the capabilities of this weapon and its reputation for being extremely accurate and devastating in the hands of the right shooter. Everybody knew if Garrett had to take a shot from that distance he wouldn't miss. A hundred-and-fifty yards for him with that rifle was nothing but a warm up to longer ranges. He could put a round in a man's ear at that distance.

Doug went on to explain he, Conway, Rocco and Mike would be doing dynamic entries into both of the two buildings. From the hilltop they would make a determination at the time as to which building they would hit first. Their primary choice would be to enter the building with the greater population of the two, and then, after clearing, restraining and gagging the occupants of that building, go on to the next and do the same.

Everybody had brought their gear in, and it was all laid out in the entryway of Carter's house. After a little more than forty-five minutes, Doug completed his briefing and answered all questions. He next had everybody pair up and double-check each other's gear. Fortunately, they all had suppressors for their rifles and they'd use them in the night's mission along with their night-vision gear.

By 11:10 p.m., they checked their gear, including a radio check, and were out the door. Carter, with Mick and Garrett inside his truck, was following Doug and the others as they headed down Carter's driveway on their way to San Miguel.

Friday Morning, 1:15 a.m.

Other than the sound of the idling engines, it was a silent, moonless and cloudless cold night in the January desert. Under the cover of a heavily star-blanketed night, Garrett quietly got back into Carter's truck, after closing the gate separating the United States from Mexico on the X-7 Ranch. The two blacked-out vehicles then continued on through a cloud of dust. With his night-vision goggles on, Carter followed Doug's SUV down the dirt road leading to San Miguel and watched as he pulled off to the right in the same spot as last night. He followed, as they both went back a couple-of-hundred yards to hide their vehicles. When they came to a halt, the occupants of both vehicles quietly opened and closed their doors. Everyone put on his gear and slung his rifle. They all turned on their red-dot optics, inserted a thirty-round magazine in them and yanked down on it to ensure it was secured and then quietly racked a round into the chamber.

With Rocco and Garrett leading the way, they moved through the desert and up the west side, (back side) of the hill. Once at the top and overlooking the town, all seven went to a prone position on the ground. To ensure that everyone knew which two buildings would be their focus, Doug had Rocco illuminate them with his PAC4 infrared laser device. With the infrared illumination marking both buildings, they could all easily see the two targets through their night-vision gear. As planned, they did a quick radio check before everyone but Garrett began going down the front side of the hill toward the fence line that separated the road and the two targeted buildings.

Insertion

When the group was within twenty-five yards of the fence line, following Doug's plan, Carter broke off to the right on a forty-five-degree angle, with Mick doing the same to the left. Both of them were able to take up their positions separated by seventy-five yards.

Upon reaching the fence line, Doug and the other three each went down on one knee, taking the time to do further recon of the two key buildings. Now, with only sixty feet separating them from the buildings, it was easy to see through the tattered drapes of the front window on the larger one on the left. There were at least two individuals moving around inside.

Carter's ear bud came on. Doug wanted to confirm if he, Mick or Garrett, from their vantage points, could see anyone outside the buildings in the immediate area. With a "negative" coming back from all three, Doug and the others moved north along the fence. From his backpack, Mike pulled out his suppressed Ruger 10-22 rifle, took aim and shot out the only street light illuminating the area in front of the two buildings. Next, Conway cut the four strands of barbed wire strung between the two wooden fence posts closest to them, using a pair of wire snips. One by one, they dashed through the opening between the fence posts and crossed the road into the shadow of a building just to the north of their primary objective.

The plan was to enter and subdue all the occupants in the two buildings. The Americans would deliver their message: no more threats or harm to Americans and no more crossing the border with their drugs or human cargo. If their warning was ignored, they'd be back. But the next time they would kill them. They wanted to make sure the cartel knew they were no longer untouchable.

Once they reached the larger of the two buildings, Mike and Conway went around to the back, with a quick peek in the windows as they went, reporting in whispers on their radios. As they came around the back corner, a rear door was cracked open a couple of inches. The two of them listened and could hear voices talking in Spanish in another room. Conway motioned to Mike that he was going to continue on around the far side of the other building. Mike stayed by the back door, stepping back to give another position report to Doug and the others.

Conway worked his way around to the second building, peering in windows as he came to them. There were no lights on, and he couldn't see or hear anyone in inside. He keyed his radio, giving a quick report, and returned to where Mike was waiting by the cracked door. Doug came back on the radio and told Conway to come back to his and Rocco's position in the front. Mike, staying by the back door, reported he still could hear only two different voices coming from inside. Looking through the thin opening, Mike could make out only a few of the details of the room, but it was enough to be able to tell it was the kitchen and that no one was in it.

Off to the right of his position, Carter could see the glow in the dark night of the Pemex gas station in the distance. His vantage point allowed him to see the front and right side of both of the targeted buildings. From the radio transmission, he knew Conway would be coming around the south side of the second building, and he watched in anticipation. He was impressed by how smoothly Conway moved down the side of the second building, pausing only momentarily to look in the two windows in the back and front of that side of the building.

Both buildings were typical Mexican-style dwellings, with the larger one on the left maybe fourteen-hundred square feet and the smaller one to right around nine-hundred square feet. Both had flat roofs with parapet walls and rebar jutting upward at the corners. And both had a front porch roof extending out eight feet to provide cover from the sun and weather.

Conway came back around the corner, joining Doug and Rocco near the front door they were about to breach. Rocco would be the first one in and would slant to the right, rifle raised in a ready position. Conway would follow, button hooking to the left, with Doug immediately after, slanting to the right in Rocco's direction. Luckily for them and particularly for Mike, the rear door was ajar.

Upon Doug's command through the radio, Mike squatted down and quietly slid the flashbang he'd pulled out of his vest through the door and on the tile floor. Then leaned back out of way of the blast and stood up. On the radio, Mike called out, "Set!" Doug and the others waited for the explosion and flash.

Carter could see the flash through the windows and could hear the muffled thud of the explosion. To him it looked as if someone popped a giant flash bulb inside. Immediately, Rocco kicked in the front door, disappearing to the right, with Conway behind him going to the left, followed by Doug going right. The two startled men inside were stunned and confused. Mike called out, "coming in" and quickly entered the back door through the acrid smell and smoke of the flashbang. He slung his rifle, joining Conway in putting each of the two dazed men on the floor onto their stomachs and zip-tying their hands behind their backs. Rocco and Doug had already gone through the open doorway into a hall, with Doug turning left to cover and Rocco going right, opening a door to what he assumed was a bedroom. The hallway and room were both dark, and Rocco flipped down his night-vision goggles so the darkness turned into a well-lit, glowing, green-room.

As he entered, he saw a heavy-set man in a bed, pulling his hand back from a nightstand and swinging the barrel of a gun in Rocco's direction. With the speed and accuracy that only a former Spec Operator could deliver, there was a "thump, thump, thump" noise as Rocco squeezed off three rapid shots, hitting the man twice in the middle of his chest and once just above his left eye socket. Out in the main room the other three could hear the muffled sound of Rocco's suppressed weapon and the concussion of the bullets smacking soft tissue.

In front of Doug was a bathroom with the door open, so nothing to be concerned about. A few feet behind him and to his right, there was a partially opened door. Rocco called out, "coming out" and emerged from the bedroom. He swiftly moved down the short hallway to where Doug was standing in front of the door with his rifle raised to his shoulder. With night-vision goggles still in place, Rocco turned away from the light of the living room and went through the open door, slanting right, with Doug behind him slanting left into the small room. Finding nothing, Rocco called out, "clear," and both came out to the larger room, joining Conway and Mike and the two bound men lying on the floor.

With their goggles removed, Doug instructed Mike to stay with the two men. "Coming out," crackled through the radios of Carter, Garrett and Mick, still positioned across the road. Rocco, Conway and Doug came out of the first building and moved to the smaller one next door. Conway went to the back of the building to cover the rear door.

Doug keyed his microphone, checking in with Carter, Mick and Garrett to make sure they hadn't seen any movement outside in either direction. After getting a "negative" from the three watching from a distance, Doug keyed his microphone again and let Conway know they were ready. Conway checked the rear door: it was locked, so he put the flashbang in his left hand back in his vest. With the flat of his hand, he then hit the door hard; this was the second-best choice to use as a distraction in case anyone was in the building. Upon hearing the thud out back, Rocco again kicked in the front door, and they repeated the same entry procedure. With their night-vision goggles deployed, when they entered they were immediately engulfed by the pungent smell of marijuana. The room was stacked with three-by-two foot bales of the stuff. Doug maneuvered around them to get to the rear door to let Conway in.

Conway covered both doors while Rocco and Doug entered the short hallway. Rocco again went to the right and through an open door. Through his night vision goggles he could see no one was in the room but there were more of the stacked bales of marijuana. In the far left hand corner something caught his attention. There was something on the floor with a faint glow around it, coming from what appeared to be some sort of canisters. There were four of them in all.

"Coming out," Rocco said, exiting the room and joining Doug as they went down the short hallway and entered the other room. This room, like the main one, and the one Rocco checked, was also loaded with bales of marijuana.

After confirming no-one was hiding in this room, Rocco said, "Sir, there's something weird in the other room that we need to check out."

"Roger that," Doug responded, as they went down the hallway and back into the other room. The glow in the corner was hard to miss, looking through their night-vision gear. Doug pulled out a flashlight with an infrared filter.

Hot Discovery

Doug was careful not to hit the light switch in the room. That could alert anyone who might be looking in their direction that someone was in the building. He clicked on the flashlight and pointed it at the four canisters on the floor. Both men could easily make out the labels on each one: "Cobalt-60"

This label was the international symbol for danger:

"Holy fuck!" Doug said softly.

His mind raced to try and make sense of what they were looking at. He thought to himself... *Why is there radioactive material being stored here and for what purpose?* He felt the hair on the back of his neck rising.

"What the fuck?" Rocco said, looking at his commander.

"I haven't a clue. Let's get back next door and see if our two friends lying on the ground can enlighten us!"

Doug radioed the others that they were coming out and going back to the other building.

"Carter, Mick and Garrett, stay sharp. We're going to be in the first building for a little bit. Let us know if you see anything."

"Roger that!" Carter replied, speaking for the three of them.

All four of the operators had been in places where sometimes things just didn't seem right; for Rocco and Doug, this was definitely one of those times. They understood the neatly wrapped small bales of marijuana, but the four containers of cobalt-60 were a mystery to them. They intended to find out what they could from the two men now gagged and hog tied on the floor.

When Doug and Rocco got back to the first building, they couldn't help but smile at the sight of the two cartel members lying there helplessly.

"Who speaks English?" Doug asked, looking down at the men on the floor.

"Habla ingles?" Still no response.

Doug looked at Rocco with a nod at the men. Rocco went to one knee next to the man closest to him, and with his left hand holding the man's head down, he used his right index finger to press into the small, soft spot below his ear.

"OK, OK," the man cried out, trying unsuccessfully to wriggle his head out of Rocco's grasp.

"Wow, see how easy that is?" Doug said, looking at the man wincing in pain and then at the other one. "How about you, do you need some persuasion too?"

"No." Both of the men knew these four Americans were not to be fooled with. These four Americans had a certain kind of hard edge and confidence the cartel members had never witnessed before.

"Do you know who we are and why we're here?" Doug asked.

The man who Rocco persuaded to speak English said, "I don't know who you are, but I know you're here to steal from us – to take our drugs."

"Wrong; we don't give a fuck about your drugs. We are here to warn you not to cross our border anymore, and if you ever fuck with another American again and we find out, we will be back. And you'll end up dead like your fat fuck amigo in the other room. Comprende? You tell your piece-of-shit boss we were here, and we're coming for him if he crosses our border or sends anyone over it. There will be no place for him and the rest of you to hide!" Doug said, now visibly pissed off. The man nodded.

"Good, glad you understand. Now tell me, what's with the four radioactive canisters in the other building? Why do you have that?"

"No, we know nothing," said the man closest to him.

Doug thought for a moment about the previous night and started to see the pieces coming together. What did they take out of the other building last night and put into the Suburban? Why did the three men that got into the Suburban go north and then return back across the border so quickly? Who was the person they met up with just south of I-10?

243

Why did he head east on I-10, and where was he headed? There was nothing but questions with no answers. Deep down in his gut all of these un-answered questions left him with a feeling of impending doom.

His concern was that last night's delivery wasn't drugs, but rather cobalt-60. Further heightening his apprehension was the question, "If it was cobalt-60, what type of person would want such a lethal item and for what?" He didn't believe for a second that the two men sprawled out before them didn't know what last night's activity was about. He was going to get some answers and get them now! There was too much at stake otherwise!

"Bull shit, you know plenty about it. Now tell us about the red-and-yellow canisters over in the other building. And who was the guy you delivered some of them to last night on the other side of the border?"

"Please, señor, we know nothing."

Without waiting for a signal from Doug, Rocco reached down again, holding the man's head down with his left hand while pressing even harder into the soft spot below his right ear with his right index finger. He held it there for a few seconds before letting up, as the man screamed and writhed in pain.

Doug squatted down, putting his face close to the man's face. "OK, tell us everything you know, and if we think for one second that you're lying to us, it's going hurt much worse for you and your amigo! Comprende?"

With tears of pain and fear rolling down his cheeks, the man nodded his head in the affirmative.

Doug was surprised how easy it was to get this man to talk with just a bit of persuasion. These may be ruthless men, but they weren't tough. Their loyalty went no further than the bling around their neck and their fear that either they or their families might be tortured and killed by their own people. He was grateful for their shallow loyalty to their boss and fellow cartel members.

Unlike Al-Qaida, the Taliban and ISIS, who were driven by ideology and fanaticism, the Mexican cartel members were driven by greed and the need for power over others. Individually, they were cowards, finding false courage only when surrounded by their own kind and terrorizing the weak. Islamic extremists, on the other hand, will die for their beliefs, making it hard not only to take them alive but also difficult to interrogate. Many times, interrogation sessions of Islamic extremists ended in an unsatisfactory outcome. In that regard, Doug and the rest respected them as fighters. But as far as he was concerned, the two men sprawled out before him were cowards who hid behind drugs and guns. The one thing both groups had in common was that they were both evil, and they should be exterminated!

Looking at their height and body type, Doug wondered if these were two of the men from the previous night who crossed the border. The fact he wasn't sure didn't matter; he was going to assume they *were* two of the three men he saw get in the Suburban and head north last night. Remembering what happened to the Grimms, all Doug could feel was contempt for the two terrified men lying in front of him.

"OK, did you two with a third man go across the border last night to meet someone up near I-10 and give him some of those canisters in the other building? Who was it you met, and why?"

The man hesitated, so Doug, making sure the man could see him, gave Rocco a nod with his head. Rocco again started to push the man's head down.

"OK, OK, it wasn't the two of us. All I know, it was someone who came from Tucson, gave mi amigos money, and they gave him four of those canisters."

"What's the name of the person your amigos met with, and how much money did they get?"

"Boss, got something here!" Mike said, as he walked out of the kitchen into the main room. He had been rummaging around in there and found a pad of paper with some phone numbers on it. Two of the numbers started with 520 area codes, the area code for southern Arizona and, in particular, Tucson. Written next to one of the numbers was the name "Ammar" and next to the other number was the name Imam Mohammad Abdullah al Hamadan. Doug and Mike looked at each other. Though neither of the men knew the two names, they did know they were both Arabic names. Keeping his poker face on, Doug turned back to the bound men on the floor while holding the pad of paper up for Rocco and Conway to see.

"Tell me again, why did you turn over the cobalt-60 to the man from Tucson?"

"I told you, please, all I know is we gave him the containers and he gave us much money."

"How much money did you get, and where is the money now?" Doug asked.

"I don't know how much, maybe two million or more; it was given to our boss when they got back here."

"Who's your boss?"

The man knew giving up his boss's name with his fellow cartel member hearing him do so could be a death sentence for him and his family. He felt like a trapped rat

– either cooperate with these men and hope they won't hurt him anymore, or take his chances with his friend ratting him out.

The second man looked at him, shaking his head "no," which was followed immediately by a stiff boot kick into the man's ribs, delivered by Conway. The man cried out in pain, gasping for air. Both men knew who ever these four gringos were, they weren't U.S. law enforcement of any kind, and they weren't fooling around.

"Señor, please, if I tell you, he will kill me and my family," the man pleaded, looking for some sort of sympathy from Doug. Doug again gave Rocco a look.

"OK, OK, his name is Juan Ortiz."

Doug gave Rocco another look, only this time it was a nod for him to follow him outside. It was recognized by Mike and Conway that Rocco was second in command, and Doug wanted to have a conversation with him out of the earshot of the two Mexicans. Over the years of working together, Doug trusted Rocco's intuitive and common-sense point of view. Whenever he could, he liked to use him as a sounding board for his thoughts.

In the meantime, Carter, Mick and Garrett were waiting for Doug and the others to exit the building and return to their vantage point. It seemed like a long time, but in reality was only about fifteen minutes since Doug and the others had first breached the two buildings.

Don't Tread on Us!

Carter wondered why they were taking so long and what was going on inside the larger of the two buildings. In the middle of his thoughts, his ear-bud crackled, and Doug announced he and Rocco were coming out. Carter watched as the two men came outside.

"Something is really wrong with this picture. I lay money that the cobalt-60 went to one of the two names associated with those phone numbers, and if that's the case, we've got a much bigger problem than just dealing with these piece-of-shit cartel members coming across our border," Doug said to Rocco, with a grave look on his face.

"You're right; this is not good. What the fuck? That stuff would be good for only one thing to Islamic terrorists. It's perfect dirty bomb material!" Rocco answered.

"I'm afraid you're right. OK, I say we downplay our attention on the cobalt-60 to the two on the ground in there. We should just re-focus our threat of retribution to them if they come across our border and especially if they mess with any Americans living on the border. What do you want to do with those guys?"

"I'd just as soon put a bullet in their heads and let their boss figure out what happened to them. I think our discovery of the cobalt-60 changes everything. If we leave the two of them to talk, and if there's a plan for a dirty bomb, they could warn them we're on to them! Boss, I know we're not cold-blooded killers, but the truth is, if we leave those two alive it could eliminate whatever chance we might have of interrupting their plans. I don't trust law enforcement to handle the problem. Hell, they're too afraid of getting into trouble if they do their jobs, and they're scared to death of being called racist. Hundreds, if not more, of American lives are at risk!"

Doug weighed the gravity of what Rocco just said. Although he didn't like the thought of it, he knew he was right. The possibility of a dirty bomb going off in the U.S. was beyond serious. He thought about his wife and children. To dispatch the two men inside grated against the core values that Doug and the others believed in. He knew in war sometimes a few have to die to save more lives. Though it was not politically correct to say it, the United States is in a war, a war declared by Islamic terrorists' hell bent on killing American citizens and destroying their way of life.

"OK, you're right. Let's give Conway and Mike a heads-up, and then we'll take care of the problem and get the hell out of here!"

"What do you want to do about the remaining four canisters of the cobalt-60 in the other building?" Rocco asked.

"We leave them. One reason is we know they're leaking radiation; we could see it through our goggles. I don't want it around any of us. The other reason is if we took it with us, they'll realize we know about it. Then they could tip off whoever they sold it to. I think it's better to leave the stuff and let them wonder what happened here."

"OK, makes sense. I'd still like to somehow leave a message dealing with the reason we came here in the first place. Hey, Conway used to carry a small Gadsden flag in his pack. If he still has it, let's pin it inside the front door. I think it's the message we wanted to send in the first place."

"I like it!" said Doug, and he keyed his microphone to let everyone know they were going back inside the building.

Extraction

From across the road, Carter watched the two men go back inside. Less than a minute later he saw four rapid flashes from inside the building, and then all four of them exited, coming back across the road and through the cut in the fence.

Doug and the other three silently made their way up the slope to Garrett's position, with Carter and Mick trailing. All six constantly checked to the rear and to each side as they came up.

Garrett stayed in his position until all six of them made it to where he was still lying prone and scanning below for any threats. When Doug tapped him on his shoulder, Garrett quickly got up, backing away from his position and joining the others as they moved down the back side of the short hill, angling right to the north on their short trek back to where their two vehicles remained hidden.

Quietly they all got in the vehicles, and with Carter leading the way, drove out of the wash. Both trucks turned left for the short five-minute run to the border and the gate separating the two countries. Once there, Garrett got out and opened the gate, waiting for Carter's and then Doug's vehicle to pass. Once the two vehicles were through, Garrett closed and latched the gate and trotted to Carter's truck. Then they sped off to the north, still in blacked-out condition, back through the Grimm's ranch and on to I-10.

Carter looked at his watch – it was quarter after three. He was surprised that two hours had passed since they went through the gate into Mexico.

Friday Morning, 4:58 a.m.

They reached Carter's house without incident and, without saying a word, all seven went inside Carter's house. Even though Carter, Mick and Garrett didn't know exactly what happened in the two buildings, they knew it was something serious, and that something big was up.

On the way back, Doug, Rocco, Mike and Conway discussed their concern that radioactive material crossed the border and their assumption that it was now in the hands of an Islamic terrorist who was heading to who-knows where. The only question for the four of them now was what to do about this latest development.

Doug told them about a close friend of his who worked in the National Security Administration. He planned to call him in a few hours but wanted to wait for the sun to come up on the east coast before doing so.

Alex Watson and Doug went all the way back to boot camp and been through a lot together. Ten years ago, Alex sustained an injury that negated the possibility of his continuation as a Delta Force member. He had taken a desk job, but Alex was not a bureaucrat kind of guy. Doug knew he would do anything he could to help out, including bending a few rules if needed.

With all seven of them assembled in Carter's living room, Doug looked at Carter, Mick and Garrett. "I know I speak for all four of us when I say the three of you were essentially invisible during the mission and frankly performed beyond our expectations. A chorus of "Hooah," echoed from Rocco, Conway and Mike.

Doug then went on to explain the discovery made in the second building. Because of interrogation of the two cartel members, they now understood that what they'd witnessed on Wednesday night was the delivery of four canisters of cobalt-60 to someone by the name of either Ammar or Imam Mohammad Abdullah al Hamadan. He also told them why they choose to silence the two Mexicans. Carter, Mick and Garrett nodded their heads in understanding.

"There's only one reason a guy named Ammar or Imam Mohammad Abdullah al Hamadan would want radioactive material, and that would be for the making and detonation of a dirty bomb on U.S. soil. I'm going to contact a friend of mine who might be able to help us with this. If we're right, then we're going to need to move on this, and do it right away – like possibly tonight. Is there anyone who can't be available?" Doug asked.
It was dead quiet. Every man in the room understood the gravity of the situation. Each answered in the affirmative that he would be available.

Mick and Garrett stayed after Doug and the other three left. The three of them talked about the previous evening and how they felt about it. They appreciated Doug being straight forward with them and his including how everything went down once they entered the two buildings. They understood the reason for dispatching the three cartel members.

"I have to tell you guys, I don't have any issue with what Doug and the others did. I understand it and I agree with it. We're in an undeclared war with the Islamic extremists and that includes the Mexican cartels. Terrorizing the Grimm's was reason enough as far as I'm

by that kind of evil. The second issue
igger one is the possibility of a dirty
n our country. If they didn't silence the
floor, it's likely that whoever is
erial would find out we know about it.
about what we're going to do, but
hopefully, somehow, we can prevent something really bad from happening to our country. For better or for worse, it looks like it's falling on the seven of us to act. I certainly wouldn't trust the Feds, especially with the sympathy towards the Islamics that comes out of the White House," Carter said.

"I'm with you, brother. Agnes and Harold have been like a second set of parents to me. I guarantee you, if I'd been in that building, I would have gladly pulled the trigger on those two assholes. I swear to God if anymore of the cartel fuck with them, I'll personally hunt them down and kill every last one of them! This is all happening because of our government's unwillingness to protect our country. And you're right, if the feds knew about this, I wouldn't trust them to do anything about it either. I'm definitely on board about hunting down whoever's got their hands on the cobalt-60. Just tell me when and I'm there!" Garrett said.

"You took the words out of my mouth. You both can count on me; I'm all in!" Mick said.

After another ten minutes Mick and Garrett left and went to their homes to get some rest. Fortunately, all three of them set it up so they could be off work for the next few days if needed. Carter took a shower and hit the sheets. He noticed that the old fears of freezing up hadn't surfaced, but then again, he wasn't in a position where he had to pull the trigger.

Friday Morning, 7:14 a.m. – Eastern Standard Time

Alex had left his home and was en route to NSA headquarters when he got a call from his longtime friend, Doug Redman.

"Doug, you desert rat, how the hell are you?"

"If I was any better, I'd be you! How the hell have you been?"

"I'm good, same old bull shit here in D.C. Just a different day. What's cooking, brother?"

"I need a favor, and I need it fast. Last night we ran an op on something in our neck of the woods. I need to know if you can zero in on some cell-phone activity on Thursday, around two a.m. our time. If I send you the coordinates, can you do this for me? I don't want to give details over the phone, but I can tell you, this is urgent and hot, and we need to act on it ASAP! I believe thousands of American lives are at risk and maybe our whole way of life!"

Given his position and length of time employed by the NSA, it was natural for Alex to want to know more as to the nature of Doug's request. However, he knew Doug well enough to know by the urgency in his voice that he wouldn't be calling him asking for help unless something really bad was about to happen. He also knew better than to interrogate him over the phone. The capabilities of the NSA went far beyond what the news reported, including going much farther than what most of Congress was aware of. Because of Alex's position in the NSA, he'd have no problem getting the information for Doug if it was available. *I'll have to bend a few rules, but so be it,* he thought to himself.

"Roger that, send them over to me and bracket the time of day and location you need me to look at. If there was any chatter over cell phones and who it belongs to, I'll get it for you; shouldn't be difficult at all. After sending it give me a few hours before I get back to you. I've got a bureaucratic bull-shit meeting till noon our time."

"Copy that. Thanks, brother. Info will be on its way to you in ten minutes or less."

"It will cost you a steak dinner next time you're in DC, and I don't mean a cheap one either!"

"You got it. I'm anxious to hear what you find out. Talk with you then."

The two hung up. Alex thought to himself… *How I wish I could be back in the field rather than riding a desk here in Washington in this cesspool of liars and corruption.*

After pulling up Google Earth, it was easy for Doug to copy the coordinates into his text to Alex of the location of I-10 and the on ramp from the other night. He remembered Carter calling him on his cell phone and looked up the exact time, knowing this would help Alex in nailing down the location. It was just a hunch, but over the years he'd learned to trust his hunches. He was a firm believer in *if there's any doubt there is no doubt!* Doug wanted Alex to check on any cell-phone activity within a five-mile radius of Carter's call to him. Then he would ask him to bracket fifteen minutes before and thirty minutes after the time of Carter's call. He hit the send button on his phone and thought about how thankful he was to have a friend like Alex.

By the time Doug got to his house, he realized he was exhausted. Liz was up and moving around in the kitchen. He thought about her daily routine of getting the kids off to school, and then heading to the gym to work out. They greeted each other with a kiss and a hug. Liz trusted her husband completely and didn't need an explanation about where he'd been all night. Besides, she'd notice he'd taken all his gear with him the night before. Doug took a quick shower and then laid down. In case they were rolling out later on, he wanted to get some rest.

Friday, 6:00 a.m. –
Islamic Training Camp, New Mexico

Ammar awoke and was anxious to get his SUV fixed and be on his way. After he completed his prayers, there was a knock on his door. It was Qulaib asking him to join him for the early morning meal. Qulaib knew Ammar was on a mission for Allah and regarded him with reverence. He therefore understood why Ammar was nervous and anxious to continue his mission. Qulaib assured Ammar that Tameez would be calling the auto-parts store in Albuquerque as soon as they opened to locate the part needed to get him on his way.

At a quarter after seven, Tameez came to inform Qulaib and Ammar that the part they needed was nowhere to be found in Albuquerque, but he'd located one in Farmington. Since Farmington was almost a four-hour drive one way, Tameez said he'd leave right away and be back as soon as he could. Ammar thanked him, resigning himself to the fact that the earliest he could leave would be that evening. He phoned his contact Tahmeed in Michigan again, informing him of the further delay. Tahmeed was not happy about it but had no choice but to accept the circumstance. He too felt this was all part of Allah's plan. After years of planning, he was confident that everything was coming together.

Tahmeed thought to himself… *The detonation of the dirty bomb will kill hundreds, maybe thousands, of American's and create havoc in the U.S. economy and send fear through the entire population. Through the grace of Allah we will bring the infidels to their knees, kill the men, enslave the women and children. Sharia law will rule the land. Allah Akbar!*

Friday, 1:30 p.m. – Mountain Standard Time

Somewhere in the distance, Doug could hear something he couldn't quite make out; it kept getting louder and louder, like it was getting closer to him. He was warm and comfortable and had closed the blinds in his bedroom, making it almost completely dark against the sunlight. *Where was he?* he thought. *What the fuck?* Suddenly he realized it was his cell phone ringing. Coming out of a deep sleep, he grabbed it, looked at the time and saw it was Alex calling. Over six hours had passed since they last talked.

"Hey, brother, find anything out?" Doug asked.

"I did. Within the five-mile radius you requested in that time frame, there was a call from a Carter Thompson at 2:48 a.m. to your phone. Prior to that, there was a call made about a mile away from your location at 2:44. It was placed from a phone registered to a company called Eastern Educational, LLC to another phone registered with the same company name. I thought this was odd, given the time of night. Digging a bit, I discovered that Eastern Educational is registered in a New Mexico trust by the name of The Guiding Light Brotherhood Trust. It was setup to be a dead end. However, I dug deeper and found the mailing address of the trust is in Tucson. I cross referenced the address with whom or what the address belonged to. I don't think you're going to like this – the Madkhal Mosque in Tucson. Whoever answered the phone that night was in that mosque. What the fuck dude, what's going on?"

"Son of a bitch. Are you able to tell the direction of travel of the caller to the mosque that night?" Doug wanted to know.

"Thought you'd never ask. Eastbound, and I've tracked the cell phone to a location in northeastern New Mexico, north of Santa Fe. It took the individual about eleven hours from your location the other night to get there. Just north of Albuquerque the movement stopped for about an hour and a half and then started again. The subject then went in a northeasterly direction for a little more than an hour. The phone associated with that individual was there overnight and is still there as we speak. I just checked on its location before you called. Ready for this? The user and cell phone is inside of one of the Islamic training camps that our government, including our agency, isn't monitoring or doing anything about. If there's any movement of the phone outside of a radius of one mile of that compound, I'll know about it and give you a heads up. I've got a tracking alert set on it," Alex reported.

"You're the man! Thanks, brother. I'm not sure exactly what's going on, but I have my suspicions. I'm concerned something very bad is in the works. I'll keep you posted. In the meantime, if you can, let me know which direction calls are being made from that phone – time, location et cetera."

"Will do, out!"

It went without saying between the two of them that the conversation they'd just had never happened. Doug knew that because of Alex's high position at the NSA, he had the freedom to track and eavesdrop without any worry that someone would ask questions.

The passage of the Patriot Act, shortly after September 11, 2001, gave law-enforcement agencies increased, broad powers under the guise of bringing terrorists to justice. Under these obscure and gray guidelines, the doors were opened for agencies like the National Security Agency. The Patriot Act basically gave them carte blanche when it came to surveillance; under the pretext of preventing terrorism, it was no longer necessary for a law-enforcement agency to go before a judge and get permission to do whatever it wanted. All an agency needed to do was make an assertion that their claim had something to do with suspected terrorist activities, and they got a free pass. Many believed it was a clear violation of the Fourth Amendment of the Constitution. The American public, in its usual dumbed-down fashion, lacking information and aided by the media, was naively trusting the powers given by the Act wouldn't be abused. Outside a small percentage of individuals who understood the temptation for abuse, the rest of the public was oblivious.

While Doug talked with Alex, he opened the blinds, letting the Arizona sunshine light up the bedroom. It didn't take Doug long to become alert, and the light in the room accelerated the process. After hanging up with Alex, Doug went down to the kitchen on the other side of the house. With every step of his bare feet on the hard, cold, stone-tile floor, he could feel his body coming back to life. Once in the kitchen, he gave the Mr. Coffee maker a hard look. "OK, let's get some going!" he said out loud."

He grabbed the coffee pot, filled it to the halfway mark and poured fresh water in the reservoir. Grabbing the coffee canister, Doug started counting out one, two, three, and when he got to six he decided to throw in one more scoop. The next course of action he would take was getting clear to him. He just needed a little coffee right now to gather his thoughts.

2:42 p.m. Central Standard Time – Islamic Training camp, N.E. New Mexico

After finishing his afternoon prayers Ammar nervously looked at his watch. *Where's the mechanic, I need to get going.* He thought to himself. As he walked out of the house into the bright New Mexico sunlight he felt the warmth on his face. It was January in the high desert, and the contrast between the sun on his face and the cold, dry breeze wafting through the compound felt invigorating to him. Somehow it calmed him, but just for the moment. He felt a gentle but firm hand on his right shoulder.

"Be at peace, my son. Tameez called and is on his way back. He should be here in less than three-hours. It is Allah's will," Qulaib said.

Turning to look at him, Ammar was comforted by the gaze of the old man's eyes. In spite of this, he couldn't shake off a feeling of uneasiness about not moving forward and completing his task.

Training at the compound was an ongoing event throughout the year. Every other Saturday, at least thirty to forty believers would show up. All of them were die-hard adherents of Islam, and at least a half of them were turning into home-grown American terrorists. This particular group had the potential to become the most devious and dangerous to the American way of life.

Both state and federal prisons were fertile grounds to accomplish conversions. Most converts were young, African-American men who believed that the United States was a racist country. This mindset was strongly promoted by the current administration with the aid of the media. The idea of Sharia law appealed to them, along with the thought of bringing white America to its knees.

Though this point of view was held by a very small percent of African Americans, and the majority of all Americans did not necessarily subscribe to this idea, the media made sure it was presented as being a widely held belief. Coupled with this notion, there were some white people who somehow felt guilty about the way black Americans were treated. An extreme example of this occurred when a white woman, the head of an African-American group in Washington state, passed herself off as being black in order to advocate for black Americans.

The irony is that black men in prison who convert to Islam while serving their time become ideal, role-model prisoners. They follow the rules to the letter because they know becoming model prisoners will help them when they came before the parole board. Even though the parole board members understand their motives, they have to go by the guidelines that determine if parole is warranted or not.

Over the last ten years, it was proving harder and harder for parole boards not to grant parole when confronted with the display of good behavior from a black Muslim. Recently, many parole board members worried about being accused of being racist. Unfortunately, because of this concern, many inmates were being paroled when further incarceration would have been appropriate.

More so than the white or Hispanic prison populations, the black Muslims were learning how to beat the system by simply following the rules. They were all anxious to get out and do the bidding of Allah!

1:53 p.m., Mountain Standard Time – Tucson, Arizona

The coffee tasted good, and Doug felt the caffeine going to work and winding him back up. It reminded him of the multiple times over the years when his sense of wellbeing and purpose was amplified, just before going on a mission. It was an old familiar feeling, and he missed it. Grabbing the phone, he hit the speed dial.

"Carter, Doug here. We're heading out. I'd like us all to meet at four o'clock at your place. Get all your gear ready – change of clothes, plus bring an extra twelve magazines each."

"Roger that! I'll get a hold of Mick and Garrett. We'll see you at four."

Because of the events of the last two nights, and with the discovery of the radioactive canisters, Carter and Mick and Garrett were prepared to tell those who needed to know that they'd be gone for a few days to a week. Because it was January, it was easy for them to use the excuse of going to New Mexico on a depredation cow elk hunt on a private ranch as a last-minute reason to go. They'd hunted elk before at a place an hour-and-a-half east of Reserve, New Mexico, and within their small circle of friends, nobody would question them.

"Rocco, get hold of Conway and Mike. We're heading out. We'll meet at Carter's place at four o'clock. Combat load out!"

"Roger that! Out!"

Rocco, along with the other two, anticipated Doug's call and knew from past deployments what to expect. There was no need to tell them to bring all their gear, and the term *"combat load out"* was military speak for, *"be ready for a gunfight."* Rocco, like Doug, felt his senses start to come alive, he loved it! Nothing like the dump of adrenaline and doing something for their country again – and in this case on their home turf – to heighten that feeling. Rocco hadn't bothered to unload his vehicle; all he needed to do was add the extra twenty magazines to the pile, and he was good to go. He knew Conway and Mike would be doing the same.

3:50 p.m., Mountain Standard Time

While looking out the living room window down the long driveway and sipping on a cup of coffee, Carter saw Doug driving up the driveway. It didn't surprise him Doug was arriving early. As Doug came in the house, they both turned to see Garrett and Mick rolling up the drive and right behind them Rocco, Conway and Mike in another vehicle.

Once assembled, Doug began by bringing them up to speed on what he discovered from Alex (without naming him or the agency) and where he believed the individual transporting the cobalt-60 was. In the time between calling everybody and getting over to Carter's, Doug had done some homework on the Islamic training camp in New Mexico. Everyone in the group was aware of the thirty-plus Islamic training camps in the U.S. from conversations in the past. That there was one located just one state away was news to them.

One morning over the campfire at their training facility, they'd talked about Islamic training camps. They were all surprised that no law enforcement agency anywhere in the country had raided any of them and taken the terrorists into custody. It was yet another example of their government failing to protect the citizens of the United States. It was obvious what the Muslim jihadists are doing in the camps. Guaranteed that if it was an American "militia" group meeting and training, the Justice Department, ATF and FBI would be all over it, arresting American citizens and making news headlines. It would be one big photo op.

Doug had everyone go out to his vehicle and bring in his gear so they could do a double-check with each other one more time. As Carter looked at the gear laid out on his living room floor, he felt a great sense of pride and purpose come over him.

Just like the last two nights, they'd be going in two vehicles, with Doug taking the lead. The estimated time to the compound was approximately ten hours. It was decided not to use any credit cards, short of an emergency. They would use cash for everything, and all seven of them brought more than enough. After they were done checking and double-checking each other's gear, Doug pulled them all together in a circle.

"To be honest with all of you, I haven't a clue where this journey is going to take us or what the end result will be. My gut tells me something bad is going to happen if we don't catch up to this guy with the cobalt-60. I will tell all of you, though; I trust you, and through the grace of God, we'll do the right thing when it comes to it."

He then led them in a prayer for a safe return and accomplishment of their mission. By four-fifteen they were heading out of Carter's driveway, going east.

5:25 p.m., Central Standard Time

Tameez opened the box containing the fuel pump for Ammar's SUV, assuring him and Qulaib that it would take only an hour and a half and then Ammar would be on his way. Qulaib suggested to Ammar, since it was going to be late, that perhaps he should spend the night again and get off to a fresh start in the morning. Ammar thanked him for the offer but explained to him he would be on his way as soon as possible. He was anxious to get to the safe house in Michigan and deliver his lethal cargo. He called Tahmeed and let him know he would be on his way soon. Though it took a little longer to install the fuel pump and relay, Tameez was able to have Ammar on his way by 7:25 p.m.

7:35 p.m., Central Standard Time

They were about a half-hour west of Lordsburg, New Mexico, when Doug's phone rang.

"Hey, brother, what's up?"

"Your target started moving east about ten minutes ago on State Hwy 85. Since we last talked, he's made two phone calls to a cell in Dearborn, Michigan. I was able to do a little eavesdropping on the call. He mentioned something about the package was in good shape and heading their way. I'm expanding my surveillance to include that new number. I'll watch and see what it connects to," Alex said.

"Thanks for the heads-up and your help. This is really a hot item, if you get my drift."

"I do, and I'll keep you posted to let you know if he changes direction. I assume from your position you're on his tail. Well, at least by eight hours behind you're on his tail. Assuming your target is inbound to Dearborn, are you going to stay with it all the way?"

"We're going to do whatever it takes to catch up to him and see what he and his friends are up to. If at all possible, we will stop him and his fellow goat-humpers before something bad happens."

"Roger that. Talk soon." "Out."

After his phone call with Alex, Doug was quiet. Rocco, Conway and Mike knew when Doug got quiet they should let him be with his thoughts. Doug called back to Carter and let him know they they'd stop at Lordsburg, fuel up and talk. Carter figured Doug must have gotten some updated information on the whereabouts of the individual they were trying to catch up to.

Both vehicles rolled into the truck stop in Lordsburg with Carter's SUV pulling up behind Doug's in the well-lit fueling area. All seven men got out of the two vehicles at the same time, and everyone except Doug and Carter went into the store and the warm bathrooms inside. Doug and Carter both started fueling up.

"What's the latest?" Carter asked, while zipping up his jacket.

"Our target left the compound about half an hour ago and is heading east. My guess is he's heading to Dearborn, Michigan, and it shouldn't be a problem to track him all the way there. He did make a phone call to a contact there about ten minutes after he left. What I don't know is if he has all of the canisters with him or just some of them. If we avoid turning off and heading north through Albuquerque to the compound, we could keep heading east on I-10 and then head north in about six hours. If we did this, we might be able to intercept him by this time tomorrow. But if we head north as originally planned and assuming we have minimal problems at the compound searching for the canisters, it would probably put us behind him around ten hours or so. Our advantage is there are seven of us, and we don't have to stop except for gas and stuff. If he's by himself, he stops to rest or maybe he drives through with no rest. Assuming he drives all the way through, we'll just have to do the best we can when we get to Dearborn. My gut feeling is, we need to search the compound and interrogate anyone there first. There's too much at stake with this cobalt-60 on the loose. What are your thoughts?"

"There's just too much at stake. Assuming there are a total of four radioactive canisters, we don't know if all of them were left at the compound, two were left or all four are traveling with the Islamic heading east. If we somehow were to leave it up to the Feds to search the camp, it would never happen without a search warrant. It really does come down to us. I don't see any other way than to be thorough in eliminating the possibly that some of the canisters are at the camp. You're right; we've got to cover all bases. Let's do it," Carter said, watching as some of the guys came back to the gas island.

As they were pulling out, Carter brought Mick and Garrett up to date on the conversation he'd had with Doug. They too agreed on making sure none of the canisters were left behind. There was a McDonald's just a mile down the road and both vehicles used the drive-through. They were hungry, and all of them were used to eating on the run. Mickey Dee's would do for now.

After turning left onto I-25 heading north to Albuquerque, Carter took a deep breath of air in and slowly let it out.

"What we're doing is the right thing, and I'm glad you two are with me. And I feel good about the guys in front of us! Love you guys!" Carter said to Mick and Garrett as the headlights revealed snow starting to fall.

10:45 p.m., Central Standard Time

Up ahead, Ammar could see the lights of a truck stop and turned on his right-hand indicator just before he pulled into it. His progress was slowed by the weather. He hated cold weather, especially the snow, and thought about the beautiful, warm nights he'd spent in Yemen. Growing up there, snow was something you saw only on TV. The truck stop was busy, and he was always nervous pulling into one like this late at night. He first fueled his car up and then pulled into a parking space in front of the store and went inside. He used the bathroom, got some coffee and then walked back to his vehicle. As he opened the door, he quickly glanced back at the covered pile of his deadly cargo. Smiling, he got in and continued on his way. He was tired, but he didn't want to stop. He wasn't foolish enough to risk falling asleep at the wheel, and the coffee would help. He continued down the road, with the wipers doing their methodical thing of back and forth, back and forth, back and forth, cutting through the snow at fifty miles per hour. He cursed under his breath but resigned himself to it. He was determined that no matter what, he'd get to Dearborn and deliver his cargo. Allah Akbar!

Friday, 11:50 p.m., Central Standard Time

"Hey, my eyes are starting to float. What do you say we get some gas and hit the bathrooms when we hit Albuquerque?" Rocco said to the others.

"I second that. Between the Mickey Dee's coffee and Big-Mac I'm about to burst. Anybody want to pull my finger? Ahh, relief is just a flush away!" Mike said, ripping off a large fart. The rest started laughing and hurling obscenities at him. They were all used to his locker-room humor, and deep down they appreciated his ability to always lighten up the mood.

"Fuck you and pulling your crap-ass finger. Yes, by all means, let's get some gas and get this stinky motherfucker out of the truck. Nobody light a match!" Conway said from the back seat, pointing at Mike. All of them were now laughing even harder while rolling down the windows at the same time.

Doug picked up the radio and let Carter and the other two know the plan, which sounded more than good to them.

After fueling up and doing the usual other things, they pulled away from the gas island where they could talk. Alex called Doug about a half-hour before, giving him an update on Ammar's direction and location. Doug repeated this to the group and then opened the door to his SUV. Rocco had a laptop out with a Google Maps picture of the compound, where it sat off a rural road out in the high desert northeast of Santa Fe. From what they could tell, there were scrub oak trees with open areas. *Thank God for a moonless night and crappy weather,* Doug thought to himself. There was a driveway, close to a half-mile long, with a few slight turns. But other than that, the image revealed that it was a fairly straight shot to the main building of the compound. Another hour-and-a-half or so, and they'd be there. Doug decided that when they got to Santa Fe, he'd pull everyone together again to go over the approach and positioning of everyone.

Doug told Carter the plan to stop in Santa Fe and top off their fuel tanks, providing an opportunity to go over the plan for the night. They hit the road, and it wasn't long before they could see the lights of Santa Fe up ahead. Turning into the gas station, they could all see the snow starting to drift against the curbs.

They topped off their tanks and pulled to the side of the convenience store. Doug went over the plan for their approach to the compound. Essentially, it would be identical to the plan from the previous night, with the exception of a lack of pre-surveillance. They'd have to figure it out on the fly in this case. For the four Special Forces guys, this was not a big deal. More than half the time in combat they were confronted with the same problem. "*Improvise, Adapt and Overcome!*" Even though it's the motto of the United States Marine Corps, it was utilized by all branches of the Special Forces, and these four seasoned warriors lived by this principle.

From what they could see on Google Maps, as well as the downloaded topographical map Garrett put into his Garmin GPS handheld, there was a slight elevation right up against the compound. The front of the main building faced the approach. How many occupants, if any, were at the compound was unknown. Doug's main concern, given it was a Friday night and the weekend was upon them, was that there could be a sizeable force of jihadists at the compound. Even though their main target was moving away from them and eight hours ahead, Doug couldn't risk just rushing in and the possibility of one of his men getting hurt or killed. They would take their time and do a proper recon of the area first. Then, if possible, they would initiate entry and overpower and interrogate whoever they came upon. If there proved to be too many men and guns at the compound, they'd bypass it altogether and go after their target heading east. Given what was at stake, they all hoped they'd be able to do a thorough inspection of the whole compound, insuring whether or not there were any cobalt-60 canisters to be found. After that, they'd continue their cross-country pursuit.

I've been waiting for your call...

Jamal had been back in Chicago for a few days after he picked up the RDX2 from his nephew down in Chattanooga. Now, when his phone rang, it was the call he'd been waiting for. It was Emran, another Black-Muslim convert and cellmate of Jamal at Joliet Prison. Emran was the first of Jamal's friends to convert to the teachings of Muhammad, and after much encouragement, Jamal joined him. Because they became model prisoners, both were paroled a few years ahead of their scheduled release date.

"Hello, my brother, I've been waiting for your call. I have everything," Jamal exclaimed.

"Can you get up here by tomorrow afternoon with your items?"

Jamal assured him he would be there and assumed it would be at the same place they'd always met in Dearborn. Emran confirmed the time and location, then declared "Allah Akbar!" and hung up. Jamal felt a sense of destiny and pride; it was time to bring America to its knees and start initiating Sharia law.

1:00 a.m., Eastern Standard Time – Dearborn, Michigan

Jamal started to knock on the door of the row house again when the door opened. A short, stocky man in his fifties waved him in. The room was dimly lit with a TV on in the corner. Jamal could see two long tables to the right in a well-lit area next to the kitchen.

"Come in, brother," Saad said.

Saad al Humaydah came into the country the same way most other Islamic terrorists have done since 9/11, through the open and porous southern border of the United States. He'd come across near the New Mexico/Arizona border two years ago. Saad was a bomb-maker who learned his trade in Yeman as a young man. Their plan was in the making for a long time, and he would be the one entrusted with the task of building the suitcase bomb. A suitcase bomb normally evokes the image of a large Samsonite. While a Samsonite type could be used, it tended to be a little too delicate for the job. In this case, a large Pelican case was the preferred choice to hold the explosive material along with the cobalt-60. It could all be packaged in a Pelican case, which comes with foam material that can easily be cut to customize for the contents. The Pelican cases were known for their robust design and solid latches, plus they had a handle and a set of heavy duty wheels attached.

Jamal hoisted the gym bag he was carrying onto one of the tables and unzipped it. He slowly pulled out the four pieces of RDX2 – all forty pounds of it! They both knew this amount was enough to level the building they were standing in along with the ones surrounding it.

Saad picked up a piece and admired it. He'd knew about it and its efficient explosive qualities. For a bombmaker like him, it was the Holy Grail of explosives!

Saturday 12:42 a.m.,
Central Standard Time

About a mile before the compound, there was a rural road that intersected the highway Carter and the others were on. It angled away to the southeast of the compound. However, it would serve as a good spot for them to leave their vehicles and approach from that direction.

With everybody out of the two vehicles and with full gear on, Rocco did a quick radio check to confirm they were all good. Just in case the Islamists in the compound were monitoring radio frequencies, Rocco devised a short and simple code to mimic the chatter of truck drivers.

"Hey good buddy" was code for "roger that," "smoky in the area" meant a tango was spotted in the compound and so on. Doug issued standing orders to maintain radio silence unless it was absolutely necessary to communicate.

With the snow softly coming down and no wind, it was dead quiet as they spread out in a "V" formation, with Conway at the point. They stopped every fifty yards or so and listened for any unusual sounds as they proceeded. Also, they looked for trip wires or listening devices that might be planted to discover their approach to the compound. Fortunately, the four Special Forces men were skilled in this area, having had to deal with it in Afghanistan. They were all operating under the assumption that multiple devices were set up on the perimeter of the compound.

The falling snow made their walking almost soundless. From a quarter-mile out, Conway held up his hand for everybody to stop. Simultaneously, all went to one knee. Carter felt the softness of the wet ground underneath his knee pad and was grateful for the protection and comfort the knee pad provided. He'd never felt so alive and alert and was very glad to be on this mission, doing something to help his country.

Doug moved up to the right of Conway with Rocco on his left. The compound lights were shining ahead through the blackness of the falling snow and cover of night. Doug lifted his binoculars and could make out the main building and the drive leading up to it. They all waited for a few minutes, looking for any kind of movement. Seeing none, they stood up and kept moving forward, stopping short of the main entrance a hundred yards away.

When Doug last checked in with Alex a couple of hours earlier, Alex reported picking up only four cell-phone signals, indicating the possibility of at least four individuals occupying the compound. Even terrorists all seem rely on cell phones. It's one of the devices that enables them to be as effective as they are at disruption and inflicting harm on both civilian and military personnel. Modern-day technology has become an important tool for the jihadists to carry out their murderous missions.

Slowly, silently and carefully moving forward, the seven arrived within twenty-five yards of the entrance – still no sign of life.

Complacency can affect anybody, and the inhabitants of the compound were no exception. With so many Islamic training camps around the country, it is astonishing that none of them has ever been investigated by local or federal authorities or molested by local citizens in any way whatsoever. Those practicing Islam around the world regarded Americans as cowards who were afraid of them. They knew that the local citizens, including law enforcement, were fearful of being accused of either profiling or being racists. That kept them from doing something about the clear and present danger these camps and their inhabitants represented. With the administration and the Justice Department running cover for them, they were able to carry out their planning without any fears of being wiretapped or having listening devices planted inside the buildings. Under the current regime, they'd become untouchable. So complacency was a predictable outcome. The jihadists never considered the possibility that some of the citizens of the country were sick of their bullshit and were willing to do something about the problem, since law enforcement wouldn't.

Although there were only four of them at the compound, the elder Qulaib still maintained the protocol of having at least one sentry on duty overnight. Tameez, the mechanic who'd repaired Ammar's vehicle, had the duty that night. To him, walking around the grounds in the falling snow was a cold and useless task. He justified his thinking because there were cameras and motion detectors surrounding the main building, giving him the ability to monitor all approaches to the buildings.

Because of the falling snow that night, the motion detectors gave false alerts at least a half-dozen times. It was known this could happen, so because of this and the weather conditions, Tameez turned off the volume on the detection system.

By the time the Americans worked their way to within twenty-five yards of the main house, it was apparent to all of them that they'd gone undetected. They had even tripped a motion detector, but it didn't seem to make a difference.

While maintaining radio silence, Doug motioned everyone to his position. He deployed Garrett to cover the left, fifteen yards from the main house on a forty-five-degree angle. There was a dirt drive on the west side of the house, running from the front and down the side of the house all the way to a barn which was forty yards north of the house. Once in position, Garrett would be able to see all the way down the west side of the house, including down the west side of the barn. With the forty-yard separation, Garrett was also able to see a slice of the open area between the house and barn.

On the east side of the house, there was a three-and-a-half-foot-wide walkway between the house and a large garage. Doug next sent Rocco and Carter to move down the east side of the garage until they reached the back. From their position, they would be able to see the large open area behind the house and garage. Once the two of them were in position, they were to break radio silence and give everybody a position report since they would now have the advantage of eyes on the back of the two buildings as well as being able to see the front, east side of the barn.

On the right side of the house was a doorway leading to the walkway that ran between it and the garage. He motioned to Conway and Mick to go down the east side of the house to the doorway. So far, all was still quiet. Once in position at the door, Conway keyed his microphone to let everyone know they were in position and ready to breach the doorway. Doug told him to hold his position until he gave the signal to blow the door. Many times during a dynamic entry by both law enforcement and military, nobody bothers to turn the door handle to see if just by chance it's unlocked. Conway was not one to miss an easy entry, but he didn't want to touch the door knob first just in case it was wired to an alarm system. Before trying the door knob, he would first line the door with thirty-grain det cord. If the door was locked, then he would blow the door.

Carter and Rocco smoothly and quietly worked their way down the east side of the garage to the northeast corner. Both of them stopped a couple of feet short of the corner of the building. Watching Rocco in front of him, Carter knew he'd first take a quick peek around the corner to the left and the open area adjacent to the barn. Carter watched him as he did just that. Meanwhile, Carter kept his eyes forward to the right and behind them.

Rocco could see all the way to the barn as well as being able to look straight down the north side of the house. There was an open-air patio running the whole length of the house with the roof extending out fourteen feet. A porch light was on over a door of the house on the back patio.

The barn, unbeknownst to the Americans, was converted by the ragheads into a barracks and communications center. Straight ahead and a bit to the left of Rocco and Carter's position, there was another rectangular building roughly eighty feet in length. This was a new building being utilized as a kitchen and mess hall for the compound. It was capable of feeding fifty at one time.

From their position, Rocco didn't see any lights on in the mess hall. Looking back in the direction of the barn, he noticed a door on the south end of the building. As he was watching, suddenly a light came on inside at that end of the barn. He keyed his microphone and alerted everyone that there was movement in the south end of the barn.

Trolling

On the other side of that door was a communications and camera-monitoring room. Inside of this twenty-two-by-sixteen-foot room was a fourteen-foot-long table running along the south wall. This was where multiple monitors were set up to display the views of the ten different cameras positioned around the compound. Along with the video monitors, there was a police scanner, CB and a ham radio station. Also on the bench were chargers for ten two-way radios, of which eight were in the chargers. Tameez had one which he'd put next to one of the video monitors as he sat down. Qulaib had the other one on the night stand next to his bed in the main house where he was sleeping. Undoing his belt and the zipper on his pants, Tameez brought up Internet Explorer and started trolling for kiddy porn.

The inside door of this room opened into a large assembly and meeting area. The north end of the barn was converted into barracks where the other two extremists were sleeping. This area could sleep up to thirty-six. It was set up military-barracks style, with rows of bunk beds, eighteen in all.

Normally, a middle-of-the-night raid on a compound this size would be carried out by at least eighteen to twenty-four operators hitting all the buildings simultaneously. After their view of the recent Google Maps photos, Doug decided to take their best shot with their limited resources. First they would assault the house, keeping all seven of them together as a squad, and then move on to the other buildings one at a time. The good news was that the photos from Google Earth were recent and that his friend Alex detected only four cell phones in the compound.

Even though Carter, Mick and Garrett were proving themselves, Doug and the other three operators recognized they had to carry the load. Doug knew that operationally, the negatives outweighed the positives by at least three to one. In spite of this and because of the danger to the country, he saw no other option but to go for it. He'd rather put his trust in the seven of them than turn this over to law enforcement who most likely would do nothing. Besides, there was that little nasty incident the previous evening just south of the border, and he didn't want law enforcement tying the common threads together.

As Doug thought through everything, he came to the conclusion that putting the negatives aside, the seven of them did have a few critical things going in their favor. One was the cover of darkness coupled with some really crappy weather; and, most important, the element of surprise.

The plan was straightforward and simple. After Rocco and Carter cleared the garage, they would move down its east side, giving them a view of the open area to the rear as well as the barn and the mess-hall building. From this position, they'd be able to cover the complete backside of the house as well as the open yard area.

Once Doug, Mike, Conway and Mick blew the doors, Garrett would go to the west side of the house. This would put him directly across from the barn and afford him the opportunity to view the open yard from the opposite angle of Rocco and Carter, while also covering the south and west side of the barn. If he had a clear field of view, he would go to the west side of the barn. Garrett would then provide cover for Doug and the other three after they'd cleared the house and exited to the back.

Simultaneously, Rocco and Carter would move to the mess hall. Once assured that the mess hall was empty, the two would go to its north side, to the end adjacent to the north end of the barn.

Doug hadn't sugar coated anything in his conversation with his men. He told them to expect a gunfight. He and the other three operators knew the Islamic extremists well from their time in Iraq and Afghanistan. The men here were most likely hard-wired jihadists who would relish the idea of killing some Americans on U.S. soil. The primary mission and focus, though, was to determine if any of the cobalt-60 canisters were in the compound. After that was accomplished, they were then to move out ASAP and get back on the trail of their primary target who was heading northeast. They all understood the clock was ticking.

1:38 a.m., Mountain Standard Time – Colorado Springs

Ammar had been driving for three-and-a-half hours, and the snow was starting to let up. He was on the outskirts of Colorado Springs which would be a perfect place for a quick stop to fuel up and get some coffee and a bite to eat. The closer to his objective the better, as far as he was concerned. He could hardly wait to see the expressions on his brothers' faces when he pulled in and handed them his deadly cargo. He knew the planning for this attack had been in the works for a long time, and he hoped all of the other elements would come together quickly. Ammar wasn't aware that Jamal had already delivered the RDX2 to Saad the bombmaker. Now all that was missing for him to put the bomb together was the cobalt-60. Saad, Jamal and Tahmeed anxiously awaited the arrival of Ammar and his cargo.

1:39 a.m., Mountain Standard Time

Mike set the det cord around the hinges of the door and stepped back, giving Doug a thumbs-up. Doug clicked his mike three times, signaling the impending explosion as he and Mike moved behind the stone corner of the house to avoid the blast. They knew Conway and Mick on the east door would do the same as soon as they heard the boom. Mike hit the ignition button and instantly, with a large boom, debris, smoke and dust blew outward. Doug and Mike immediately came around the corner through the debris cloud with Mike kicking open the surgically cut door. The door fell inward off its hinges hit the concrete tile floor with a loud slapping sound. This was quickly followed by a second explosion from Conway and Mick's door being blown open.

Mike went in first, slanting to the right, with Doug button hooking to the left and into what looked like a great room with a fireplace in the middle. Through his night-vision goggles, Doug could see embers glowing brightly. To his right, he could hear soft footsteps and the crunching of wood and glass chards as Conway and Mick moved into the house from their end. They entered the kitchen, cleared it and proceeded to the entrance hall that Doug and Mike came through. Mike was coming out of a doorway to their right; it was a small bedroom which he'd cleared on his own.

Qulaib awoke at the first blast and was further startled by the second one. In his sleepy, confused state, he fumbled around for the AK47 leaning up against the night stand on the right side of the bed. Qulaib's room was large, serving as his bedroom as well as office. He always kept the AK47 ready to go with one in the chamber and the safety off. Leaning over from the bed he grabbed it, raising it just as Conway kicked the bedroom door open and slanted left with Mick button hooking to the right, followed by Doug again slanting to the left. With the quick movements of the three going in opposite directions, Qulaib struggled to take aim in the darkened room. He didn't feel anything after squeezing a burst off his AK47, as nine rounds hit him simultaneously – two on the left side of his head and one in his forehead.

With the muffled sounds of the first and second explosions, Rocco again peeked around the corner, looking through his night-vision goggles at the open space between him and the barn and to his right toward the mess hall. Reaching back with his left arm he tapped Carter's left thigh to indicate he was moving. The two of them had already discussed what direction they'd take, and Carter knew from all his training to lean into Rocco and move with him like a shadow. Rocco spoke into his mike, "Moving to north building."

Then they were off, smoothly moving forward, Carter with rifle up and scanning to the right one hundred and eighty degrees, while Rocco with rifle up scanned left as they moved to the southeast corner of the mess hall. Just as they covered the distance, Rocco noticed the light went off on the south side of the barn. They made the corner, with Carter taking a quick run down the side of the building to clear the backside.

Pervert Interruption

Inside the communications room in the barn, Tameez was stroking himself while watching a video of a ten-year-old Christian girl being raped by four of his ISIS brothers in Syria. With the little girl screaming as one of the men penetrated her, he pounded away on himself. Caught up in this perverted moment, he didn't hear the explosions but rather felt the concussions hit the side of the barn. Alarmed, he stopped jerking off and reached up, muting the computer. With his pants down around his knees, he listened while pulling them up. Tameez thought to himself... *Something wasn't right; what was that?* He turned to his left, grabbing the AK47 at the end of the counter, got low and walked over to the light switch, turning it off.

Then he came back to the long counter, grabbing a hand-held, two-way radio. He keyed his mike, "Qulaib, Qulaib!" He waited and repeated it again. Nothing; the elder's voice didn't come back to him on the radio. This was unlike him because Tameez knew the old man was a very light sleeper. Alarmed, he went through the door leading out to the large open area inside the barn, walking in the dark to the other side where the barracks were occupied by the other two men.

The men were asleep, three bunks away from each other. He shook the first one and then moved on to the second. At first, they were both annoyed with Tameez waking them. Tameez told them in a loud whisper what he heard and that he couldn't reach Qulaib. They both jumped up, grabbing their rifles which were leaning against their bunks. Tameez motioned them to be quiet and listen. It was dead quiet. The three of them flicked off the safeties to their rifles.

Tameez thought to himself... *What could be happening? Did that young little Ammar betray them? What's going on?* He then remembered he'd left his cell phone in the communications room. He wanted to alert the others who were not in the compound as to what was happening. Tameez turned to the other two and told them to move to the back side of the barn in the middle. He was going back to get his phone. The taller of the two men grabbed his arm while pulling out his cell phone. "No need, brother." All three then moved to the back of the large open area. This would allow them to oversee the entire middle inside of the barn while affording them cover.

1:42 a.m.

Upon hearing the sound of the door breaches, Garrett moved down the west side of the house as planned. He was now on the northwest corner of the house and had a clear view down the back side of the barn, the south side of it and all the way across the open area to the mess hall. He also could easily look down the back side of the covered porch attached to the house. Through his radio, he'd heard Rocco call out that the two of them were moving to the north. Just as Garrett got into position on the corner of the house, he looked through his night-vision goggles off to the right and down the far corner of the mess hall where he saw Rocco and Carter arrive at their new position. Raising his rifle, pointing in the direction of Carter and Rocco, he tapped his Pak4 laser, toggling the infrared beam in their direction. He knew that with their goggles on, they'd be able to see him. He wanted to make sure they knew his position. Within a couple of seconds there were three quick flashes from Rocco's Pak4, coming back in his direction.

Garrett took a deep breath and sighed; though Doug and the rest were using suppressed weapons, he was still able to hear the muffled sound of the nine rounds striking Qulaib. They were on the opposite side of the wall from where he was standing.

Three-minutes after breaching the doors and now back assembled in the hallway and looking at the doorway opening out to the back porch, Doug keyed his mike, "Coming out!" With Rocco and Garrett giving them an all-clear report from their respective positions,

Doug and the other three knew they were covered while coming out of the house onto the back porch.

Garrett, Carter and Rocco, from their two positions, watched as Doug, Mike, Conway and Mick emerged onto the porch. All four went into a combat-kneeling position with Mick on the right corner and Conway on the left. Rocco gave them three quick clicks of the Pak4 and Garrett did the same, letting them know their relative positions. Doug and the others then moved over to the southeast corner of the barn, adjacent to where Garrett was. With them in position and as planned, Garrett turned and moved back to front of the house to keep watch for anyone approaching up the drive.

"In position," Garrett said through his radio.

Rocco and Carter were in a good spot to observe the east entrance points to the barn. Over the radio, Rocco called out a door just fifteen feet to their left in the front. Fifteen feet to the right of that door was a large set of double barn doors. There was another door on the front, south end of the barn.

On the radio everyone heard Rocco say, "Moving," as he and Carter went down the back side of the mess hall. There was no need for them to come down the front because Doug and his group had that area covered. Once at the northwest corner of the mess hall, Rocco peeked around again, tapping his Pak4 laser three times to let everyone know they were in position. From the end of the mess hall to the north end of the barn was only around twenty yards. Rocco again called out,
"Moving," as he and Carter hustled across the opening between the two buildings to the northeast corner of the

barn. The door on that end of the barn was now only about six feet away.

Doug made a decision that could turn out to be a disaster if it didn't go well. He turned and whispered to Mick, telling him to stay in position on the corner of the barn. From there Mick could easily look to his right and see the back side of the house, or he could look straight ahead at the open space and to the left to the mess hall and all the way down the front side of the barn. Normally, Doug would want four men on each corner outside a building like this; however, it was time to improvise and work with what they had. They now covered the outside leaving Doug, Mike, and Conway on the south end of the building and the door close to them with Rocco and Carter on north end of the barn ready to breach the other door. He wasn't going to worry about the two large barn doors. Because of their size, it would be too difficult for anyone to open them hastily.

On the inside of the cavernous barn, Tameez and the other two were in back at the center of the main room, huddled behind crates piled up to a height of roughly six feet. The taller of the other two men was eyeing the loft which ran in a "U" shape around the main room of the barn. The ladder going up to it was only ten feet away.

"I'm going up there," he said to Tameez and the other man.

With as much training as these ragheads had been through, they never planned for an assault on their own compound. Everything they were doing was a spur-of-the-moment decision that would give an edge to Doug's well-thought-out plan. The only smart thing these three were doing now was getting one of their guys up onto the loft.

This position would be a strategic advantage. High ground is always preferred in a gunfight. But in the complete darkness of the interior of the barn, without any night-vision goggles, their one advantage was neutralized against the men about to storm building. The terrorists had no idea who or how many they were up against.

Tameez motioned to the man standing next to him to give him the cell phone. Tameez knew if he could reach the Imam at the Madkhal Mosque in Tucson, the Imam would mobilize fellow brothers in the area to come to their aid. They just needed to hold out for a while. He punched in the number and hit send, put it up to his ear, but nothing happened; just a low, humming noise came through the phone. Tameez hit "end" and then "re-dial' and again got the same result.

When there's a threat to the body, the first thing that happens is an adrenaline dump into the system, then auditory exclusion, tunnel vision and loss of finite motor skills. As Tameez started to call a third time, he had difficulty holding the phone and dropped it. When he bent over to pick it up, the door to the communications room swung open, and something landed on the floor in the room. Through the doorway he saw a bright flash and heard the loud thump of an explosion. He next saw three shadowy figures silently and quickly come into the communications room. He and the other man raised their AK47s and fired off multiple bursts in the direction of the room, just as Rocco and Carter burst through the north door.

Doug checked the door knob and to his pleasant surprise, it was unlocked. On the opposite side of the barn, where Rocco and Carter were, Rocco also felt an unlocked door. Doug pulled out a flashbang, opened the door, chucked it in and closed the door all in one motion. He and the other two waited momentarily for the flashbang to do its thing.

"Going in," Doug said, keying his mike. Conway entered first, going straight ahead through the open door and then slanting to his left. Mike followed, button hooking to the right, with Doug immediately following him, again going straight ahead and left behind Conway. Just then, fifteen to twenty rounds tore through the walls, hitting one of the computer monitors on the counter. The wall between the room they were in and the large room of the barn was made of particle board and fragments of it were flying throughout the room. Through their night-vision goggles, it looked like it was snowing inside the room. All three men immediately got down low behind a couple of metal desks that were positioned against the particle board wall. More and more rounds kept coming into the room.

For the time being, they were pinned down. While staying low, Doug crawled his way over to the partially opened door leading to the inside of the barn and looked around it into the cavernous main room. Just then he saw flashes of light straight ahead and to his right; it was Rocco and Carter dispatching the two men who had been shooting at them. They'd seen and heard Doug and the others breeching the door on the opposite end of the barn.

A moment earlier, leaning into Rocco and about to breach the doorway Carter thought of the old woman yelling at him in the doorway at the mall. "*Do something!*" he heard her say, as he felt the ice-cold tingles of fear going down his spine.

Just then Rocco reached back and gave him a squeeze on his left side, bringing him back to the present. Carter returned the squeeze. Rocco twisted the door knob, opening the door just slightly, paused, and then swiftly he and Carter went in. Rocco slanted to his right and Carter button hooked left, both with rifles up to their shoulders. They would stay back against the wall so that if they engaged anyone it would be on a forty-five-degree angle and not directly across from where they believed Doug and the others were. They trusted they'd be doing the same – no need to be hit by friendly fire!

Rocco and Carter made their entrance into the barn just moments after Doug and the others did the same at the opposite end. Carter, scanning with his rifle up on his shoulder and looking through his red dot with his goggles, saw within seconds the two men at the back center of the barn, firing their weapons in the direction of Doug and the others. At twenty feet, it would have been hard for Carter to miss as he brought his rifle to bear on the shooter on the left, putting two quick rounds in his left side and then one dead center to the head. Carter missed with a fourth round that hit the wall behind the man as he slumped to the floor. Rocco moved to the right side of Carter, picking up the silhouette of the second man on the right and putting three quick rounds into his left upper torso and two to the head.

"Two tangos down!" Rocco yelled out.

With their night-vision goggles on, the flash of the weapons temporarily blinded both Carter and Rocco. On the other end of the barn Doug and the others slowly peeked their heads up from behind the metal desks. Conway was bleeding from his left arm as a result of shrapnel from the desk cutting into him. It was a miracle that none of the three of them had been hit by rounds from the two AK47s. There was no need to return fire because of the quick and decisive action of Carter and Rocco. A ghostly cloud of smoke with its acrid smell of cordite hung in the air. Rocco and Carter remaining in their positions could hear the last gurgling gasps of both terrorists as they lay on the ground.

Doug worked his mike, calling for a "SITREP" from everyone. Quietly, Rocco gave Doug a report on their position. All agreed for the time being to stay put. From Rocco and Carter's vantage point, they could see a loft running in a "U" shape around the interior of the barn. They stayed low, not knowing if anyone was up in the loft waiting to ambush them.

After a minute or so, Carter's and Rocco's eyesight started to return to normal, and both of them put their night-vision gear back on, scanning the glowing green interior of the barn. The smoke from the weapons continued to hang in the air like a thick fog. They looked in all areas and from their position they could see up to the front edge of the loft across from them and three quarters of the way down the middle of the front of the loft. What they couldn't see was the area directly above them.

Across the way, Conway and Mike ducked walked their way to the door which was cracked open by Doug. Looking straight ahead, he could see Carter and Rocco and the area just to his right along with the front side of the loft and down the middle of it. He saw no one else. After years in combat zones, most soldiers develop a sixth sense when something doesn't feel right. Doug thought for a moment, reflecting on Alex's report of four cell-phone signals. One terrorist was down in the house and two were lying on the barn floor; gut feeling told him there was at least one more to go.

Lofty Tumble

Behind Rocco and Carter were the barracks. Rocco quietly radioed that they were going to clear the area. Both were impressed by the size of it with the thirty-six bunks. After clearing it, which took no more than a couple of minutes, they returned to their original position. Comfortable with the knowledge that no one would come up from behind them, Rocco keyed his mike, giving Doug and the others an updated report.

As he thought through the situation and after hearing the far end of the barn was a barracks, Doug started to put together a possible scenario. Maybe there had been two men sleeping with one at this end of the barn in what appeared to be a communications room. It would be reasonable to assume he heard the explosions inside the house and gone to the other end to alert men in the barracks area. If there was a fourth man or more, the only place left to look for him was up in the loft.

There were two ladders going up to the loft; one on Rocco and Carter's side and the other on the side where Doug and the others now were.

"Rocco, do you have any flashbangs on you?" Doug asked, keying his mike.

"Roger that!" Rocco came back quickly.

Doug had one left and figured between Conway and Mike they had a least one more. Doug turned around just as Mike finished dressing the wound on Conway's left arm.

"Are you good to go?" Doug asked, looking at Conway. Conway gave a thumbs-up. This was one of the common characteristics of Delta group members along with all other Special Forces units; they stay in the fight no matter what until it was over.

The plan was a simple one; have Rocco jump out, turn around and throw a flashbang to the area of the loft above them. At the same time, Mike would do the same on the other side. Rocco and Mike would then each climb the nearest ladder to the loft, with Doug and Conway covering above for Rocco and Carter doing the same covering for Mike.

In the loft above, the remaining terrorist could hear movement below him and knew his two brothers had been killed by the infidels. He didn't care what happened to himself, as long as he could kill as many of them as he could. He figured it was some of the locals who'd harassed him and his other Muslim brothers in the past in town. They were lucky they got Qulaib and Tameez and his other brother, he thought to himself. He was crouched down and being as still as possible and prepared to die in the name of Allah. Just then he heard something hit the floor of the loft a few feet from him, and then and a sizzling sound followed by a thunderous explosion, flash and shock wave, knocking him over. All he could feel was a ringing in his head and intense pain shooting through his entire body; he felt like he was floating in a sea of pain.

Following the lobbing of the flashbangs and their detonation, Rocco and Mike scurried up the ladders across from each other. With their night-vision goggles on, they turned away after throwing the flashbangs so as not to be blinded by the flash. They slung their rifles as they climbed up their respective ladders. Carter on Rocco's side and Doug on the other side stepped out, barrels pointing up above each position while Conway moved, with rifle shouldered, to the two lifeless bodies lying on the floor. He poked each one in the eye with the end of the barrel to make sure they were dead.

As Rocco got to the top of the ladder with his head now level with the loft floor, he could see the third man fifteen feet away and to the left. He heard him before he saw him; the man was rolling around in obvious, excruciating pain. Rocco bounded up to the floor of the loft and quickly was on top of the man, rolling him onto his stomach and grabbing his right hand and then left. Rocco put the terrorist's hands behind him, while placing his right knee on the back of the man's neck. As he reached with his left hand for the handcuffs he carried in the pouch on his vest, the man screamed and jerked hard, throwing Rocco off him. Then he started flailing at Rocco with both his arms and his feet, catching Rocco across the head and pushing him onto his back.

Carter, hearing the ruckus above him, slung his rifle and quickly climbed the ladder. As he got to the top, he saw Rocco's goggles go sliding across the loft floor, He could see they were locked together side by side in a fight. Just then, the terrorist hit Rocco in his sternum with his knee, hard. As the man pulled his arm back to hit Rocco again, Carter grabbed it, pulling him back with such force that the man went over the edge and fell the fifteen feet to the hard floor below. Everyone could hear the sound of bone breaking.

Conway, though injured, was starting to come up the ladder to help out when the man almost hit him as he flew by, smacking the barn floor hard with his face. His head snapped back on a ninety-degree angle. You could almost feel the impact when he hit the hard ground below. Carter moved to Rocco, who was a bit dazed by having the wind knocked out of him.

"You OK?" Carter asked, reaching his hand out to Rocco to help him to his feet. Rocco grabbed Carter's extended hand and pulled himself onto his feet with a grimace on his face.

"I'm good! Thanks, brother!"

To Carter, it was inspiring to watch these incredibly tough and resilient these Delta Force guys in action. He felt really good about being able to help Rocco. They both stood on the edge of the loft floor, looking down at the crumpled and twitching body of the now-dead terrorist.

"Fuck, dude, nice job throwing him off the edge; looks like he broke his neck! You are one crazy, nasty motherfucker. Glad you're on my side; thanks, man!" Rocco said, looking down at the lifeless body below and laughing hard. "I don't think we're going to be able to interrogate that one." Carter looked at him with a goofy smile on his face, and they gave each other a hug.

Doug keyed his mike, checking in on Garrett and Mick positioned outside. Both reported back that all was clear and quiet. Doug called up to his three men in the loft that they were going to handheld lights and to remove their night vision gear. Since they were already up there, he told them to do a search for anything out of the ordinary such as any cobalt-60 canisters.

In only took a few minutes for Carter, Rocco and Mike to search the loft since there wasn't much up there. They found nothing out of the ordinary, so Doug told them to come down. He wanted to bring them together to start their search of the buildings to see if they could find any canisters here.

Mick heard the shooting inside and was grateful to hear everyone was OK and that there were three tangos down inside the barn. Doug radioed to Mick to come into the barn, but he kept Garrett in his sentry position. Inside, with all six of them together in a huddle, he outlined his plans for a fast and thorough search. And then they should get the hell out of there.

Doug was unaware that eighteen hundred miles away, Alex had activated NSA jamming on the four cell phones he'd detected at the compound, thus negating Tameez's attempt to call the Iman in Tucson.

Before leaving Tucson, Conway picked up a Geiger counter at an Army-surplus store, anticipating they might need it. Pulling it out of the pouch he was carrying it in, he flipped the switch on and started moving it back and forth as he explored the dark recesses of the barn. Though it was a used one, it was sensitive enough to pick up any kind of radiation with in fifty feet. Methodically, he worked the inside of the barn which was full of equipment, boxes et cetera. After fifteen minutes, Conway came out of the barracks area and gave a thumbs-up. Two more buildings to check – the mess hall and house. Carter looked at his watch which now read 2:22 a.m. To him, it seemed like they'd been there only a few minutes.

2:51 a.m., Central Standard Time

A little more than an hour passed since they'd launched their assault on the compound, and Doug was anxious to exit the area. He didn't know if any of the terrorists had been able to send for outside help during the raid, but it would be smart to assume they did. They all felt an urgency to get on their way. But first, he wanted to make sure they sanitized the compound and left no trace they had been there. It was decided that torching all the buildings was the preferred method to accomplish this. Rocco noticed a couple of five-gallon cans of gasoline in the barn, along with several fifty-five-gallon drums of what looked and smelled like diesel fuel.

Putting a match to the place would handle a couple of things. First, it would confuse the jihadists and law enforcement as to who did it. The local people in the area were well aware that this place existed and that it was being used by radical Islamic men. The neighbors were pissed off and angry because neither the local or federal agencies were doing anything about it. It was a common topic of conversation in the local bars and restaurants in the area. So it was predictable that law enforcement would concentrate their investigative effort on the neighbors at first. The second thing it would accomplish would be to deny the other members of this Islamic terrorist training camp any kind of compound to return to.

As they got into their vehicles and headed for the highway, the glow of the blaze from the three buildings was strangely serene in the diminishing snow falling in the dark of the night. Now it was time for them to get back on the trail of the man driving northeast ahead of them. They assumed he also was an Islamic terrorist, transporting the cobalt-60 canisters. Forty-five minutes after leaving the compound, with Mike at the wheel, Doug pulled out his cell phone and punched in a quick text to Alex. He asked for any updates he might have and also asked if he could get a position report of the person they were chasing.

Doug knew the guy had a good eight-hour lead on them. He hoped they would be able to intercept him and secure his deadly cargo before he reached his destination. The Americans had an advantage with the seven men and two vehicles versus what Doug hoped was just one person in one vehicle. They could take turns driving while others slept. If the terrorist they were pursuing was alone, then sooner or later they hoped he'd have to stop and rest.

6:00 a.m., Eastern Standard Time, Saturday Morning in Columbia, Maryland

The smell of fresh coffee brewing met Alex's nose just as the alarm went off. Through the thin cracks in the bedroom-window blinds, he could see it was still dark outside. He liked waking up early, ahead of the sun coming up, and the smell of coffee always made the transition from being asleep to fully awake much easier. In earlier years, he'd spent too much time taking short catnaps on hard ground which went along with being a Delta Force operator. He had come to cherish every night in a warm bed since those nights' years ago. He reached over, feeling the soft, warm skin of his sleeping wife. He pulled her in close to him and kissed her.

Swinging his legs out of bed, he saw the green light flashing on his cell phone, indicating a message of some sort. As he stood up, putting weight on his legs, he grimaced from the now all-too-familiar shot of pain up his right leg. If not for this, he would have finished out a twenty-five-year tour with Delta Force. But he was one of the lucky ones who got to come back home alive. He had more friends tha he wanted to remember who he'd lost over the years. He reached over and grabbed the cell phone as he limped his way quietly down the hallway to the kitchen, the smell of coffee getting stronger with each step.

Reaching the coffee pot, he looked at the cell-phone screen and saw the text from Doug, requesting any updates on the progress of their eastbound target. Doug grabbed the Coffee Mate and put a heaping teaspoon of that plus a teaspoon of honey into the cup and then poured the steaming coffee into the mug. He walked to his office where he'd have access to his secure computer and satellite-tracking information. Once the satellite zeroed in on a cell phone number, the hardware and software were capable of tracking it continuously, along with up to another fifty-million cell phones at one time if needed. Alex had set up an alert to notify him if any of the cell phones he was tracking was activated, if calls were made to another phone or if calls came in, along with an audio recording of every call.

Alex entered his password which allowed him to go into the NSA-secured tracking site. He entered the project number, bringing up a high-resolution satellite image of the location of the cell phone Ammar was using. This gave a visual rendering and also displayed the longitude and latitude coordinates of his current location, direction of movement and average speed. From the flashing red dot on the map, it showed that Ammar was an hour west of Salina, Kansas, eastbound on I-70. He then checked Doug's location; he was about two hours north of Santa Fe, heading north on I-25.

Just as he was lifting up his coffee for another sip, the flashing red light turned to flashing green, indicating Ammar was placing a phone call. Alex grabbed his headset, muting the loudspeakers so as not to awake his wife. Putting the cursor on the flashing green light, he then pressed the right mouse button and selected the "eavesdrop" icon on the screen. Immediately, he could hear a phone ringing and then a man answering. The conversation he was listening to was in Arabic and in a dialect he recognized. Though Alex wasn't totally proficient in the dialect, he understood enough of it. He listened as Ammar gave a report to the man on the other end as to where he was and his expected arrival time.

Alex used the wheel on the mouse to give a bigger view of the map, showing another flashing green dot located in Dearborn, Michigan, along with the current address of its location. As he listened, he could hear the annoyance in the other man's voice because Ammar had not yet arrived. The man in Dearborn also asked Ammar if everything was going OK, making sure the package was in good shape. Ammar assured him in the affirmative and let him know he'd be there as soon as he could. The conversation took no more than three minutes and the two men agreed to be in contact in the next four hours.

4:30 a.m., Mountain Standard Time

Doug felt his phone vibrating in his pocket before he heard it. Pulling it out, he hit the "answer" tab.

"How are you doing, brother?" Alex asked. "Your target is an hour and twelve minutes west of Salinas, Kansas, traveling eastbound on I-70. Fortuitous, as it was just after I received your text and opened up my program, I was able to eavesdrop on a conversation between him and another man located in Dearborn, Michigan. The whole conversation was in Arabic. I was able to understand a mention of a package he was carrying with him. The guy on the other end in Dearborn sounded like his panties were all wadded up because it wasn't there yet. I assume your concern is for whatever the package is more than the guy transporting it."

"Roger that," Doug answered. "We're very concerned about the nature of the package. I have no doubt this could have bigger and longer-lasting consequences than the attack in New York on 9/11. We've got to get this guy and intercept what he's got with him. How far are we behind him?"

"You're a good eight hours behind at this point. At his current average rate of speed, he could be in Dearborn by twelve noon tomorrow, local time. I'll keep you updated every few hours or sooner if anything interesting happens."

"Roger that. Thanks, brother. Out!"

Doug hit the "end" button and then called Carter to let him know they'd stop in Colorado Springs to fuel up and get a SITREP eye to eye rather than over the phone.

Carter, Garrett and Mick had calmed down from the adrenaline rush they experienced during the events at the compound two hours ago. Garrett said, "I'm tired, but I've never felt so focused and alive than right now." Carter and Mick agreed.

4:44 a.m., Central Standard Time

After hanging up the phone with Tahmeed, Ammar stretched in his car seat as best he could. The snow had let up, and he hoped he'd be able to pick up the pace. He'd been driving for over eight-hours and was relieved when he saw the highway sign that said "Salinas 28 miles." He would stop there, fuel up and maybe walk around a few minutes before getting back into his vehicle. He knew he needed some sort of exercise, and it would help keep him alert. While driving, out loud he prayed to Allah to speed him on his journey. He knew he was tired, but he didn't want to stop and rest more than ten minutes, if at all possible. He opened the top to the small cooler sitting on the passenger seat and took out a bottle of water. Unscrewing the cap, he took a long drink; he hadn't realized how thirsty he'd become. "Salinas 18 miles" appeared on another road sign. Before too long, he was rolling into a truck stop in Salinas. Unbeknownst to him, Carter Thompson, Doug Redman and the rest were doing the same thing in Colorado Springs.

5:15 a.m., Mountain Standard Time

Carter was flipping through the stations on the radio as a sign showing eighteen miles to Colorado Springs flew by the window. He was listening for any kind of report on their activities just a few hours before. Carter wasn't a religious man, but he did believe in a higher power. He thought he and the others had been chosen to intervene on the events that were unfolding. He felt it an honor to have such friends as Garrett and Mick, and nothing but the utmost regard and respect for the men traveling in the vehicle in front of them. Carter thought to himself that at no time in his life had he felt so sure about what he was doing.

He knew he was in partnership and in the presence of great men; these were men among men, no-nonsense individuals who you never wondered where you stood in their eyes. He'd learned, after the weeks of training with Doug and his three friends, that if he made a mistake, they'd let him know it, as well as praise him when warranted. He had no regrets about their foray into Mexico or last night's events. As Carter thought about it, he felt good they'd killed those men. Both the cartel and the Muslim extremists had one thing in common – they were pure evil! For God, family, and country, he was ready to take care of some more of these cockroaches in the same manner. He'd had enough of his own government standing by doing nothing while his country was under attack from outside forces.

The lights of Colorado Springs lit up the sky in the last remnants of the night. Carter slowed down as Doug's vehicle made a right turn into the Quick Mart. He was anxious to hear any updates there might be on the man they were chasing.

Sunday Morning, Tucson

FBI Special Agent Rebecca Harper had just stepped out of the shower when her cell phone rang.

"Becca Harper here."

"There was an incident last night over in New Mexico just north of Santa Fe at an Islamic Educational Center. We've got four bodies and the place was burned to the ground; someone hit it and hit it hard. Washington is in an uproar about it and wants us to take over the investigation from the county sheriff. They're thinking it was probably some locals who wasted the place. I need you and Blake to get over there ASAP. I've got a plane waiting for you on the runway at Tucson International Airport. You'll meet up with a forensics team in Albuquerque and follow them up to the camp. See what you can find. I'll text you the GPS coordinates to the camp. Call me when you get there," ordered Ben Nottingham, Agent Harper's thirty-eight-year-old supervisor.

He loathed the idea of having to deal with Agent Harper. On more than one occasion she'd told him to go fuck himself, she just didn't care. He knew she was beyond full retirement age and didn't care what he thought. He hated how she always answered her phone with "Becca Harper," rather than "Special Agent Rebecca Harper."

"'Islamic Educational Center' my ass; stop with the politically correct bull shit, you know as well as I do it's a jihadi training camp. OK, I can be out of here in forty-five minutes. I'll swing by and pick up Trevor on the way to the airport."

Special Agent Trevor Blake had just returned from his five-mile morning run when his cell phone rang.

"Trevor, Becca here. Hey, pack your bags, we're heading over to New Mexico, north of Sante Fe. It seems someone or persons whacked a bunch of ragheads at the Islamic Educational Center last night. I'll pick you up in forty-five minutes. I'll fill you in on the details en route"

"Islamic Educational Center?"

"Hello! That's the politically correct term for a jihadist training camp. You know, as in ISIS affiliate. See you in forty-five minutes," Harper said.

What the fuck? Leave it to Washington to jump the gun for a photo op. I'm sure there'll be a White House press conference – long before the facts are in – calling it a local militia attack long and vowing to bring the perpetrators to justice! Becca thought to herself.

4:45 p.m., Central Standard Time

Doug checked in with Alex every three hours. After the last one Alex told him they'd gained an hour on their target. By the time they'd passed through St. Louis, they'd gained almost another hour. They were now headed in a northeasterly direction on I-70 toward Indianapolis. Doug, Alex and everyone else assumed at this point that the destination for their target and his package was Dearborn, Michigan. Since leaving the terrorist training camp in New Mexico, all of the calls made by the target went to a cell phone in Dearborn located at the same address as before. Given that Dearborn, a suburb of Detroit, holds one of the largest Muslim populations in the United States, it made perfect sense. This fact and the significance of what they suspected the target was carrying created a constant sense of urgency for everyone in the group. They needed to get this guy and relieve him of his suspected cargo; what to do with it if and when they got it, they'd figure out later.

6:35 p.m., Central Standard Time

Even though Ammar figured he had a little less than five hours to go, once he passed Indianapolis, he was having a hard time staying awake. Just fifteen miles outside of Indianapolis he saw a sign for a rest stop two miles ahead. He promised Tahmeed he'd be in Dearborn as soon as possible, but he was so tired he was afraid of falling asleep at the wheel again. He'd already started to fall asleep, snapping out of it just in time to avoid hitting a guard rail. Up ahead he saw another sign for the rest stop – just one mile ahead now.

"Why not just take a quick break, thirty minutes; just something to help me make the rest of the drive safely," Ammar thought to himself. As he turned on his right signal marker, heading off the freeway, he could see at least twenty cars and trucks parked in the area. There was steam coming out of many of the exhaust pipes. Obviously people were keeping the engines running to ward off the cold. He looked at his watch; it was 6:42 p.m. He'd sleep for a just a little bit.

7:05 p.m., Central Standard Time

Since Mike was driving, Doug had dozed off, with the sound of the engine and wheels on the pavement steadily droning away, when he heard his phone ringing. It was Alex, informing him their target had been stopped in a rest area for over thirty minutes, and he'd let him know as soon as he was moving again. Doug radioed Carter to give him a heads up. This was a break for them, and they hoped their target would stay put for a while, giving them precious time to continue to close the gap. All seven of them had agreed never to exceed ten miles per hour over the posted speed limit when driving; the last thing they needed was to draw attention to themselves. They also knew some of the weapons they were carrying were illegal in certain states. This didn't bother any of them on a personal level, for as far as they were concerned they were going to do whatever was necessary to stop what they believed was an imminent terrorist attack. They just didn't want to be sidelined by some local law enforcement.

9:15 p.m., Central Standard Time

What is that buzz-like noise coming from? Ammar thought to himself; he just wanted to sleep. The buzzing and ringing finally stopped. He was so tired. *Oh shit,* he thought as he pulled himself out of a deep sleep and grabbed his phone. It was Tahmeed. He looked at the time display which read "9:15" and hit the "answer" button.

"Yes! Yes, I'm OK! I just took a quick break," Ammar groggily said to Tahmeed. He assured him he was moving and should be there sometime after midnight. Ammar hit "end," rubbed his face and started his car up, heading on his way and cursing himself for sleeping so long. After completing the call, Tahmeed was angry. He told Saad to expect the package around ten o'clock, and he didn't like this interruption in their grand plan. Saad looked at him and turned away, shaking his head.

9:20 p.m., Central Standard Time

"Your target's moving again. He just left the rest stop and is continuing northbound on I-70. Looks like you gained another two and a half hours or so on him; you're now only about four hours behind. Also he called his guy in Dearborn again; same address. I could tell from the Dearborn's guy's tone of voice that he was pissed," Alex said.

"Thanks, brother, for the update. That's good news! If his destination is Dearborn, that should put him there sometime after midnight. Does that jive with your reckoning?"

"You're right on the money, barring no more stops other than for fuel. I would assume he'll make another phone call when he gets in the Dearborn area. If he does, I'll give you the location of the cell he's calling at that time."

"Roger that. Talk with you then; out."

Needless to say, the Americans in both vehicles were now wide awake and happy with the news that they'd shortened the gap. They figured they'd top off their tanks in Toledo, Ohio, putting them just about an hour away from Dearborn. By that time, they hoped they'd have the exact address. Alex had assured Doug he'd stay with them even if it meant all night. With their long history together, Alex and Doug were used to doing whatever it took to support their fellow brothers; it was part of being a Delta Force member.

Alex recognized, without getting all the details from Doug, that this mission was deadly serious. He didn't question why Doug or the others hadn't contacted law enforcement. He assumed the reason was that somehow it could implicate them in something they wanted to keep quiet. But then again, it could be just a complete lack of confidence in law enforcement to eliminate the threat. Or it could be both reasons. Whatever the reason, as far as Alex was concerned, it didn't matter; what did matter was that his friend and brother, Doug, needed help. And Alex was there to answer the call.

Alex saw a report come through that an "Islamic Educational Center" just northeast of Santa Fe had been burned to the ground the previous night, and four Muslim men who were on the watch list were found dead on the property. Smiling, he thought to himself... *What a coincidence, that was the same area where Doug and his buddies were last night. Whoever it was they'd wasted, it was good riddance to bad rubbish!*

The only reason the radical Muslims had training camps inside the United States was for the purpose of teaching their believers how to do bad things to Americans. They wanted to murder every U.S. citizen they could. Alex knew that if the administration, infiltrated by the Muslim Brotherhood, were to discover who killed the Islamic extremists and burned their compound to the ground, it would make sure the perpetrators paid dearly. The event would immediately be turned into a race and civil rights issue by the president and attorney general.

Oh how I wish I could have been there, Alex thought to himself. He missed the days of the constant adrenaline rushes.

Sunday, 12:33 a.m.,
Eastern Standard Time

As he entered the outskirts of Detroit, Ammar called Tahmeed. "I'm here, brother, and should be at your place in about fifteen minutes," Ammar said.

Tahmeed answered, "Allah is great!"

Ammar was able to park just a block away from the house where Tahmeed and Saad were waiting. He got out, stretching. Carefully, so as not to slip on the ice covering the sidewalk, he walked to Tahmeed's place.

Sunday, 12:46 a.m., Central Standard Time

Alex felt confident the target had arrived at the location of the cell phone in Dearborn where he'd placed several calls on his journey there.

Doug answered his ringing phone.

"He's arrived, brother; ready to copy the address?" Alex asked Doug.

Tucking his phone between his ear and shoulder, Doug was ready. "Roger that, go ahead," he said, as Alex started giving him the information.

"I put us around four hours or less to the target area. Does that confirm your figuring?" Doug asked.

"It does. I've got a pot of coffee going, I'll let you know if there's any movement. Other than that, give me a shout when you're in his area."

"Will do; out." Doug said.

Sunday, 12:47 a.m., Eastern Standard Time, Dearborn

The house was in a cluster of row houses about a mile or so east of I-94. All the houses in this neighborhood were built in the 1950s. They were modest homes, the largest being no more than sixteen-hundred square feet. Typically, they had two or three bedrooms and were basically a downsized version of the larger homes in the suburbs. Over the years, this neighborhood, along with many in Dearborn, was taken over by Muslims. Sharia law was practiced, and many of the women in the community covered their heads. Honor killings were not an unusual event in the area, and recently local law enforcement didn't investigate or prosecute very aggressively for fear of being accused of racial profiling. How many of the members of the Muslim community in Dearborn were actually in the United States illegally was not known. What was known by both local and federal law enforcement agencies was that it was a hotbed for indoctrinating young Muslim men into becoming jihadists.

Previous administrations had done little to thwart this. However, the current administration covertly encouraged these behaviors and beliefs. The Muslim Brotherhood, Al Qaida and ISIS had their tentacles deep into Dearborn. These groups, under the guise of a balanced administration, had a number of members of local mosques serve as advisors to the White House. This was all done to promote peaceful co-existence with the Muslim community. It was in this community that Tahmeed had set up the staging point for what they planned would be an act of aggression against Americans that would make the attacks on 9/11 look like child's play.

Final Assembly

Ammar was glad to be off the road and away from the steady hum of the engine. He hadn't eaten a decent meal since he'd left the New Mexico compound. Tahmeed had lamb and rice on the stove and scooped up a generous helping onto Ammar's plate.

Saad was anxious to get the containers of cobalt-60 out of Ammar's SUV and into the house. After Ammar finished eating, the three men went out and retrieved the canisters. They brought them into the house and put them in one of the bedrooms which was being used as a workroom. There was an eight-foot-by-three-foot workbench with a stool against one of the walls. Everything Saad needed to assemble the dirty bomb appeared to be ready, including a thirty-four-by-twenty-four-inch Pelican case which would house all the components. As he stood just inside the doorway of the room, Ammar could see a soldering iron, four unopened cell phones, wires and something that looked like three tan-colored pieces of clay, each about the size of a coffee can. Off to the side, he also recognized from his training in Yemen a number of blasting caps.

Above the bench was a three-foot florescent light fixture which Saad reached over and turned on. They placed all four of the cobalt-60 containers on the workbench. Though Ammar wasn't an expert on bomb making, he could see this was to be a very simple device. Ammar smiled to himself at the thought of the carnage and terror it would inflict on the infidels, and rendering a large swath of the area uninhabitable for decades to come.

Saad noticed Ammar looking at everything laid out on the workbench. Softly putting his hand atop the tan clay-like material, he asked Ammar if he knew what it was. "I assume it's the explosive material, but exactly what kind I don't know," Ammar said.

"This is a gift from Allah himself, young one; it is RDX2. This is what the infidels have on the inside of the missiles and bombs they rain on us, killing our women, children and elderly. Now it's time for us to use it against them."

Jamal emerged from one of the bedrooms, yawning and rubbing his eyes. He walked into the workroom, stopping to take in everything he was seeing on the work bench. He quietly walked over to it, looking at label on the cobalt-60 canisters; he knew what it was. During his incarceration in prison he had access to the prison library, and he remembered reading about it. Though it was low-grade plutonium, he knew it would kill a person if he was exposed to it over a period of time. He turned and looked at Saad, Ammar and now Tahmeed, who was standing in the doorway. "Allah Akbar!" he said, with the other three men echoing his cry.

It was now one thirty in the morning, and it was obvious Saad wanted to get to work on putting the components together. Saad, like many of the bomb-makers who'd come before him, was minus some digits on his hands. Two fingers were missing on his left hand and his thumb on the right. Since he was in his mid-fifties, he was ancient by bomb-maker standards. He had very thin hair with a receding hair line. Most of his right eye brow was missing, and a long jagged scar ran from just above the top   of   his   right   eye   to   the   left side of his forehead. As Ammar turned and walked out of the room, he wondered if the missing fingers, thumb and scar on his head happened at the same time.

"With Allah's help, I will have this ready to go in about an hour," Saad quietly said, as the other two men followed Ammar through the doorway.

The three men went to the kitchen and sat down at the table, discussing their intended target of Chicago's financial district. Jamal, a native of the Chicago area, knew it like the back of his hand. All three of them, Ammar, Tahmeed and Jamal would go. The dirty bomb would be placed in Ammar's 4Runner and Tahmeed would travel with him. Jamal would lead the way in his vehicle. The only question now was where to place the bomb for the greatest effect, and that would be determined by the direction of the wind. Jamal had checked the forecast for the Chicago area. As usual, the "Windy City" was living up to its name. The forecast was for strong winds for the next day, coming from the northeast off Lake Michigan at twenty-three miles per hour. Perfect conditions for a wide spread disbursement of the radioactive material upon detonation of the bomb. Jamal smiled at the thought of all those non-believers who would be maimed and killed near the blast area, and of how an area up to one hundred square blocks would be shut down for decades to come.

As soon as Saad was done, the three men would be on their way to Chicago.

What's Next?

Carter figured at this time of night there would be very little traffic. He looked at his watch just after they passed the sign saying, "Toledo 20 miles." Once they arrived there, it was only an hour's travel time to Dearborn. They'd fueled up two hours ago, and even though they could comfortably make it to Dearborn, he thought it might be wise to fuel up again in Toledo. Carter thought to himself... *No telling what will happen when we get there.* The idea of an almost full tank gave him a level of comfort. At the same time, he'd learned to trust in Doug's judgment of things which up to this point been pretty much flawless. Working and fighting along such men as Doug, Rocco, Mike and Conway went beyond impressing him. He liked the idea of being around men that ran towards trouble instead of running away from it. He knew these were the kind of friends that would never let him down. He was grateful not only to be with them on this mission, but also to call them friends. These were the best of the best America had to offer on the battlefield. Carter hit the mike key on the radio to offer his idea of stopping at Toledo to fuel up. He'd learned to anticipate Doug's decisions on things and wasn't surprised to hear Doug come back in the affirmative of his idea.

Doug and his crew pulled up behind Carter's truck, and the doors on both of the vehicles opened up. The men all got out to stretch and do what for the last day and a half had become routine; bathroom, coffee, et cetera. It felt good to Carter as his feet hit the pavement, and he took a few steps to loosen his stiff, cramped muscles.

327

Ten minutes out from their pit stop, Doug contacted Alex to get an update. So far, so good; their target hadn't left the location, and that allowed them to gain a lot of ground. They were now slightly more than an hour away from Ammar and the cobalt-60. Carter was pleased to hear this from Doug and at the same time thought to himself; *What's next?* Even though they'd been driving for over twenty-four hours everyone was able to sleep while someone else was driving. Carter was tired yet exhilarated at the same time. Maybe it was because of the company he was in, or maybe because it was his time and their time to make a difference for the safety and security of the country and its citizens. Whichever it was didn't matter to him. God willing, they'd find a way to stop the impending attack.

4:18 a.m., Eastern Standard Time

Ammar felt some one kicking the bed as he slowly emerged from his deep sleep. It was Tahmeed, saying, "Ammar, wake up! It is time, brother. Saad is done, and we're ready to go." Ammar slowly sat up, confused at first as to where he was and the time of day. It started to come to him where he was and what he was doing. Once remembering, he immediately swung his feet onto the floor and stood up.

"It is time; we must go," Tahmeed said again.

"Give me two minutes, and we'll be out the door," Ammar said as he headed to the bathroom.

Ammar, Tahmeed and Jamal were in the workroom. They watched Saad affix a four inch by five-inch Red Cross *First Aid Decal* to the top lid of the Pelican case. Saad stood there for a moment like he was about to unveil a great piece of artwork. He then slowly opened the Pelican case. All the components were neatly placed in the custom cutouts in the foam rubber that Saad meticulously shaped with a heat gun. Ammar could see wires running from the cell phone to the blasting cap which were placed in the middle of the three coffee-can sized pieces of RDX2 in the Pelican case. On both the right and left side of the RDX2 were two canisters each of the cobalt-60 for a total of four in all. Once the RDX2 was detonated it would scatter the radioactive material contained in the canisters, allowing the prevailing winds to spread it far and wide.

Saad handed one cell phone each to Ammar, Tahmeed and then Jamal, along with the number for the phone inside the Pelican case. This was a failsafe means in the off chance one of them for whatever reason couldn't make the call on the cell phone, or if by some freak accident one of the cell phones didn't work. All three of the phones plus the one in the case were cheap flip phones easily purchased at Wal-Mart or other similar stores. All of the phones were untraceable. They were also small, which allowed them to be put into a pocket, and because they were flip phones, no keys could be pressed accidently. The older Saad looked at the younger men and said, "Allah Akbar!"

"Allah Akbar!" the three men answered back in unison.

They would leave now, going first to Jamal's apartment in Chicago. Once there, they would change into business attire before heading out to place and detonate their dirty bomb.

4:36 a.m., Eastern Standard Time

Doug knew it was Alex calling as he answered his phone, and he was immediately concerned. They'd just spoken an hour before.

"Your target is moving, and they just got on I-94 heading west. You're now only about thirty-five minutes behind them. I'm tracking two cell phones in the lead vehicle and five cell phones in what I think is a second, following vehicle. One of the phones in the following vehicle is the one you've been trailing since Arizona and another one is the Dearborn phone. I'll keep you posted."

"Roger that. Out," Doug said, as he hit "end".

"Fuck!" Doug thought to himself. They were going to have to proceed to the location in Dearborn first and make sure none of the cobalt-60 is sitting there. Again, just like in New Mexico, Doug didn't want to risk assuming that the two westbound vehicles had all the radioactive material. Doug quickly grabbed his phone, calling Alex back.

"Are you picking up a cell phone located at the house in Dearborn?"

"Yes, there is. I'll let you know if it leaves the location."

"Thanks, brother!"

Doug thought, *OK, five phones in the following vehicle. Two were the phones they'd been tracking. Why were there three other phones in the vehicle?* He pondered that briefly and then considered their options. He called Carter, telling him to take the next exit and pull over. He made a decision to send Rocco with them to stay in pursuit of the two westbound vehicles while he,

Mike and Conway would go clear the house in Dearborn, making sure there were no canisters there. Once stopped, Rocco got into the right front seat of Carter's SUV, along with his gear. He looked at the three of them and said, "Let's go, brothers! I'll fill you in as we're rolling."

Carter, Mick and Garrett liked Rocco and were happy to have him riding with them. Doug passed on Alex's number to Rocco, as well as letting Alex in on what they were doing. Alex assured Doug he'd stay in touch with Rocco and keep him apprised of any changes. Doug didn't like the idea of splitting the team up, but had no other choice but to – adapt, improvise and overcome!

Monday, 4:59 a.m.,
Eastern Standard Time, Dearborn

Doug, Conway and Mike parked a block away from the house in Dearborn where the one lone cell phone was located. The streets were quiet, although it was obvious people were starting to move about as a few lights came on inside other houses. They still had about another hour and a half of darkness, more than enough time for what they needed to do; that is, as long as everything went according to plan.

When they got to their target house, Doug sent Conway around to the back while he and Mike would breach the front door. First they looked in and saw only a faint light somewhere that appeared to be coming from a hallway.

Saad didn't hear them enter the house. He'd been up over twenty-four hours and was dead tired. Within minutes of Ammar, Tahmeed and Jamal leaving, he'd gone to bed. Very quickly, he fell into a deep sleep. He woke up with the barrel of a gun tapping on his forehead. Saad slowly opened his eyes, squinting in the now-lit room. He wondered who these men were, but it didn't really matter; he was trapped and would just have to play along with them.

While Conway rolled Saad over on his stomach. putting the plastic flex cuffs on him, Doug and Mike finished clearing the house.

"Boss, you better come and see this," Mike said from inside the room with the workbench. As Doug entered the room, he saw Mike holding a blasting cap in his right hand and in his left was some tan clay-like material. Behind him he could also see empty phone packages, soldering iron and wire.

Doug and Mike looked at each other and then back at the phones. This validated their initial worry about a dirty bomb. Blasting caps, clay material and cell phones – all the hallmarks of a typical IED make-up of the kind used in Iraq and Afghanistan against American troops.

This explains all of the extra phones, Doug thought to himself.

They were now convinced a dirty bomb was going to be detonated; the only question was when and where? Mike grabbed the stuffed wastebasket under the workbench. Inside there were wiring clippings, receipts and a bunch of dark-gray foam rubber which had been cut from something else. Then he noticed, in the bottom of the trash can, a printed label which read, "Pelican Case."

The piece of tan clay was no bigger than a jawbreaker, Mike sliced off a little piece, putting it on the workbench. He pulled out a lighter and put the flame to it; immediately it started burning just like C4 or Semtex would. They realized it was some sort of plastic explosive. Mike put the rest of the substance in his pocket, along with the blasting caps.

Conway hadn't said anything to the man lying face down on the floor with his hands cuffed behind him. He noticed the man was missing some fingers and a thumb and saw the scars on his forehead. Conway was more than familiar with the telltale signs of a bomb-maker. During his time in service he'd heard enough tales from EOD (Explosive Ordinance Disposal) buddies and briefings to understand who and what he was looking at.

Doug and Mike entered the room.

"I think what we have here is an old bomb-maker," Conway said, while pointing his barrel in the direction of Saad lying quietly on the floor. Doug clicked on a flashlight and grabbed both of the man's hands. He looked at his fingernails with a small magnifying glass he always carried with him. As he closely examined Saad fingers and nails, Doug could see small traces of what looked like the same tan material they had found. There was now no question in Doug's mind as to what these guys were up to. Finding all the components in the workroom validated his fear. The only thing missing was the cobalt-60. They assumed it was in a Pelican case.

"Conway, take a quick scan of this place with your Geiger counter, and let's make sure no cobalt-60 has been left behind. In the meantime, Mike and I are going to have a little talk with our friend here," Doug said.

Out of the corner of his eye, Saad could see Conway pull something out of his pack and leave the room. Then they could all hear a faint tone as he moved around the other rooms. Saad then felt strong hands pulling him up to a sitting position on the floor, with his back leaning against the bed.

"Where are the rest of the men that were here earlier, and where are they going?" Doug asked Saad. Although Saad didn't speak English very well, he understood enough of what Doug was saying, but he just looked at Doug with a puzzled look on his face. Suddenly, Saad felt a sharp jolt to the right side of his head, knocking him over onto the floor. He could feel the warm drip of blood starting to trickle down his face. Again strong hands sat him up right. Although Doug didn't speak Arabic fluently, he spoke enough, letting Saad know he could understand whatever Saad might say. Again, Saad looked at him with a puzzled face, trying his best to put on the appearance of not understanding what was being said. Both Mike and Doug knew the likelihood of this bomb-maker giving up any information was slim to none. Looking at Doug, who nodded, Mike pulled his suppressor out of its pouch and screwed it on the end of his AR15 barrel, putting against Saad's forehead. The bomb-maker from Yemen just looked at him and then smiled. "Allah Akbar," Saad said just as Mike pulled the trigger.

They weren't cold blooded killers, but they knew, just as in San Miguel, that too much was at stake for them to leave any chance of Saad alerting the other men with the bomb. Conway found no cobalt-60, so all three men quietly closed the back door of the house behind them and went back to their SUV. Doug called Rocco, letting him know they were on their way out of Dearborn. He explained about the materials they'd discovered and the bomb-maker they'd found it with. All seven of them now knew, beyond a shadow of a doubt, that they had to catch up to these terrorists at all costs. Somehow that bomb must be defused."We're about an hour-and-a-half behind you. Stay with them, and do what you need to stop them," Doug said. Rocco acknowledged the information and told Doug he'd just spoken with Alex. Their targets were still westbound, heading in the direction of Chicago.

Chicago, Monday, 8:30 a.m., Central Standard Time

Ammar slowly pulled behind Jamal's vehicle as they came to a halt in front of Jamal's apartment house. They'd put a blanket over the Pelican case when they'd left the Dearborn house, to conceal it from prying eyes. Ammar stretched as he walked behind Tahmeed and Jamal, entering the building and walking up the flight of stairs to Jamal's second-story apartment. Jamal's apartment was on the north side of Chicago, about two miles away from Lake Shore Drive. It was a nice, upscale neighborhood and very quiet at this time of day.

Jamal learned how to work the system while in prison and had more than enough money coming in from government entitlement programs to be able to afford to live in a neighborhood like this one without having to work. After all, he served his time in prison, was a minority and therefore should receive the generous handouts that both the state of Illinois and federal government provided. Since he'd lived here the past few years, he'd made a point to keep a very low profile. None of his neighbors really knew him at all. If you were to ask them about him, they'd say, "He seems like a nice young man."

It was a modest two-bedroom and one-bath apartment. Jamal unlocked the door and showed them where the bathroom was. After having showered and shaved, Ammar felt refreshed. As he came out of the bathroom, Jamal was standing there holding a dark-blue suit, with shoes, socks, belt, tie and shirt. He looked at Ammar and motioned his head in the direction of one of the bedrooms. Months ago, Ammar wondered why he'd been asked by the Imam in Tucson for his shirt, pant and shoe size. Tahmeed stepped out of the other bedroom, putting on his suit coat and smiling at Ammar. Five minutes later, Ammar appeared in the living room in his new business outfit. He looked in the mirror and thought the two of them looked like the businessmen he'd seen in Dubai on his visit there a few years earlier. Tahmeed gave Jamal and Ammar a nod toward the door, and the three of them were off. Tahmeed would ride with Ammar and the bomb, following Jamal.

Since Jamal knew the Chicago streets well, he would lead them to a downtown parking garage close to their target area. Once there, the two of them would remove the Pelican case and exit the parking garage, meeting Jamal outside as he would not be parking in the garage.

On the way there, Jamal made a right turn, with Ammar following him. Ammar noticed the sign, "LaSalle Street," and another large sign below it that read "Chicago Federal Reserve and Money Museum 1 mile" with an arrow pointing straight ahead. Ammar looked up at the towering buildings and then over at Tahmeed. They both knew what utter catastrophe they were about to inflict, not only on Chicago, but on the entire country.

"Allah is great," Tahmeed said. The two of them didn't fully understand the power and force of the RDX2 sitting inside of the Pelican case, surrounded by the cobalt-60 canisters, but they knew it would be devastating. Along with the energy and shock wave, there would be the deadly radioactive fallout, which would appear as debris dust from the explosion. The death and injury toll could be easily in the hundreds if not thousands. They wanted it to go off between ten fifteen and ten thirty that morning. Monday mornings,

338

financial districts around the world were always packed with people moving up and down the sidewalks and going in and out of buildings, eager to get started on the work week. After the explosion, emergency personnel would hurry in to help the injured, news broadcasters, and curious onlookers would also rush to the afflicted area. No one would understand the nature of the dust they'd encountered until a day or two later, when people started showing up in ERs with symptoms of radiation poisoning.

Stupid, Simple, Boom!

"Fuck, they're moving again," Rocco said, after hanging up the phone with Alex. He called Doug to find out their progress. Doug said they were about an hour east of Chicago. Carter, Rocco, Mick and Garrett were just ten to fifteen minutes from the now-mobile terrorists. Alex had called Rocco an hour earlier to report they'd stopped, and he also relayed Jamal's address to them. They were on the move again and from what Alex could tell, they were heading in the direction of the Chicago Loop, home to Chicago's financial district.

"We'll stay with them. I hope we can wait until you guys get to our position," Rocco told Doug.

"Roger that, but do what you have to do; don't wait for us. As far as we could tell from our visit to the Dearborn house, we should assume the bomb is "hot" and ready to go. Also we're fairly confident the device is in a Pelican case."

He went on to describe what else they found: cell phones, wiring and a blasting cap. Rocco, Doug and the other two operators knew from their experience in Afghanistan and Iraq that this was a typical profile of an IED. They were always simple devices; no digital read-outs like in the movies. Nothing like that, just stupid-simple devices – explosive material, containment vessel for the device, detonator, wire, a cell phone and in this case, radioactive material. Stupid, simple, boom!

Everyone, including Carter, Mick and Garrett, was familiar with Pelican cases. Over the years, it became the industry standard storage device when traveling with weapons. Foam-rubber cushioning, hard-polymer case, secure latches for padlocks, pressure valve for airline travel and wheels for easy transporting. "Does anyone have bolt cutters?" Rocco said out loud as Mick took the exit off the expressway that would lead to Chicago's Lake Shore Drive.

"I don't, and I'm sure you're referring to the potential padlocks on the Pelican case. I do have a high-temp butane torch and one refill. It'll take longer, but we could use it to cut around the polymer," Carter said.

"That'll work; assuming we get to these guys and the bomb in time, we won't need it, but good to know if we do," Rocco replied.

10:02 a.m.,
Central Standard Time

As Ammar watched Tahmeed pull the Pelican case out of his SUV, he put his hand in his pocket to reassure himself that the cell phone Saad gave him was there. He'd nervously checked it about ten times in the last hour. Tahmeed grabbed the case by the handle at one end and the other handle in the middle, lifting it up and out away from Ammar's vehicle. He heard the wheels touch the dirty, oil-stained concrete of the parking garage. He reached over and pulled the rear lift gate shut. Tahmeed and Ammar looked at each other and then at the exit sign, directing them down to the street level and out into the daylight. As they walked, the wheels on the Pelican case being pulled by Tahmeed made a smooth, nonresistant sound on the concrete.

Jamal was already waiting for them as they came out of the garage with the case in tow. By sheer luck, he'd found a parking spot around the corner on the street. He took one last draw on his cigarette and flicked it into the street. Jamal stopped smoking four years ago, but the day before he'd bought cigarettes, anticipating the tension.

What if he got caught? What if the bomb went off prematurely? What if, what if? I'm not going back to prison, Jamal thought to himself.

He nodded to the two men and turned, staying in front of them about ten feet, heading off in the direction of the Federal Reserve Building located at the end of the block at LaSalle and Jackson. As anticipated, the sidewalks were packed with hundreds of people walking in both directions, in and out of buildings. The sound of car horns, sirens and people whistling for taxicabs added to the chaotic mix; it was a typical, busy Monday morning in Chicago's financial district. The wind was coming from the northeast across the lake at twenty-eight miles per hour, better than expected. It was typical weather for the town well known for its nickname, the "Windy City."

10:16 a.m.,
Central Standard Time

As Carter's truck rolled off the Lake Shore Drive exit, heading in the direction of the last-known location of their target, Rocco's phone rang.

"Rocco, it looks they went into a parking garage, because I lost their signal for about five minutes. Then I picked up on all five of the cell phones we've been tracking. They're now all clustered within a few feet of each other, moving two to three miles an hour which indicates they're walking, going south in the direction of LaSalle and Jackson. Rocco, that's the heart of the financial district and at that corner is the Chicago Federal Reserve. I've already alerted Doug so he knows what's up. You guys are only about ten minutes away from the targets. Better step on it!"

Even though Alex still didn't know exactly why they were after these men, his gut feeling, given the origin of at least two of them, was that something really bad was about to happen. All the pieces were falling into place for a major terrorist hit.

"Thanks, brother! Keep me posted. We're going to park ASAP and go on foot, getting as close to the subjects as possible and hopefully overtaking them," Rocco said and hung up. He then called Doug, Mike and Conway.

"Where are you guys?"

...

"We're about twenty-five-to-thirty minutes out from your position. I just spoke with Alex and he gave me an update – doesn't sound good. I hope we can get there to support you four. However, if Alex reports they've stopped moving, you're going to have to act

quickly. There's too much at stake here. Do what you have to do; Carter, Mick and Garrett will back you up. If it's a dirty bomb, I sure hope you can get to it and defuse it before it goes off. Otherwise this whole effort of ours has been a waste for us and our country. Oh, yeah, and if that happens, it's been nice knowing you!" Doug said, and both of them laughed.

"Roger that; out!"

10:19 a.m.,
Central Standard Time

This is happening way too fast; breathe, Carter told himself, feeling his gut tightening. He was grateful Rocco was with them. If they got a chance to get to the bomb before it went off, he was very glad Rocco would be the one to disarm it.

Unknowingly, Carter turned into the same parking garage where Ammar and Tahmeed left their vehicle. He looked for a parking place and Rocco went over their impromptu plan. First, they'd have to dress down, leaving their rifles in the vehicle and just taking their handguns, concealed, with two extra magazines each. As they pulled into a parking place on the second level, Rocco grabbed the butane torch as he got out and put it in his coat pocket. Since it was winter and cold out, it would be easy to walk down the street with their weapons concealed. No one would notice that they were all carrying handguns. They knew Chicago had some of the nation's most restrictive gun-control laws, even though it had the highest murder rate in the country. Anyone spotted in this town carrying a firearm would immediately cause alarm for the "sheeple" who inhabited the "Windy City." But given what was at stake, the four of them didn't care.

Best-case scenario was they would catch up to the bomb and diffuse it in time. Dispatching the individuals responsible would be a bonus but wasn't their primary concern. Besides, if it was indeed a dirty bomb, they were now all at ground zero!

10:26 a.m.,
Central Standard Time

Jamal crossed the street at LaSalle and Jackson. Directly across the street from the Chicago Federal Reserve building, between the curb and sidewalk, was a row of eight ten-foot-long-by-three-foot-high concrete planters; each was separated by a three-foot space. As he scanned the area with all the people bustling around, to his relief he saw no Chicago Police or any type of security, which was unexpected. As planned, he stopped walking and lit a cigarette, standing in between two of the large planters, directly across from the entrance to the Federal Reserve. Ammar and Tahmeed, with the Pelican case in tow, stopped across the street on a forty-five-degree angle from where they saw Jamal. The light turned green and they crossed, turning left and heading towards Jamal. Tahmeed, towing the case, saw one of the nooks in between two of the planters, right where Jamal was standing. The two of them walked the fifty paces to where Jamal was. He stepped three paces away from the nook. To anyone passing by, the two dark, sharply dressed Middle-Eastern men fit right in with the other similarly dressed people in the financial district.

It had been a decade plus since the attacks on 9/11. With the continued dumbing down of America encouraged by our government, partnered with the mainstream media, leaving something as obvious as a Pelican case marked with a large first aid sticker, unattended, across the street from the Federal Reserve might not raise any immediate concerns. Tahmeed wheeled the case in between the planters, laid it down, and then he and Ammar turned and headed back in the direction they came, passing Jamal. Jamal looked right and then left and flicked another cigarette out into the street. Then he turned, walking in the same direction thirty seconds later.

10:31 a.m., Central Standard Time

Rocco got another call from Alex, informing him that four of the cell phones, presumed to be two or three individuals, were heading in their direction about a block and a half away. The fourth cell phone was stationary, right across the street from the Chicago Federal Reserve. They both agreed it had to be the bomb and would be detonated via a cell-phone call. Both Rocco and Alex witnessed this method of detonating an IED remotely in Iraq and Afghanistan. IEDs were not set up to be suicide devices, but rather an individual would set them off with a phone call from a safe distance. They'd just lie in wait for an American military convoy to come by, and then, boom! Since in all likelihood this one contained radioactive material, the terrorists would want to get up wind before placing their deadly call. Alex told Rocco to keep him on the line as they caught up with their target.

With his phone to his ear, Rocco updated Carter and the other two and described who to look for. Carter and Rocco were walking abreast of each other, with Mick and Garrett ten feet behind. Looking straight ahead, Carter could see two sharply dressed Middle Eastern-looking men walking toward them about a block away. He watched as they crossed at the light at LaSalle and Jackson.

"Your targets are closing in on you at twelve o'clock about three hundred feet away," advised Alex over the phone.

Alex could hear Rocco instructing Carter to stay with him. They'd pass the two men and go directly to the bomb. Alex knew that Rocco, being a former Delta Force brother, had a basic understanding of how to diffuse a bomb; it was part of their overall training. Alex understood the decision not to intervene with the two men approaching them. He then heard Rocco tell Garrett and Mick that ten seconds after the two approaching men passed them, they should turn around and trail them. Once inside the parking garage, when the terrorists reached their vehicle, Garrett and Mick were to overpower them, keeping them from grabbing their phones and setting off the bomb.

The two men passed Rocco and Carter and then Garrett and Mick. Jamal, who was trailing his cohorts about a hundred feet behind, saw two men do a quick about-face and start following Tahmeed and Ammar. He kept walking as he watched Ammar and Tahmeed turn right into the parking garage; and he saw the two men following them do the same. Rocco, still on the phone with Alex, was now informed of the approaching African American man, who was one of the three targets.

Jamal was good sized, standing at six-feet-two and weighing about two hundred pounds. In a split second, Rocco weighed whether to have Carter turn and follow Jamal and overpower him, taking his phone, or to do it himself. Rocco realized this was one of those moments of damned-if-you-do/damned-if-you-don't. They could be

screwed either way. Rocco decided to go after Jamal, and he just hoped Carter, with the help of Alex on the line, would be able to defuse the bomb on his own.

Rocco slightly elbowed Carter, who was on his right. "See that black guy approaching us? He's our third target. I'm going to go after him and relieve him of his phone and then double back as fast as I can to help you. If I hear a big boom, it's been nice knowing you," Rocco said, with a wry smile.

"Alex, I'm turning you over to Carter. Call him on his phone."

"Roger that!"

With that, he quickly handed the butane torch to Carter. "Remember what I told you, once you have the case open, you should see two wires running from the cell phone to the detonator. Carefully lift up the phone and remove the battery in the back of its case as fast as you can."

"Will do," Carter replied, as he thought to himself about the task at hand. *Defuse a bomb! Holy shit! But what the fuck, it sounds simple enough. And if not, might as well kiss my ass goodbye! Lord, please don't let me freeze up.*

As he walked forward he had an insight; he noticed his fear of freezing up was greater than his fear of the bomb going off in his face. *Interesting!* he thought, walking on with his feet starting to feel like he had lead shoes on.

10:39 a.m.,
Central Standard Time

Ammar and Tahmeed, breathing hard and fighting the urge to run, didn't notice the elevator and stairs to their right nor the two men who just entered the parking garage behind them. They were walking at a brisk pace and lost in conversation about how ecstatic they were to have gotten the bomb planted. By the time they realized they could have taken the stairs, they were well past them and decided to keep walking up the vehicle ramp. It really didn't matter if they hurried or not.

They knew that sooner or later someone would become suspicious of the unattended Pelican case and call 911. The dispatcher would then send a police officer to investigate. The officer wouldn't touch it, but instead would call his supervisor, who in turn would call the bomb-disposal unit and start dispatching more officers to cordon off the area from pedestrians and motorists. The two terrorists both knew all this was going to take time, and they didn't want to be conspicuous by running or walking too fast. They also wanted to make sure Jamal had sufficient time to get away from the blast area. Since the wind was blowing from the northeast, they were going to move in that direction to get up wind and away from the financial district. The three of them agreed that once they were ten minutes away from the blast area, Tahmeed would have the honor of using his throwaway phone to call the phone in the Pelican case to detonate the bomb. As they topped the ramp to the second level, they turned left and could see Ammar's 4Runner parked one-hundred-and-fifty feet away.

Garret and Mick, not too far behind them, turned right and saw Ammar and Tahmeed stop, look back toward the stairs and elevator area, and then turn left to take the vehicle ramp up to the second level. Both Garrett and Mick realized this could be a break for them to get ahead of the two terrorists. It was obvious that the two were lost in conversation and were going to walk up the ramp. Garrett and Mick made a quick right to the stairs and, skipping two steps at a time, both men were on the second floor before Ammar and Tahmeed were even halfway up the ramp.

Both men stayed low, hoping nobody else would come up the stairs and discover them hiding almost at the top of the stairs. Directly in front of them was the ramp, putting them in a good spot to see the two men coming up the ramp. Crouching low on the steps, they could hear them talking and laughing and see the tops of their heads bobbing. They both continued to watch as their two targets rounded the top of the ramp, moving to their left and toward the next ramp leading up to the third level of the garage. As soon as the targets were fifty feet away from the stairs, on cue Garrett and Mick both stood up, took the next few steps to the second level and followed them. They made a point of making small talk and acting as natural as possible so as not to alert the two in front of them. Either way, Garrett and Mick would get these two guys, but ideally they wanted to make sure they knew which vehicle was theirs before they made their move.

Ammar and Tahmeed looked back when they heard the two men behind them emerge from the stairwell. They turned back around upon hearing the two Americans in the distance talking casually, and Tahmeed said to Ammar, talking in Arabic, "Infidels!" smiling as he did so.

Garrett and Mick kept walking, but quietly picked up their pace so as to cut down the distance as much as possible. When the two in front started veering to their right at the row of cars, it was now obvious which one was theirs. Without saying a word, both Garrett and Mick broke into a sprint, with Garrett going for Ammar on the left and Mick after Tahmeed on the right.

Just as they got to the back of Ammar's SUV, Tahmeed turned to look back in the direction of the two men as he headed to the right front car door. As his head turned to his right, he felt the massive force of Mick's fist hitting him, slamming him up against the side of the SUV. He could feel and hear his ribs crack as they smashed against the right-rear door handle. Less than a second later Ammar was thrown hard onto the concrete floor of the garage. He yelped as his left hip and skull made the forceful impact with the concrete. Before they could respond, both men were forced face down, with their arms being pulled behind their backs. They felt the plastic zip ties tightening.

"Fuck you! You little goat humping mother-fuckers!" Garrett said, laughing, as Mick stood up, glaring at their captives.

"Too bad we don't have some bacon to shove down their throats. Bad planning on our part!" Mick said, as he started to laugh as well.

Ammar and Tahmeed felt the two infidels patting them down, grabbing everything that was in their pockets, including their cell phones and wallets. The two phones had the number to the cell phone in the Pelican case already pre-loaded in them. Tahmeed, turning his head up and looking at Mick, yelled out, "Fuck you!" Just as he got out the word "you," Mick's fist connected with Tahmeed's face and blood instantly started gushing out of his flattened nose.

"I really like the hard-polymer knuckle insert on these gloves we're using … really made a mess out of this little goat-humpers face," Mick said.

Garrett had Ammar's keys and unlocked the door, hitting the automatic unlock button so Mick could open the door from the other side. Both men hastily searched the vehicle and found nothing of interest. Garrett folded down the back seat, smiling at Mick as he said, "Let's have some fun with these two assholes."

They hoisted Tahmeed and Ammar into the back of the vehicle, hogtied them, and then zip-tied both of their hands behind their backs to each other. Next, Garrett opened the lift gate so they could get at the two men's feet and zip-tied those together. Mick pulled a roll of duct tape out of his small pack and taped each man's mouth. He then smacked their heads together, taking the duct tape and wrapping it five times around both their heads. They then closed the doors, leaving just the right rear door open and looking at the two men, now gagged and motionless. The windows on the SUV were darkly tinted, and it would be impossible for either of the two men to move or kick from the inside to draw anybody's attention.

"Hey, assholes, don't breathe a lot, you'll use up your air too quickly. I think after thirty days someone will consider this vehicle abandoned, and maybe they'll find you," Garrett said, as he closed the right rear door and hit the lock button on the remote. They walked off, taking the batteries out of the phones they'd removed from Tahmeed and Ammar, rendering them inoperable.

"Good Lord, that was fun! Let's see how Carter and Rocco are doing." Mick said as they walked away. Both men did a fist bump and started laughing uncontrollably. They squinted from the bright sunlight glaring off the street and windows of the buildings as they came out of the parking garage onto LaSalle Street. They turned left and picked up their pace as they headed toward the traffic light at Jackson. When they'd last seen Rocco and Carter, they were heading in that direction. They knew the bomb was somewhere on the other side of the street to the left. Since they hadn't seen Rocco turn around to follow the black man, they assumed he was with Carter.

Out Cold

Since he had spent over a decade in prison, Jamal had become very street wise and cautious. While in prison, he'd learned always to be looking over his shoulder and, whenever possible, always to be around some of his brothers when doing anything. As he reached the end of the sidewalk, he turned right and looked back to where he'd just been. He saw that one of the two men he'd passed going the other direction was now heading toward him, but not looking at him. In prison, men survive by developing a sixth sense and trusting their gut feelings. Jamal felt that old familiar gut feeling that he'd experienced on so many occasions while incarcerated.

He picked up his pace a bit, going to his car which was parked three-quarters of the way down the block. As he approached it, without turning his head, he eyeballed his two Black Muslim brothers who he'd asked to cover his back. They were standing just off the sidewalk, fifteen feet behind his car. Both these men served time at Joliet at the same time Jamal had, and over the years they covered each other's back. As Jamal passed them, he discreetly raised his right hand, pointing his thumb to the rear in the direction of Rocco.

Rocco sprinted to the end of the block to close the distance between him and the black man who he knew had one of the phones on him. Coming around the corner he slowed to a fast walk. He assumed one of the phones the man was carrying could be used to detonate the bomb. Rocco knew from his experience overseas that usually the terrorists had at least one if not two or three additional people with cell phones to detonate an IED.

Even though it was broad daylight with many people walking around, he had to take this guy down, get the phone and his ID if he had any on him. He noticed that as the man passed two black men on the right, he lifted his right hand; maybe they were there to protect him, or maybe it meant nothing. Rocco closed the distance to around thirty feet. He could see the man veering off toward what Rocco assumed was his car; he broke into a sprint.

Jamal, hearing footsteps closing in on him, quickly turned to look just as Rocco was about to tackle him. Instead, one of Jamal's two friends, six-foot-four and all three-hundred-twenty-pounds of him clocked Rocco, taking him off his feet with other man immediately on top of him. The second man then kicked him a couple of times in the head. They looked at him and then at Jamal. It was obvious the man was out cold. Both men turned and walked away from the unconscious and bleeding Rocco. Jamal got to his door, unlocked it, calmly looked back at the man lying and bleeding on the sidewalk, got in and drove away.

The instructions were that after fifteen minutes of having left Ammar and Tahmeed, as a backup Jamal was to use the throw-away phone to detonate the bomb. This was an additional fail-safe mechanism they'd put in place in case something prevented Ammar and Tahmeed from doing so. Jamal wanted to wait, making sure he was far away from the dirty bomb before he hit the speed dial to the Pelican case.

What Are You Doing, Mister?

Carter had kept walking as the black man passed him on his right. Five steps later, Rocco turned around to go after him. Carter crossed the street at LaSalle and Jackson, ignoring the red light and flashing "No Walk" sign. All sorts of doubts and fears were racing through Carter's mind, so when he answered his ringing phone, it was comforting to hear Alex's voice at the other end. Alex heard everything that was said and knew his job now was to support Carter as best he could. Since Alex was a former Delta Force operator, he understood the ins and outs of diffusing a bomb. On the plus side, he'd been assigned to a EOD unit for two weeks in the early part of the Iraq war and picked up some nuances about the dangerous craft.

Watching the green dot on his monitor, representing Carter cross the street, Alex instructed him to turn left. "You should now be able to see it on your left about one hundred feet straight ahead," Alex told him.

Without saying a word, Carter kept walking, looking to his left. Up ahead, he could see a long concrete planter, then a gap and another concrete planter starting up. Carter got to the end of it and stopped dead. On his left was a black Pelican case, lying on its side between the two planters. He tried to look as calm as possible, but he could instantly feel a surge of adrenaline run through his body. His legs started to feel weak.

So this could be it; My last day on the planet, fuck! he said to himself.

He resisted the urge to turn and run. His hands started to shake, his head was pounding and felt his gut tighten up. He felt that familiar dread and fear overcome him as he froze, staring at the Pelican case sitting on the ground right in front of him.

"Are you there?" Alex's voice came through the Bluetooth.

"What? Yes, I am; I've got it. It's a Pelican case, lying on its side."

Being relieved beyond all belief, Carter saw just two zip ties securing the latches. He quickly went to one knee, pulling out his Leatherman on his way down, and snipped the two plastic ties. Conscious of people walking by, he did his best to position his body in a way to shield people from seeing what he assumed was in the case. Slowly, he flipped up the two latches on the right and left side of the case and raised the lid up an inch, doing his best not to make any sudden, jerky movements. With his Surefire light in hand, he looked inside to see if there were any trip wires that Alex warned him about. Letting Alex know he saw nothing, he continued to raise the lid until it was fully opened.

Looking inside, he could see the four canisters of the cobalt-60, three tan pieces of RDX2 and then what he figured was the top of a detonator. The detonator was in the center of one of the pieces of clay.

Suddenly, he was paralyzed with fear, just like in the doorway at the mall and the many times in life when he had gotten into a dangerous situation. All he wanted to do was run in the opposite direction, but he was afraid if he tried he wouldn't be able to move.

"What are you doing, mister?"

Carter turned his upper body to the left and saw a young boy standing there, looking at him and the bomb. Somehow the sound of the young boy's voice, the innocence and sincerity which can come only from listening to a child, brought him out of the morass of his cowardly thoughts. It was like a splash of cold water, yet he was still confused. He still wanted to run from it all – the bomb, the child and all the evil that was now permeating his country. His head was swimming; he looked back at the bomb and then at the child again.

"What?"

Carter could hear himself asking the question as if he wasn't the one who'd asked it. He looked back down at the bomb and then back to the little boy. In a nanosecond an insight came to him about the source of his becoming paralyzed with fear when physically threatened. He remembered a time when he was a teenager with the innocence of being unafraid of getting into a fight, especially if was he was sticking up for the little guy or one of his friends; then one day that all changed.

It happened during his junior year in high school at lunch in the school's cafeteria. Carter had never been one to be pushed around, and he frequently put himself in situations where he had to use his fists. One day at lunch he saw a much bigger kid bullying a smaller and younger student. Seeing what was happening, Carter moved between the crowded lunch tables and chairs and confronted the larger, aggressive kid, who had the smaller and younger one by the throat. Carter's grandfather had been a professional fighter in his youth taught him how to fight from an early age. By his junior year, Carter had been in a number of altercations and earned a reputation of being someone not to mess with. When he got into fights, he had always prevailed, without as much as a scratch on him. Because of this and his quick athletic ability, Carter wasn't intimidated by anyone and their size didn't matter to him.

The bully, upon seeing Carter approaching and ordering him to let go of the younger kid, did just that. Carter and the bully's eyes were locked on each other, but as Carter came toward him in between the tables and chairs, he slipped on a sandwich wrapper just as the as the bully let go of the younger boy. The bully took advantage of Carter's imbalance and hit him with a right hook to the jaw, sending him backwards into the tables. Carter was instantly knocked out, falling and hitting the left side of his upper lip and nose on the edge of the table as he fell. He landed with a thud on the hard linoleum floor, and his head hit the floor and bounced, leaving him completely still. The larger kid, seeing this, started kicking him in the head. If not for the intervention of some other kids pulling him off, the unconscious Carter could have been killed. He recovered after spending three days in a coma in the hospital.

In the midst of his insight, Carter saw that while he was physically healed, emotionally he'd never been completely the same... until now, that is! As silly as it seemed, he realized that what happened decades ago wasn't important and had nothing to do with now. He then thought about the old woman at the doorway in the mall, pushing him and telling him to do something. He finally could let go of the past and really live in the present. He saw it clearly; this young boy and possibly the country was depending on him to be fearless and get the job done.

Suddenly, an attractive woman in a business suit grabbed the boy's hand and walked away with him. He could hear her scolding the boy for not keeping up with her and for talking to strangers. Strangely, he felt very calm. Remembering what Rocco told him, he turned his attention back to the bomb.

"OK, Alex, let's do this!"

Coming out of the detonator were two wires that went into a cutout in the foam material. He cautiously slid his right hand to the spot where the wires disappeared into the foam. Feeling the wires with his fingers of his right hand he pushed down into the foam feeling something metallic and cold – it was the cell phone. Very carefully, using his index finger and thumb, he grasped the phone, pulling it straight up.

"Alex, I've got the phone. It's got two wires coming out of it going to what I believe is the detonator."

"Good! Don't cut the wires; turn the phone over and remove the battery; then after that, cut the wires and remove the detonator."

"Will do."

Carter took his right glove off, turned the phone over and maneuvered his finger nail into the cover on the back of the phone, lifting it up and exposing the battery. With the cover removed, he lifted the battery out. The phone, along with the bomb, was now useless! He put the battery in his left pocket and the phone in his right pocket. Then he pulled out the detonator from the tan, clay-like substance and put it in his left pocket.

"Done!"

"Good job! Now, it would probably be a good idea for you to get the hell out of there. I'm going to contact a friend of mine with the Chicago P.D. who will keep things on the QT. I'll let him know he's got a defused dirty bomb sitting across from the Federal Reserve."

Carter eased the lid down on the case.

"Thanks! Good having you backing us up. Take care and I hope I can meet you in person sometime and buy you a beer!"

"You got it, brother," Alex said as he hung up.

10:47 a.m.,
Central Standard Time

Doug called Rocco, anxious to stay abreast of what was happening. He listened as the phone rang a number of times and then Rocco's voice came on saying the usual, "I'm not available to talk right now; please leave a message." Doug hung up and called again, getting the same recording. He next punched in Carter's number.

10:48 a.m.,
Central Standard Time

Carter got up and looked around, seeing people continuing to walk by, oblivious to what might have just happened. He turned and went back in the direction of the light at the corner. Just as he did so, he saw Mick and Garrett walking toward him. Carter gave them thumbs-up. He'd never been so happy to see his friends.

"Let's get the fuck out of here," Carter said to Mick and Garrett, nodding his head back in the direction they came.

"Where's Rocco? We thought he was with you," Garrett asked with concern.

"No, there was a third guy, a black guy who passed Rocco and me. Rocco turned and went after him. Alex walked me through defusing the bomb. Fuck, something's not right; he should have been here by now," Carter said, just as his phone rang.

"Carter, Doug here. Is Rocco with you?"

"No, he's not," Carter answered. He explained the sequence of events he'd just told Mick and Garrett, including that the bomb was inert.

"The three of you head back in the last direction you saw him heading; we're only a couple of minutes out from your location. We'll rendezvous with you. I'm going to contact Alex and see if he can track his cell phone. I'll call you right back. Out!"

Alex had just finished looking up his Chicago P. D. friend's number when his cell rang and he could see it was Doug.

"Hey, brother, we have a problem. Don't know where is Rocco is. Can you get a fix on his phone?"

"Stand by," Alex said, as Doug looked at his watch. "Got him; he's a block east of LaSalle on Jackson, or at least his phone is, and it's not moving."

"Got it; I'll be back in touch. Out," Doug said as he hit the "end" button and immediately called Carter.

Carter, Mick and Garrett jogged their way down to the end of the block and just as they got there, Carter's phone rang. It was Doug again, relaying the information he'd received from Alex. The three of them turned right and towards the end of the block they could see people gathered around something and looking down. The three broke into a sprint.

As typical in most cities in America and especially a town like Chicago, people had become de-sensitized to violence, even when someone was hurt and lying on the ground. It was rare for anyone to stop and offer aid, let alone trying to help someone if they were in the middle of being attacked. When the two men went after Rocco, it happened so quickly that those passing by just kept on walking.

Mick, who was the fastest of the three, got to Rocco first, and just as Carter and Garrett arrived a few seconds later, they heard the squeal of braking tires. It was Doug, Conway and Mike. Doug could see them squatting over Rocco, who was out cold with blood running down the side of his face. Doug grabbed the medical pack as he jumped out. He grabbed one of the ammonia smelling salts ampules, breaking it open. He got to Rocco and waved it under his nose. Suddenly, Rocco sat up.

"What the fuck?" Rocco said, looking at the group of familiar faces.

They could hear sirens in the distance.

"Come on, brother; let's get the fuck out of here," Doug said to Rocco, as he and Conway lifted him up. Carter, Mick and Garrett, seeing Rocco was in good hands, turned and walked quickly, heading back to their vehicle in the parking garage.

"By the way, how did it go with the two assholes?" Carter asked Mick and Garrett as they walked. Laughing, Garrett and Mick explained, with distinct pleasure, the details of how they subdued the two terrorists.

The three of them got in Carter's truck and left the garage. They knew there'd be no stopping. They would go to the expressway, heading west to rendezvous with the others and start their trip back to Tucson.

About ten minutes later, Carter's phone rang; it was Doug.

"Hey, brother, Alex told me what you did with the package. I'm proud of you. Are you guys on your way?"

"Thank you. It was a team effort and, yes, we're out of the garage and heading to the freeway. How's Rocco doing?"

"He's a little worse for wear, but he'll be OK. Conway is putting a few stiches in his head right now. How are you doing on gas? We're good, so if you can make it, there's a truck stop at Elk Grove Village. We can rendezvous there."

Carter answered in the affirmative. He, Mick and Garrett were still coming off their adrenaline rush. After hanging up, Carter said quietly, but in a firm committed tone, "I'm glad we didn't just sit around and do nothing! Maybe we are Citizen Warriors after all." With Mick at the wheel they drove on in silence for about ten minutes.

Carter sat there lost in thought, realizing the fear was associated with getting hurt in his youth. His worries about letting others down vanished somehow in that moment of seeing that little boy. He smiled and felt a warm, calming sensation through his entire being. He felt free and very happy that all this was over. He was so proud of what they'd done.

"Hey, Garrett, I wonder, how do you think your buddy Eric's grandparents are doing down on the border?" Mick asked.

"Good question. I don't know; I'll give him a call and see what I can find out.

10:53 a.m.,
Central Standard Time

"You have reached a phone that is not in service at this time," the recorded message said. Jamal pulled over, double checking the number he'd written on the back of a pack of matches that Saad had given him along with the phone. He manually entered the phone number, double checking it before he hit the "send" button. Again he got the same recording.

He drove on, wondering what happened. He then wiped the phone with his coat and threw it out the window.

Monday, 2:35 p.m. Mountain Standard Time - San Miguel, Mexico

Reggie Ortiz was pissed. He was having a nice, leisurely breakfast in San Carlos at the Hilton when he got a call from his uncle wanting to know if he'd spoken with the three men they left in San Miguel to guard their stash of marijuana and the remaining canisters of cobalt-60. When Reggie told him he hadn't talked with them in a couple of days, his uncle became enraged and told him to take his two goons with him and find out what was going on.

Reggie knew better than to argue or resist his uncle's demands; even though he was his nephew, he feared him and knew him to be a dangerous man. He was thinking of all of this as they pulled up to the two houses in San Miguel, with dust from the road engulfing their vehicle. Before getting out, Reggie told the other to just wait a moment. If any of their guys were in the buildings, they'd hear them and come out and greet them. After a couple of minutes, nothing happened.

"I don't like this," Reggie said, as he pulled his gold-plated Colt 1911 pistol out of his waistband. The other two men, seeing him do this, reached back and grabbed their AK47s. They slowly opened the doors and got out of the big SUV. The three approached the larger of the two houses. The bigger of the two goons reached for the door handle and pushed open the door. A putrid smell came out of the house and Reggie could hear the sound of flies buzzing inside. They could see two men lying on the floor in pools of coagulated blood. They both had what appeared to be gunshot wounds to the head. Reggie, holding his shirttail over his mouth and nose, went by them to the short hallway and, turning right, opened the door. He could see the third man. His legs were in the bed with his upper torso turned and hanging off the bed with four obvious gun shots; two to the chest and two to the head in a nice, tight group.

"Fuck!" Reggie said, as he pushed past the other two men who were transfixed, staring down at their two friends on the floor. As Reggie was heading for the door, he noticed something hanging on the back.

Closing the door, he saw a yellow flag with a coiled rattlesnake on some green grass, with words below that said in English; "Don't Tread On Me."

Reggie told the other two men to come outside as he stepped out the door. He grabbed his cell phone and called his uncle.

"All three of our men have been killed. They're inside the main house, and they've all been shot. Uncle, there's something else." Reggie said, and he went on to tell him about the flag and the words on it.

Juan Ortiz was not the typical stereotype head of a cartel. He'd gone to college at USC. He knew from Reggie's description it was the Gadsden Flag. He also knew it was associated with Americans who were very patriotic and probably didn't appreciate the surge in illegal activity along the border. These had to be people who wanted to secure the border and maybe were sending a message meant to intimidate them. Juan Ortiz was incensed. He told Reggie to go with his two men to the rancher's house and kill the old man and his wife and hang them upside down from their front porch. He, Juan Ortiz, would not be intimidated. Just like with Mike Davis, he would make an example out of the rancher and his wife.

He let his nephew know he was going to contact Capitan Sanchez of the Mexican Federal Police to contact the American authorities. He figured it was probably the work of a militia group, and he knew the U.S. authorities would investigate who was responsible for this. He wanted to make this an international incident. Juan Ortiz knew the U.S. authorities would make a concentrated effort to hunt down who did this.

Reggie hung up the phone, calling to his two goons.

"Let's go. My uncle wants us to make a lesson and warning out of the rancher and his old wife. This will be fun."

Closing the doors to the blacked-out Suburban, they quickly headed north on the road to the Grimm ranch.

4:10 p.m.
X-7 Ranch

Harold Grimm was sitting in his usual spot on the front porch. It was a beautiful Sunday afternoon and he could smell the roast his wife had in the oven. Even though his eighty-two-year-old wife used a walker, Agnes still got around pretty well and, like him, was sharp as a tack. He was thinking about all the years they'd spent together. Through the good and bad times, other than when he was gone in the Korean War, they were inseparable. They still held hands, hugged, kissed and told each other "I love you" on a regular basis.

All the windows to the house were open to let in the fresh air through the screens, including the front door. Inside the house, Harold could hear the faint noises of his wife working in the kitchen. They'd lived a good life. Other than the problems with the illegals and the cartel, they'd loved living here. He hoped his son Eric would carry on the ranching tradition, but he knew after their passing Eric would probably sell it. His son had a good job with the city in Gallup, New Mexico, and was settled there with his family. Feeling melancholy, he was thinking about how quickly his life had passed when, in the far distance to the south, he could just hear the sound of a vehicle moving in his direction.

The front porch with a three-and-a-half-foot solid porch railing was low enough to look over while seated. But it was high enough so that anyone on the other side of it wouldn't be able to see the lower half of the person sitting in a chair, or the table beside it. It was unusual for any vehicles to be coming from the south at this time of day, especially on a Sunday. Looking in that direction, he saw the fast-approaching black Chevrolet Suburban with a large cloud of dust trailing behind it. As it got closer, he could see it was the same one that paid them a visit earlier, threatening him and his wife and killing old Sally. Harold instantly became angry.

I've had enough of this, he thought to himself, as he reached over for his Springfield M1 Garand that was leaning on the table, low enough so anybody on the other side of the railing couldn't see it. As usual, it was ready to go with one in the chamber and a full clip and an extra loaded clip sitting on the table. Then he thought about Agnes and realized it would be best to maintain his composure. He vowed to do nothing rash.

The Suburban made a hard left turn into the drive just as before, coming to a skidding halt with a following cloud of dust drifting over it. Harold remained sitting on the porch, watching them. The two front and one right rear door opened, and three men got out.

Same short little asshole and his two big thugs just as before, Harold thought.

The two larger men gripped their AK47s, while the short one with the gold chain approached him. Harold could see the short one had the pearl-handled, gold-plated Colt 1911 tucked inside his waistband.

Haven't these idiots ever heard of something called a holster? Harold thought to himself.

All of a sudden, the three of them somehow looked comical to him. After facing down hundreds of Red Chinese in the Korean War, thugs and punks like these three put a smile on Harold's face. He couldn't help but chuckle a bit, as the short one with the other two right behind him, walked up to the steps.

Just give me the slightest excuse, and I'm going to kill you sons of bitches right now, Harold thought to himself, as he felt a surge of adrenaline pour into his system.

"Hola, amigo! What's so funny?" Reggie said to Harold, as one of his two men walked past him onto the porch, raising the AK47 and pointing it right at Harold's face. The big man looked down the sights of the AK, then raised his head seeing the M1 Garand Harold gripped in his right hand. Just as the man started to turn his head to warn Reggie and the other man, there were three popping sounds from inside the house. Harold watched as the man's head jerked to the side three times and then he stood straight up, took a step forward and fell over to Harold's left, hitting the porch floor hard, face down.

Harold knew it was Agnes who shot the man in the head three times, using the Ruger 10-22 that was leaning against the inside doorjamb on the other side of the darkened screen door.

Then, another crack hit the other big man. Harold could see his shirt moving ever so slightly, as the rifle bullet hit him in the right side just below his heart. After seeing their friend hit the deck, Reggie and the other man, now wounded by Agnes, were momentarily confused, giving Harold time to stand up, flick off the safety of his M1 Garand and raise it to his shoulder. With two large, thunderous reports, he put two thirty-ought six rounds into the larger man's chest, lifting him up and throwing him backward down the porch steps. Then turned it on Reggie.

Reggie, being the little coward that he was, started to beg for mercy, pleading with Harold not to shoot him, telling him how very sorry he was. Harold smiled again as he watched a wet spot form on the front of Reggie's pants.

Harold heard the screen door open up and the sound of Agnes pushing her walker through the door opening with the Ruger 10-22 resting atop the walker.

"Oh, look, honey, looks like the little man peed himself."

Just like Harold, Agnes had enough of this. She'd listened through the screen door during their first visit, and knew why Harold hadn't killed them then; it was because of his love for her.

With the rifle still up to his shoulder, he glanced to his left at Agnes. He couldn't get the smile off his face and burst out laughing along with her.

"Something really smells bad. Hey, sweetheart, do you have any of those Depends you could give this young man? I think he just shit himself, too."

The two of them were now laughing almost uncontrollably, with Harold doing his best to keep the end of the rifle pointed at Reggie's chest, just three feet away.

Feeling the anger and rage coming back over him, Harold stopped laughing and with his teeth clenched, asked Reggie, "Well, little man, what are you going to do?"

Reggie looked at him, lips trembling, and started to whimper like a little baby.

"What's that? I can't hear your little punk ass," Harold said, as he butt-stroked him across the jaw, sending him flying backward down the steps, half bouncing over one of his dead men. The pearl-handled, gold-plated Colt 1911

376

pistol tumbled end over end onto the dirt at the bottom of the steps. Harold watched Reggie, who was now bleeding profusely from his mouth with his head facing down the steps, looking at the shiny Colt 1911.

"Go for it, you little piece of garbage, if you think you're quick enough and man enough!" Harold paused, and then he squeezed the trigger. In that one moment, all the years of frustration with the out-of-control border issues and the government not doing anything about it seemed to be over. Smiling, Harold turned around to his wife.

"I love you, honey! Hey, I'll clean up this mess, honey. When's dinner going to be ready? I'm hungry!"

Monday Afternoon
Remains of an Islamic Training Camp

"I got to tell you, whoever hit those ragheads at the ISIS training camp knew what they were doing. My guess is they took out the guy in the main house first and then, after clearing the garage and mess hall, they hit the barn, coming in through both the north and south end doors. Judging from the tracks we found in the snow, it looks like it was a small squad of six to eight men. They approached from the south, and then two or three of them went down the east side of the garage, across the open area to the mess hall and then down the north end of that building to the barn. There was also a set of individual tracks leading from the front, west side of the house going back to the barn. On top of that, it appears there were two sets of tracks leading up to the front door of the house and the same with the east door leading into the kitchen. Both of the doors were blown open; my guess, it was det cord," reported Agent Blake.

This young man never fails to amaze me with his investigative prowess, Agent Harper thought to herself. Out loud she said, "OK, that makes sense. Good to have some snow on the ground. Det cord, huh. Sounds like we need to get ATF up here also. How's forensics doing? Have they found anything that could tie someone to this?"

"I know they found shell casings inside the barn and in the house in the bedroom. One in the house and two in the barn were 5.56 rounds, and the rest were 30mm rounds which I'm sure came from the AK47s of the dead guys. All of the casings are already on the way to the lab for analysis to see if there are any matches in the data base."

"That sounds good. Hell, whoever did this made a real mess out of things. Such bullshit, this being called an Islamic Educational Center. I suppose the AKs we found next to the dead bodies were for educational purposes. What do you say we head back down to Albuquerque? It's getting late, I'm tired and we've both got reports to fill out. Let's catch a flight in the morning to get back to Tucson. I think we've done all we can here, and the forensics team looks like it's got a good handle on things," Agent Harper said as her phone rang.

She could see it was her young, ladder-climbing supervisor, Ben Nottingham. *I wonder what the hell he wants,* she thought as she answered her phone.

"Becca Harper here."

"How's it going up there with you and Blake?"

Small talk; he's always got start everything with small talk. "Good; we're good. We're about wrapped up here. Should be heading back tomorrow morning. What's up?"

"This morning, around 10:45, an anonymous call came into the Chicago P. D. about a disarmed dirty bomb right across the street from the Chicago Federal Reserve. It was in a Pelican case marked with a Red Cross first aide sticker. It had four canisters of cobalt-60 in it and thirty pounds of some sort of plastic explosive. In the news, they're just describing it as a suspicious package."

"Holy shit. Thank God for the Chicago P. D. Bomb Squad!"

"That's the weird thing; it wasn't them. An unknown person or persons were responsible for disarming it. We checked the cameras in the area, and from ten o'clock to around eleven, all the cameras in a four-block area were offline. In searching the nearby parking garages, they found two bound-and-duct-taped Middle Eastern men inside an SUV in a parking garage. They'd been beaten badly. They're not talking, though, and of course they claim they know nothing."

"Wow, close call. Good for whoever disarmed the thing. Hey, we'll see you tomorrow. We're wrapping it up here and will be on our way," Harper signed off.

"Holy shit, someone disarmed a dirty bomb across from the Chicago Federal Reserve this morning, and they found two bound and duct-taped ragheads in an SUV in a parking garage who had the shit kicked out of them. They're not talking. What the fuck!" Harper told to Blake.

"Thank God for the Chicago P. D. bomb squad; glad they got there in time," said a wide-eyed Agent Blake.

"No, it was a person or persons unknown who saved the day. Maybe one of those militia groups you don't like came to the rescue. Let's get the hell out of here; I'm tired," Harper said, laughing.

Tuesday Morning
F.B.I. Field Office, Tucson, Arizona

Agent Harper was just finishing up her report on the previous day's activities when Ben Nottingham came over to her desk. She looked up at her five foot nine, bald headed boss. "What?" She said looking back down at her report.

"I need you and Blake to go down to Douglas to the U.S. Customs main office. A Captain Sanchez of the Mexican Federal Police will meet you there. Seems someone did a number on some Magdalena Cartel members the other night in a little town called San Miguel. It's just about a mile on the other side. They think whoever did it is tied to a militia group in our area."

"Who's they? Are you talking about the Mexican authorities or ours?" Harper asked without looking up.

"Both! Apparently on the inside of the door to the house where three cartel members were killed someone left a Gadsden flag. So, I guess from that, the powers that be made the jump to a local militia group. Washington is all uptight about it. The administration wants us to check out any local militia groups. We've got marching orders to track down whoever did it. The Mexican authorities recovered a couple of shell casings and are sending them our way for analysis. That's why I need you to meet the captain, plus find out anything he might know about the incident. On your way back, I need you to go visit the rancher and his wife that own the X-7 Ranch; see if they saw or heard anything. The road on their ranch goes right past their house, through a gate into Mexico and on down to San Miguel."

"Wouldn't surprise me if the shell casings came from one of the Fast and Furious guns. Hmm, doesn't sound like a rip crew; they wouldn't have taken the time to leave a Gadsden flag, let alone to have the brains to understand the meaning of it. Doesn't surprise me Washington wants to spin this into an international incident perpetrated by an American militia group. Great fuel for the gun grabbers in the country. Honestly, I really don't give a rat's ass who whacked them. I'm glad to hear it happened, and if was a local militia group, more power to them. By the way, speaking of shell casings, did the ones we recovered from the camp come back yet with any kind of a match?"

"Not so far."

Tuesday Afternoon

What a wild three days it's been. Jihadi training camp, dirty bomb in Chicago and some Mexican cartel members whacked, Agent Harper thought, as she started watching a video recording from a convenience store on the north side of Santa Fe that was recorded close to midnight Friday local time. She watched as two vehicles pulled up to the fuel pumps, with four men getting out of the lead vehicle which was a black Ford crew cab pickup truck. Out of the other vehicle, which was a blue Ford Expedition, came three men. Five of them headed off in the direction of the convenience store, while two of the men stayed behind and talked while fueling up their vehicles. She wondered if these were the men that attacked the Islamic terrorist training camp. She watched it another five times; even though the video wasn't of the best quality because of the lighting, there was something that seemed familiar to her about the two men.

"Hey, just a bit of FYI for you. They connected one of the ragheads that they found tied up in the SUV in the Chicago parking garage to an address in Dearborn, Michigan. They got a search warrant for the place. Guess what they found? Evidence that the dirty bomb was assembled there. Had a room with all the tools, empty cell phone packages, Pelican case label in the trash can and some traces of the same tan explosive material they found in the case. Turns out it was RDX2, manufactured by Dynatherm at their munitions plant Chattanooga," reported Supervisor Nottingham, while standing over Agent Harper's desk.

"Oh, and you know what else they found?" he asked.

"A body?"

"How'd you know that?"

"Because I'm smart; you know, two plus two equals four," she answered.

"Very funny. Saad was the guy's name. Turns out he was a bomb-maker from Yeman, in the country illegally, of course. Two rounds to the head with hands zip-tied behind his back."

"Maybe whoever capped his ass was responsible for disarming the bomb. Just saying!"

"That's what they're trying to find out. Apparently, on a house a few doors down, there was a camera running, showing the possible individuals arriving and leaving."

"What kind of vehicle was it?" Agent Harper asked.

"A black Ford crew cab pickup. Why do you ask?"

"Just curious."

"Hmm, I just realized something. Right about the time the phone call had gone into the Chicago P. D. about the bomb, about a block and a half away witnesses said a white man had been attacked by two large black men and left unconscious on the sidewalk. Three men came running up to him, and just as they got there, a black Ford truck pulled up. Three men jumped out, and grabbed the guy lying on the ground, put him in the truck and took off. According to a couple of witness's the other three men turned around and went the other way, going into the same parking garage where the beat-up Middle Eastern men were found in the SUV."

Agent Harper had learned over the years to be careful in sharing suspicions with career-climbing agents. There been occasions where obsessed agents had destroyed the lives of innocent people only to be proven wrong. She wanted to double check what she was thinking, and then decide what to do about it if her suspicion's proved correct. It was late and doing paperwork all day and looking at videos was not her strong suit. She'd follow up on her hunch in the morning.

6:00 a.m., Wednesday Morning
Tucson, Arizona

It took her only fifteen-minutes to get from her house to the downtown field office. In the middle of the night, she woke up, remembering the day after the shooting at the Southwest Regional Mall when she met Carter Thompson and his lawyer. She had watched him as they walked off and got into a blue Ford Expedition. Maybe a coincidence that it looked like the same truck as the one in the video of the group at the gas station in Santa Fe. There was just one thing she had to check.

She entered her password at the door of the field office, went to her desk and pulled up the search database. She made herself some coffee. It was too early for anyone else to be in the office, and she liked it that way. On one hand, it bothered her that the F.B.I. seemed to have a file on everyone – where you went to school, how many times you'd been married, which political party you were affiliated with if any, what you did for a living, the make, model and year of the vehicles in your name; the list of personal information was extensive. She began filling in the prompts.

···

Name	*Douglas R. Redman*
Profession	*Retired U.S. Army Colonel, Delta Force Commander*
City / State of Residence	*Tucson, Arizona*

On the upper-right-hand part of the screen was a prompt that said "Search for…"

Agent Harper entered "vehicles"

It was no more than five seconds when her search query came back.

2015, Ford F150, Crew Cab, Black, Arizona License Plate Number xxx45

Leaning back in her chair she took a long draw from her coffee cup and stared at the screen. *Holy Fuck… What do I do now?*

...

What would you do next? Where do you go from here?

Make an Author Happy: Please write a review on Amazon. Thank you.

Contact the Author
contact@jthomasrompel.com.

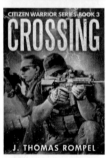

Order Citizen Warrior Series – Book 2

Order Citizen Warrior Series - Book 3

My Gift to You When You Join the Citizen Warrior Series Newsletter. Free eBook, *Citizen Warrior – Origins...* **The Prequel to the Series.**

www.CitizenWarriorSeries.com

Author Bio

J Thomas Rompel has lived in Tucson, Arizona since 1964 and understands the threats and dangers in having a porous border. He attended the University of Arizona majoring in Speech and Communication in the College of Fine Arts. J Thomas Rompel has owned and operated a number of different companies since the mid 1970's.

After the events of 9/11 he was involved in a business that dealt with U.S. military and law enforcement both at the local and federal level. This included Border Patrol agents in the Tucson Sector. As a direct result of regular contact with the above over time he observed a growing trend of the United States federal government failing in their duty to protect the Citizens against enemies both foreign and domestic.

J Thomas has been a guest and co-host on numerous talk radio shows.

Keep Up the Good Fight!

Made in United States
North Haven, CT
17 July 2022

21482014R00213